MW01470268

Meditative Rose

Lynn Gravbelle

*My Best Mail Lady
Waves to you always*

Lyn Gravbelle

Alpha World Press
Our Message to the World

2008
www.AlphaWorldPress.com

Copyright © 2008 by Lynn Gravbelle

All rights reserved. No part of this book may be reproduced or transmitted in any form or by any means, electronic or mechanical, including photocopying, without permission in writing from the publisher.

Disclaimer: This is a work of fiction. Names, characters, places and incidents either are the product of the author's imagination or are used fictitiously, and any resemblance to any actual persons, living or dead, events or locales is entirely coincidental.

Printed in the United States of America
First Edition

Alpha World Press – "Our Message to the World" – www.AlphaWorldPress.com

Library of Congress Control Number: 2008925216

ISBN: 978-0-9767558-7-6

For Joan

Acknowledgements

I would like to thank my friends Maureen and Lyn for their endless support, for their continuous backing in my decision making (whether right or wrong), and for respecting my feelings. Thanks to Dawn and Annette for opening their home to me.

To my sister Val a big thanks for bringing me home after Georgia's death.

A special thanks to my literary manager Lynn King. I owe a lot to her editing, and enthusiasm, and most of all her friendship.

Thanks Edna for all your wisdom.

And let's not forget Alpha World Press for their e-mails, phone calls, recommendations and support. Thanks Peggy and Tracey, you guys were great.

All characters, businesses, events, and some locations on these pages are fiction. They are drawn from my imagination or are used fictitiously, and bear no resemblance to anyone living or dead.

What people believe prevails over the truth

Sophocles, *The Sons of Aleus* (fragment)

PROLOGUE

In 1975 when we met, there was no same-sex marriage, no such thing as civil unions. Yet, somehow, against all the odds, Georgia and I managed to live together as partners for almost thirty years. Our lives grew entwined, like wild vines, each needing the other to survive. A day without her laughter, questioning every move I made, shaking her head as if to say, "…not again" and just being in my way was something I could not imagine living without. It had been wonderful, fun, sad, and I had only imagined, everlasting.

Georgia gave me the strength to work hard while I was on the job, and she was waiting for me every evening when I returned home, whether it was early or late. We shared everything…the good times and the bad, and when the doctors told us she was dying, we held on to every moment we had left, as tightly as we had held on to each other throughout the years. As she fought for her last breath, I placed my hand over her heart, and upon her death, my life came to a halt.

She left me, lost and alone, wondering, but not really caring, where, how, or even if my life would go on. How does anyone explain what it's like coming back into an empty house filled with only loneliness and memories?

Shortly after Georgia's funeral, I quit my job of fourteen

years as a police detective. I found I couldn't concentrate on my work, and although I didn't care that my job put me in danger, I came to realize that my lack of concentration put both my colleagues and my partner at risk.

So I left the force, and after a while decided to open an antique shop. It was something Georgia and I had talked about doing one day…and then there were no more talks and no more days.

I admit the shop ended up being closed more often than it was open. It was easy to hang out a sign that said I was out at an auction or away at a trade show. Slowly, I withdrew into myself and shut out the world, staying alone in my loft above the shop. Well, at least, that's what I tried to do.

My partner on the police force had been Detective Bobbie Kerry, and, as much as I tried, she wouldn't allow me to throw myself into despair. She called everyday. She knocked on my door several times a week, and she was, generally speaking, a pain in my ass. She was heavy-set, a heavy smoker, had sandy-brown hair with green eyes, and was always eating junk food. She was a sloppy dresser, the worst record-keeper in history, an expert shooter, close to her twenty-year retirement, and, as it turned out, a great friend.

One morning, after many months of living this same empty pattern, I decided to have breakfast at a local diner. There, I met Elizabeth, and I came to believe that I had been given that rare second chance for happiness that few people ever get.

The remorse I was still feeling about Georgia kept me from

taking the step to move ahead, but Bobbie reminded me about the many times Georgia had said that after she was gone she wanted me to move on with my life. Then Bobbie would repeat how, the night she died, Georgia had hung on, struggling for each breath, waiting for me to promise that I wouldn't hide from living and that I'd share my life with someone else when the time was right. Although I hated Bobbie for it at first, I realized that she helped me by giving me the support I desired and the kick in the butt I needed to take that first step and ask Elizabeth out.

That morning at the diner, I knew I was ready to live again, and in my heart of hearts I was sure that I had met the woman who would become my life partner. Elizabeth. The woman whom I loved from the first time I spotted her, and the woman who made my heart beat again.

But life has a way of kicking you in the teeth.

Things soon got in the way, and I walked away from her, leaving both questions and answers. My heart would never be the same, and my life would take some strange turns. Once again, my life turned dark if not black, and if it wasn't for my friend Bobbie, I might have ended up…well…I guess we'll never know, will we?

Chapter 1

So, here I am with my first case solved, looking at myself in the bathroom mirror. Besides a few bumps and bruises, and twelve stitches over my right eye, I'm alive and have begun my new life as a private investigator. All my friends are waiting in the other room to celebrate the success I have had on my first case. As I look into the mirror with my face still bruised and the stitches doing their job, I remembered the day Bobbie came in with my new license. It was an afternoon about two months ago when she popped into my loft waving a small package.

"Okay! Okay!" I said. "You've got my attention. So, what's in the package?"

"I pushed your license and registration through, so you can help me with this case."

"What license?" I replied, raising an eyebrow and squinting at her.

She had, without my knowledge or permission, fast-forwarded an application for a private investigator's license for me.

"It was easy," she said. "You already were a great detective, so I just called in a few favors."

"You did what?"

"Paula, I have this case that was dropped into my lap, and I need your input. You always had a way of solving the unsolvable. The one thing I could depend on was that you were always detached and logical. So, I hoped if I got you a license it would help you and in return you would help me."

I stared at her and slowly said, "I have a store that I'm trying to clean up and re-open. I even have some new art I need to hang."

"You have a closed store, and that art has been waiting to be hung for months. You use that excuse every time I ask you to go somewhere or help me with something. You can't stay hidden inside this loft forever. Remember, you're the one who left her."

"*She* has a name, and I'd appreciate it if you'd remember that."

"Sorry. You're right. Elizabeth. And I'm pretty sure she's not locked in her house, seeing no one and feeling sad…unlike someone else I know."

When I had been partnered with Bobbie on the force, we worked homicide cases where she steamed rolled over anyone and everyone who got in her way. We had been working a case just off Commonwealth Avenue when a call came in about a dead body found in an alley, just a few blocks from a crime scene we were working. We took over the case, and were searching the alley when Bobbie moved a dumpster. Some jerk with a gun jumped up and aimed it at Bobbie. I shot him, and because of that single moment in time, she believes she owes me…and I have been paying for it ever since. She says she believes in karma, and she thinks she must watch over me from then until (I hope she retires soon) forever. She's been a pain in my ass ever since.

"This is the case," Bobbie said. "A young lesbian was beaten to death. It looks like her partner, Carla Reed, did it, and no one cares to pursue it any further."

"So what's the problem? The case is solved. The bad guy goes to jail and the dead girl gets justice."

"I'm not sure it was the partner; although Carla Reed does look guilty."

"Do you believe she did it?"

"She certainly looks guilty, but it just doesn't feel right…you know? Yet, I guess I've been wrong a time or two."

"What makes you think the city will go along with hiring me to work this case?"

"Private Investigators are brought in by many cities."

"Yes, but only if the case has gone cold or if the evidence has dried up."

"True, but I mentioned to the captain who mentioned to the Mayor that this could turn out to be a hate crime and because it's a lesbian crime he should have all the help he can get. That way he'd be covered with the press and every liberal group out there. I also mentioned election year was coming."

"Way to go Bobbie, always looking out for the underdog."

"He agreed. I'm to back you up, and you have to share everything you find with me. I, in turn, will keep the DA and the Mayor informed."

"Alright, I'll look into it, but no promises."

"Ha! I knew you couldn't resist. You're a sucker for murder cases."

Chapter 2

I re-opened my antique shop and turned a small room in the back into an office. The space was tiny; a desk facing the left wall, a bookcase across the room, and a closet. Because my desk was so small, I had to use an end table to hold my printer. The walls were a muted beige color, and I had one small window looking onto the street. On a warm day, I could sit and listen to the traffic.

I reached for the files on the murder of Emily Fields. Emily had been a small-framed woman, thirty-eight, with dark hair, blue eyes, shiny cheeks, and a button nose that made her look like a china doll. Notes made by the first officer on the scene stated she had been dressed like a hippy. Not much else was written about her.

The files also included local information about the women who Bobbie had found were Emily's nearest friends. But, the files on the family of the deceased, on the other hand, could fill a room. I only had a minuscule amount of information at this time. The Fields were powerful, influential, and rich.

The case was already a week old. I was making notes and trying to make sense out of what the officer had written, when I noticed the date of the funeral. It was today, late afternoon.

Mentally, I flashed through my wardrobe. In the past, I had never taken the responsibility of buying my clothes or worrying about what to wear. That was Georgia's favorite thing to do. She always tried to make me look presentable when I was out in public.

(Elizabeth, on the other hand, believed I could dress myself for public appearances.) I made the decision that what I was wearing would have to do. My black slacks, pullover sweatshirt, and jacket would just have to work. At this time, I wasn't ready for anyone to know that I was investigating Carla Reed.

Chapter 3

I found a comfortable place within hearing distance of the funeral site. Dragging out my pen and notebook, I settled back and began the slow process of watching and waiting. The sky was a soft blue with a whisper of clouds. The granite stones stood silently in rows as the funeral procession drove through the winding path of death. Inch by inch the cars closed positions. Then the first car stopped next to a large maple tree. The branches shaded the faces of the women stepping from the cars. Emily's friends had begun to gather. I could identify most of them from their driver license pictures, which I had received with the case files.

Stacy and Jan shuffled their feet through the leaves, while Nancy brushed a red leaf from her shoulder. Darcie almost melted into the maple's trunk, huddling as if for warmth, while her partner Joanne moved among the other women. The wind was light as the leaves and tears fell.

Jackie looked around at all the friends who had gathered for Emily's farewell. She handed each one a white rose, then moved to the first car, opened the door, and handed Carla a red rose. Then, Jackie noticed Emily's parents were already sitting near the casket; she nodded to Carla. Carla got out of the car, and they all proceeded up the hill.

I stood back, watching. Of the women who came, I recognized three couples, two singles, the Reverend, and Carla

Reed, who began making her way toward Emily's casket. I watched as they walked up the hill, some hand in hand, others with their arms around one another. I wondered what kind of secrets they were hiding, and if one of these ladies could be a cold-blooded killer.

Carla looked the part; strong, unemotional, in charge. She never let anyone hug or touch her. She walked tall and held her head high.

From past research, I knew that the percentage of women who killed women had risen in the last ten years, approximately six percent. Most were gang-related, but some were (believe it or not) from domestic abuse. Very few deaths resulted from women killing other women because of jealously. So my list of suspects had begun.

It was difficult to stay focused. It wasn't that long ago that I had buried my own partner. She had been ill for two years, and I had to constantly shake my head and try not to remember that day in April.

I stayed within the shadows of a maple tree close enough so I could hear the Reverend speak. The unneeded tent gave off an eerie gray shadow. Baskets of flowers that sat around the tent shimmered in the sun. The banner across the casket read 'Em - Beloved Daughter'.

I watched Carla heading to a vacant chair next to Emily's parents. Mr. Fields rose, picked up the chair as Carla neared him, and placed it behind the tent post. Carla's body tensed, and her face flushed. Her eyes were wide with anger. She clenched the red rose in her left hand, thorns buried into her palm, blood drops falling to the ground. She took a deliberate step toward Mr. Fields.

I began to take a step toward them to allow myself the opportunity to step up if I was needed. Suddenly, a smirk came across my lips. Old habits die hard, proving instincts are automatic and hard to loose.

I saw Jackie move the chair next to Emily's sister. She then moved next to Carla and whispered something to her. Carla sat down, and I leaned back against the tree. I could see Carla's eyes and the clenching of her teeth, although her grip on the rose seemed to have relaxed. Carla twisted her neck in a half circle, relaxing her muscles, and her body shuddered. I could see why everyone thought she was a good suspect: she had a temper, and Jackie certainly knew about it. I also noticed that Jackie seemed to have some kind of control or influence over Carla.

Reverend Moore stood back quietly and waited for things to settle down. After a brief moment, she stepped toward Mr. Fields.

I had heard about Emily's father, a take-no-prisoners type of man. He had begun a business in building supplies and eventually owned fourteen companies and several buildings that had been built with supplies ordered only from his companies. He had friends in Washington and friends who lived and worked on the streets. His connections were public knowledge. He was a family man with three girls.

Emily had been the oldest at 38, followed by Ellen, who was now Ellen Kipfer. She seemed to be most like her father, married, controlling and possessive over her father's businesses. She had a Master's in Business, was average in appearance, and had an attitude that made her seem haughty and intimidating. And, from what I had heard, she liked being in control.

Finally, there was Lori Fields, a rather shy and submissive young woman with dull blue eyes. Her hair was lighter than Ellen's; she wore no make up, and she seemed to be the one most grieving. The report I had on her showed no work record. I thought that was a little strange for a woman not married and thirty-six.

Emily's mother, sitting next to her husband, looked frail. Her gray hair was pulled back neatly. She was dressed expensively, yet she was not overly impressive. She looked emotionally closed off, dependent upon her husband, and sullenly quiet. As Mr. Fields rose from his chair to meet Reverend Moore, Carla stepped in front of him, taking the Reverend's hand and holding it loosely.

"We are all here and ready to begin," Carla said.

Mr. Fields stepped to Carla's right. Grabbing her arm, he moved her away from the Reverend. He then spoke slowly and loudly, making sure everyone heard what he had to say.

"I told you at the wake. I did not want these perverted women at my daughter's funeral. Yet, here they are. So…get this over with and do it quickly, is that understood?"

Carla stood silently near Mr. Fields as the Reverend stepped back to the front of the casket. Mr. Fields stared at Carla then returned to his seat. Jackie took Carla's arm, forcibly seating her.

As the Reverend spoke, Beth Winslow began to sing in the background. It was a hymn, I believe, called *Just as I Am*. Carla surveyed the crowd as the eulogy continued. All the women were quiet, some wept as others held their heads bowed low. One of the women nearly fainted as her partner held her tight. It ended with the 23rd Psalm. "And I will dwell in the house of the Lord forever."

"Amen," was recited by all.

Mr. Fields took his wife's hand and stood. Carla stood and moved across him, blocking his way to the casket. She turned to face all the women. "Thank you for coming. I know Emily felt your presence today. Please say your goodbyes, and as you know, Nancy has graciously opened her house for a small but private reception. I'll see and speak to you there." Then Carla faced Mr. Fields, glaring at him.

The women walked up to the casket to pay their last respects, each laying a white rose upon it.

I was watching Mr. Fields, who towered over Carla. He was close to 6'2", muscular for his age. His hair was gray, and he wore glasses. Even at this distance, I could tell he wore a Burberry suit with a Ralph Lauren tailored shirt and vest. His tie was Armani. He was tailored down to his shoes. His stance was tall and straight.

While Carla stood solid, she looked small next to Mr. Fields. I could sense she wanted to be pushy, but guessed she knew her place and where she was standing at the moment.

Mr. Fields spoke first. "We'd like to say our goodbyes to our daughter, get out of the way."

Carla, holding onto the red rose, stepped back and took a deep breath. "Mr. Fields, your family is also invited to the reception."

I watched him push his shoulders back and bite his lip; he turned his head toward Carla, and said, "Do you think I'd step into a house filled with such deviants? These women turned my daughter into a...a...someone I didn't recognize!"

Carla began to tremble; she stepped back, making a fist. "She was my partner for ten years; we were lovers, we....."

Mr. Fields placed his left hand on Carla's shoulder and dismissively pushed her aside. "You bitch! You killed my daughter and you will pay! You'll spend the rest of your shameful life behind bars, locked in a cage where you belong! Better yet, in a dark hole, like the one you put my daughter in."

Carla stood still, both fists balled tight, her lips twitching. She thought for only a second, and then moving to the right of Mr. Fields, she approached Mrs. Fields. Carla calmly took her hand. Mr. Fields yanked his wife's hand away and pulled her to his side. Tears trickled down Mrs. Fields cheeks. She stood unaware, quiet, empty, and oblivious of the things going on around her.

"Get away from my family or I'll bury you right here and now!"

"I've taken all I'm going to take from you, Mr. Fields. If I want to speak to a member of your family, I will."

"No you will not! Stay away from my family! You've done enough all ready!"

Mr. Fields took his wife's arm, nodded to his daughters, and began walking away. Mrs. Fields tried to walk toward the casket, but her husband gave a sharp tug on her arm. Her head low, she followed the family down the hill to the waiting limo.

I noticed Lori lifted her hand to her waist and gave a single wave to Carla. I made a note of this; interesting, I thought. She doesn't seem to hate Carla. I wonder how well Lori knows her.

Carla watched the Fields enter their car. Her face was red and again she clenched her teeth; she shook, rocking front to back on the balls of her feet.

Carla hated men, and Fields topped the list. All they were to her was a mass of bone and muscle driven by egos she could live without. She knew this wasn't the last time she would see Mr. Fields, and she was certain the next time she'd be ready for him. He would never speak to her that way again. And, he certainly would never touch her again and get away with it. Carla stood alone for several minutes staring at the casket.

The walnut casket with its fancy trim and gold rails rested beneath the tent. All her friends were waiting by their cars. The afternoon sun was setting. The wind was still, and everything was quiet. Carla walked to the casket and, bending over, she brought her face close to the bed of white roses that were positioned on top. She closed her eyes and spoke slowly and quietly to herself saying, "Breathe, Carla, just breathe. You must stay in control."

I heard her as she kept repeating the words. She was lost; no one to talk to and nowhere to turn. She was just now coming to terms with the fact that this was the way it would be for a long time. Until she was cleared of the charges, she was going to be under the watchful eyes of everyone.

I watched her as she began to touch the casket, gently running her hand over the side and back to the top. I began to think maybe Carla did have feelings for Emily and that maybe she was the type who wanted no one to see them.

Then, all of a sudden, she straightened up and took a step back. Her eyes were wide in astonishment. She looked at her hand, making sure she was still holding the crushed red rose. She moved the white roses around and began pushing them off the casket, at first slowly and carefully, and then violently swiping at them.

There, on the casket, lie a single red rose under and among all the white roses. Again, she looked at the rose in her right hand, the fresh red blood showing where the thorns had buried into her palm. She picked up the second red rose and rolled it between her thumb and index finger. Her eyes darkened and her left fist once again clenched.

I watched her as she slowly shook her head…then she threw both red roses to the ground, stomping on them. She walked away without a glance back, and I heard her say, "Goodbye Emily."

I watched the funeral procession leave, then returned to my own car and headed back to my office. I needed to get my notes written and my observations down before I forgot what was important. This wasn't going to be an easy case, and I had to develop a plan.

My head was spinning as I sat at my desk, trying to get my notes in order. There had been nine women at the funeral that Bobbie thought were of interest, and if Carla hadn't killed Emily, maybe one of these women had. But then, maybe no one connected with these women had killed Emily. It could have been someone else who was at the funeral or someone no one knew except Emily. I couldn't watch everyone. I needed to get all the background that I could on Emily and Carla, and then spread out from there.

I picked up the phone to call Bobbie. She answered after one ring. "Bobbie, the information you gave me was helpful, but I need more in-depth info - as much as you can find. You've had a week already, and this information isn't enough."

"Hello to you, too. It's not like this is the only case on my desk, you know."

"This case might not even be about these women. I just need to find out all the secrets. You know how it is; I'm just guessing right now. I'll do the usual financial and credit reports, you find the dirt for me, okay?"

"I've got you covered. All the information about these

women is already right here on my desk. However, I only have what the computer brought up right now; what's between the lines is up to you. And by the way, I'll be over for supper tonight with the files. I'd like raviolis and lots of bread."

"I guess that means I have to cook. Okay, that's fair. See you around 6:30."

She knew I hated cooking, yet she always liked to discuss a case over food. At least she knew what I liked to eat, even if I did have to cook it.

There wasn't much else I could do until the additional information arrived, so I leaned back, lit a cigarette and tried to make mental notes of the things I noticed at the funeral.

Chapter 4

Mrs. Fields, her health failing, no longer seemed to care about the cold wind blowing across her face. She could barely make the stairs leading into the police station. Her husband had to hold her forearm, her leg muscles hurting, as she tried to make each step.

Mr. Fields showed no concern or emotion about the day or his wife. He was determined to put all this behind him and only concentrate on getting Carla Reed. He was single-minded and determined that that horrid woman would pay for taking Emily's life. He knew she had died because of Carla, because Carla was evil. His daughter had been brain-washed and had no idea what she was doing with that woman. Now she was dead, and Carla would pay -- one way or another.

Mrs. Fields began to lag behind.

"Pull yourself together," her husband admonished as he held her arm more tightly. Tears began to form in her eyes. "Come now, we'll have none of that."

He reached for the door. As they entered the alcove, an overpowering smell radiated toward them; a combination of bleach and sweat. The walls were a faded gray. The black and white floor tiles were worn and streaked from the heavy traffic that they had endured over the years. Mrs. Fields unconsciously held her breath. Mr. Fields quickly surveyed the room.

Several men and women were sitting on worn, stained

benches that lined the walls. One man appeared to have passed out while the one next to him was picking his pockets. Others were staring at the ceiling having conversations with only themselves. Some were handcuffed to the bench, cursing and struggling for freedom.

Mr. Fields spotted the sergeant behind the desk who was tapping the keyboard at his computer. The desk itself stood on a platform surrounded by bullet-proof glass with a small round hole through which he could speak.

Mr. Fields stopped in front of the desk, his wife moving closer to him. The sergeant was cussing the computer.

Mr. Fields cleared his throat. "I have an appointment with Detective Kerry. Could you tell me where I might find her?"

The desk sergeant paid him no attention and began pounding on the computer.

"Did you hear me? I said that I'm here to see Detective Kerry." His voice was soft but demanding.

"Yeah, I heard you. Detective Kerry. She's in the back." He pointed to a pair of black swinging doors. "Just go through and yell. Someone will hear you and point you in the right direction." The sergeant returned to the pounding on his keyboard.

"I will not!" said Mr. Fields.

The sergeant looked across the desk. "Who're you? Who're you looking for?"

"I already told you. Detective Kerry. I have an 11:30

appointment."

"Right. Appointment, gottcha! I'll buzz her, have a seat." He pointed to one of the benches.

"I will not, nor will my wife have a seat on one of those piss-covered, stinking benches. I am not one of those low-lives you babysit, nor will I be treated like one. I suggest you call or buzz Detective Kerry now." Mr. Fields tugged on the front of his coat moving his head in a circular motion to relieve the tension of his neck muscles.

The sergeant rose from his desk. "Just sit down," he said with authority.

Mr. Fields stepped forward; he was eye to eye with the sergeant, with only the glass between them. He was steady and showed no sign of fear. His voice was low and in control. "What is your badge number and name?"

The sergeant leaned on the desk and stared Mr. Fields right in the eye. "Sergeant Willows. That's W…I…L…L…O…," he began to spell his name pointing to each letter on his name tag.

Mr. Fields reached into his coat and brought out his cell phone. He opened the cover and pushed the speed dial as he raised his index finger to the sergeant. "Got it."

"Mayor, George Fields here. Actually, I'm not doing too well. I'm standing in front of a Sergeant Willows at the Central Precinct, and he seems to think I can't spell and he won't let Detective Kerry know that I'm here for my appointment. He actually told me to sit on one of those nasty benches and wait. You know how I hate to be late or wait for anything, my time is very important." There was a moment's hesitation, and then he continued. "Yes, thank you. I'll be at the club Sunday at 10 sharp, 'til then." The phone was almost in his coat pocket when the back door swung open.

"Mr. and Mrs. Fields, I'm Captain Carter. Sorry you had to wait. Please come this way." The captain pointed to the back, then turned and pointed to the sergeant. "We'll talk later."

Sergeant Willows shrugged and simply retuned to banging on the keyboard.

The captain held the door for Mr. and Mrs. Fields, allowing them to enter. The phones were ringing constantly; voices could be heard in a mixture of tones and volumes. Several desks were face-to-face throughout the room. In the back there were several small private offices. To the right of the room, there were several smaller rooms with a sign above each that read, *Interrogation..*

You could smell old coffee and bad perfume throughout the room. The captain led the way through the crowd, weaving between several people who were seated, while others just stood. A man cuffed to a chair jumped toward Mrs. Fields. The captain grabbed his shoulder and pushed him back into his seat. "Sorry," he said to the Fields.

He came to one small office and the name on the door read *Detective Bobbie Kerry.*

"Please have a seat. Detective Kerry will be right with you." The captain left them standing in the office, quickly removing himself from the Fields' presence.

Detective Kerry's desk, as well as her computer were covered with files. Several empty cups were layered over the file folders and inside the empty cups were empty Snickers bar wrappers. The two chairs that faced the desk were filled with files and several books, while every corner in the office had more file folders. There was dust and crumpled papers everywhere, even her bookcase was overloaded. The pictures and documents that hung on the walls were askew. The phone rang non-stop. There was a law book propping the window open, allowing the chilly breeze to fill the office.

Mrs. Fields wrapped her coat closer and pulled her scarf up around her chin. She started shivering. Mr. Fields went to a chair and removed the files by simply dropping them to the floor. He pointed at his wife to the chair where she obediently sat.

Detective Kerry didn't see the Fields when she entered the office carrying a pile of files. She walked into the trash can causing partially empty coffee cups and junk food wrappers to scatter across the floor. "Damn," she said as she swept the wrappers under the desk with her foot.

It was then that she noticed that she had visitors. "Oh, sorry, I didn't know anyone was here. Can I help you with something?"

Mr. Fields was standing behind his wife with his hands

resting on the back of the chair.

Detective Kerry dropped the files and went and removed the files from the chair next to Mrs. Fields. "Please, sit down," she said as the files toppled over.

Detective Kerry wiped her hands on her pant leg and held out her hand to shake Mr. Fields'. As he took hold of her hand, his eyes moved from the top of her head to bottom of her shoes. He checked her stance and the grip of her handshake. He guessed she was in her late fifties, probably waiting out retirement behind a desk.

She was heavyset; her clothes were baggy and mismatched. Her shirt was stained with chocolate and her pants with coffee. She was as sloppy as the office appeared. He began shaking his head.

"We're obviously in the wrong office," Mr. Fields said as he helped his wife to her feet.

"Really, who are you looking for?" Detective Kerry asked.

"We were looking for a Detective Kerry," he said.

Detective Kerry grinned and took a seat behind her desk. "That's me," she said.

Mr. Fields surveyed the office. "You're Detective Kerry? You look like the janitor. What's your excuse for this office? It's a disaster, a freaking mess."

No longer smiling, Bobbie said, "Look, enough! Do we have an appointment?"

"Fields, George Fields," he said.

Detective Kerry opened her desk drawer and pulled out the

appointment book and began thumbing through it.

"Do you know who I am?" Mr. Fields' voice rose.

"Should I?" Kerry asked.

She left her desk and made her way to the coffee pot. Pouring a cup, she nodded holding the cup up to the Fields offering them coffee.

"Look, Detective Kerry, my daughter was murdered over a week ago and was just buried. Damn! You had her body, doing who knows what to her, Jesus, an autopsy, collecting evidence. A week! What have you found out? What have you done? Nothing! You know that murdering dyke is out there walking the streets, living, eating, Christ, she's breathing! I want her arrested and put away!"

Mrs. Fields began to weep. Her husband pulled out a handkerchief and handed it to her.

Looking at Mrs. Fields, Detective Kerry saw a fragile lady about sixty-five. Her gray hair pulled back into some kind of French twist. She was well dressed yet not as expensively as her husband. She wasn't tall, but she wouldn't be considered short. She tried to be well poised, speaking not a word. As the tears fell, she gently dabbed the corners of her eyes so as not to disturb her make-up.

"Mr. Fields, I just got your daughter's case a few days ago, and I'm sure once I go through it I'll be able to give you an update. But until then, it's an on-going case, and I can't discuss every detail with you. I just…"

"You will discuss every detail with me. Or I'll…" Mr.

Fields stood. "Or I'll call the mayor and he'll call your captain, then your captain will explain to you…." He pointed his finger at Detective Kerry.

"Mr. Fields." Detective Kerry raised from her chair. "I know my job. I've been here a long time. Many a mayor has come and gone. I'm still here. Make whatever calls you feel you must make. I'll go over the case and I'll be in touch. Is there anything else?" Detective Kerry walked to the door.

"Sit down!" Mr. Fields yelled.

Two detectives came running to the door, but Kerry waved them off.

"Look, I know you're grieving. I'm telling you I know my job. I'm on the case. Go home. Take care of your family. I'll call you as soon as I can. You just buried your daughter, your family needs you. Getting distraught will accomplish nothing."

Mr. Fields was outwardly upset. "The mayor will be getting a call from me and you'll be walking a beat before you ever touch my daughter's case. Come, Martha. We're leaving."

He moved to the door and waited for his wife. As they left, he made sure he slammed the door.

Detective Kerry sat back, and reaching into the side drawer she grabbed a Snickers. Un-wrapping it, she took a deep whiff of the chocolate. "Ah, heavenly."

She was thinking her retirement couldn't come soon enough when the captain walked into her office. "I was just wondering how long it would take you to get in here," Kerry said. "Although, I was hoping it would be after I finished my Snickers. So what's up?"

The captain reached into Kerry's desk drawer and grabbed a Snickers bar for himself. "This Fields character has a lot of pull; he already had the mayor calling here twice. One call was about Willows. The other, complaining about you, just came in; Fields filled the Mayor's ears about you. You really pissed this guy off. He has a lot of connections; he's loaded and has friends on both sides of the track, if you know what I mean. Always gets things done and always gets his way. Just because his little daughter was a queer doesn't mean he won't get her killer before we do."

"Say, Captain, can you get me all the files on this Fields? I'd like to know exactly who I'm dealing with. Make sure you get everything."

"Sure, just tell me we're on top of this case."

"We're working on it. Oh, and Captain," she said. "...one more thing."

"Yeah"

"The word is *lesbian*, not *queer*. Got it?"

"Sure Bobbie, I got it, but you better bring in that bitch Reed and make a solid case against her before he takes matters into his own hands. I've heard he knows how and where to hide the bodies."

"Got it! And Captain, I brought in my old partner, Graham, as an independent private investigator to help me with this. I'm sure the city can afford it, and the mayor wants all the help he can get on this case. I don't want this case swept under the rug just because Fields hates lesbians and believes Reed did it. The evidence isn't overwhelming here."

The captain laughed. "Who do you think really helped fast forward Graham's license, which you signed illegally, by the way?" The captain left waving and smiling.

Kerry began looking for the case files. The clutter made her laugh as she tossed a few more files to the floor. Finding a hostess cupcake, she checked the expiration date. Then finding Emily's file, she poured a cup of coffee, shut the office door and sat back. She picked up her glasses, took a bite of the cupcake, and began reading.

Chapter 5

Nancy Hargraves was a woman that any coach would want on their basketball team. She was tall enough to slam-dunk with the best. Nancy always wore a baseball cap, jeans and tees. Her hair was brown with gray streaks beginning to show. She worked as a foreman in a plastics company that produced PVC pipe. Nancy's favorite pastime was smoking weed. She had no partner at the time and only blamed herself for that; as she always acknowledged, she was too damn independent. She owned her own home and drove, what the guys at work called a girly truck. Her house was a two bedroom ranch, white with black trim and black shudders.

Most of the women had gathered in Nancy's living room near the fireplace. It was conveniently large with a bay window seat that had cushions covered in exotic colors. The walls were painted in pastels, with several five-by-nine framed pictures of Boston in its early days, showing the old mills. The far wall in the living room had a huge fireplace and on the mantel sat several female figurines. The furniture was large and comfy.

The topic of conversation centered on the incident that took place between Carla and Emily's father. There were sodas, tea, and coffee set out on the dining room table along with finger sandwiches and a variety of cookies.

Nancy left the women and went into the kitchen looking for

Carla. Nancy's kitchen looked like a sanitized operating room. Every piece of equipment was modern stainless steel without a speck of grease or dust, yet every piece had a purpose and was used. The appliances weren't just set out for looks or used only on special occasions.

Her kitchen could have come out of one of those Good Housekeeping magazines. Her coffee maker did everything but bring you the coffee. The cabinets were all handmade, each with a built-in lazy susan. The kitchen table could easily sit eight. Her stove was a combo of two ovens plus burners. She had two dishwashers. Her pots hung from a stainless steel rack. Many of her friends wondered who Nancy cooked for.

The French doors leading from the kitchen led out to a huge deck. The deck had a large grill, a round table with a colorful umbrella and several chairs.

Nancy spotted Carla leaning on the rail. She slipped out hoping no one would see her and approached Carla carefully, placing her arm around her shoulder. Carla shrugged pulling away.

"Sorry about Emily. It must be hard on you. Ten years is a long time and to lose her in such a brutal way."

Carla clutched the rail and began pulling at it as if to pull it out. "Everyone thinks I did it…that I killed her, especially her asshole father."

"So what? You know you didn't. All your friends know you didn't. You'll get through this. Time will pass, the law will do their job and the killer will be found."

"Her father's out to get me. He doesn't care if I'm innocent. He has a lot of power and money. He'll dig into my past; he'll ruin my business. It's going to get messy."

"You've been through tougher times," Nancy said.

"You know what I mean. He'll come after me. I know it; I feel it, he's determined to get me. I know his kind; hateful, evil bastard. Gets what he wants."

"Just come in and speak to your friends. They're all inside waiting for you."

Nancy left, leaving the door ajar for her.

Looking out across the skyline Carla watched the gray clouds drifting in and the sky begin to darken.

"Damn clouds…always seem to be hanging over me," Carla whispered.

She took several deep breaths and entered the house. Jackie and Terri caught her in the kitchen, each giving her hugs and telling her they believed everything would be okay. Carla hated hugs, cringing every time. Jan and Stacy met Carla in the hallway shaking hands and giving their condolences. In the living room, Joanne and Darcie were standing by the fireplace.

"Carla," Joanne yelled. "I'm so sorry; Emily was the greatest, so full of life and her passion for art. Oh, it's so sad."

Carla acknowledged Joanne by nodding at her.

Joanne took Carla's hand. "Are you still planning on

opening up tomorrow?'

Carla pulled her hand away. "Of course I am! No reason not to. I've got customers who expect me to be open every day."

Darcie moved toward Carla. "I'm sure they would understand. After all, you just lost your partner."

Carla became infuriated. "People don't give a shit! They hate changing their routines. I need to open. I will be open; otherwise they'll find someplace else to go. I know people. They have no loyalty."

The women heard Carla's outburst, many indicated agreement, while most tried to ignore her anger. Carla noticed the reactions from the women and pulled herself together.

"Look, all of you, I appreciate your coming. I'm not usually the type to care what people think. I know everyone of you is…was Emily's friend. So I thank you. I'm going to open the gym this week. It's my livelihood and anyone who thinks that's wrong, well, personally, I don't give a sh…"

Nancy stepped forward. "Everyone understands, Carla. We all deal with grief and pain in our own way. Let's all toast Emily's farewell." Nancy raised her glass.

Carla grabbed her jacket. "I'm leaving. Have all the drinks you want to Emily, she's gone. I'm gone." Carla slammed the door as she left.

Joanne stepped forward and went to the closet to get her and Darcie's coats. "I think we'll head out, too. There's nothing else we can do now. Maybe we'll see everyone at the dance next week." She helped Darcie with her coat, then taking Darcie's hand, they left.

      Nancy finished her drink, shook everyone's hand, and thanked them as they left. After the house emptied, she pulled the rocking chair in front of the fireplace. She sat down and reached for a throw pillow, hugging it close to her bosom as she began to cry uncontrollably.

Chapter 6

I arrived at my office and was trying to get all of my notes in order and remember all the little details. I took short notes, many made no sense. My handwriting was unreadable; most of it turned into scribble. I had been in a hurry and assumed I would remember what I had written and what it meant when I was reviewing it. I'm now making a note to get a tape recorder, which, if I can remember to bring with me on my field trips, would be quite helpful.

I made notes on the strange dynamics of the Fields family. It was obvious that the father ruled the house with intimidation, followed by the oldest daughter, Ellen Kipfer. I was curious why Lori Fields had no work record. I made notes to double check on her and find out where she lived. I was assuming it was with her parents.

I made a few calls trying to set up an appointment with Ellen Kipfer, but she managed to avoid all my calls, and I received no appointment for this week. Hey, I'm patient, to a degree. I also made several notes to find information on their father. I wanted to know his story, how he made his money, and how he spent it. I've learned through the years, that it's how people spend their money that will tell you the most about their character.

I reviewed the list of things I had, giving me some information on the women who attended the funeral. Bobbie had run the names through AFIS (which is not an easy task without a good reason) to see what came up.

I needed to find the most talkative link in the group and work from there. I looked the list over again. Sometimes, I believe if I stare at something long enough, a name will jump out at me and bingo! I will know who the killer is, but, of course, we know that only works with J. B. Fletcher in *Murder She Wrote*.

The first woman on my list was Beth Winslow, age 51. She owned her own home and was self employed as a real estate agent. She obviously liked animals as she was an 'Animal Rights Organizational Member.' The city gave her a special temporary kennel license so she could keep the animals at her house until homes were found for them. She wasn't partnered with anyone at this time.

Second on my list was a Nancy Hargraves. She was 49, and worked as a foreman in a plastics company. She owned her own house, where the reception was held, so I assumed she knew most of these women really well. (Later, I learned I was wrong.) Another note, check on Nancy's work schedule. Nancy also had no partner.

Next was a couple who had been together four years. Jackie Steiner was 52. She was a bartender, an average-looking lady. Her partner, Terri Brill, taught dance and wore clothes that showed off her body. Jackie didn't seem to be the jealous type. I wrote the words 'stable relationship' next to their names. They lived over the bar that Jackie owned.

Following them was Jan Brown, 55, and Stacy Cordele, 56.

They have been together for five years. Jan was a small woman with a tiny build. She was a retired manager for the phone company. She had dark hair, was a sharp dresser and, I noticed, had a blue-tooth phone attachment in her ear the entire time of the funeral. Stacy was a little heavier than Jan with blonde hair and graying highlights. She was the Director of Disabilities at a local college. They shared a condo.

Suddenly I realized how little I knew about these women and how much Bobbie had not found out.

The last couple on the list was Joanne Adler, 45, and her girlfriend. My guess was Joanne had had a lot of surgery to keep herself in the shape she thought she should be in and the looks she believed everyone should see. Her self imagine must be way up there and her plastic surgeon must own a new home by now. Her business was a beauty salon and I'm sure she convinced everyone she looks the way she does because of her business. She's in a new relationship with Darcie Chambers, 38. Darcie's hair was already graying, and she looked about 180 pounds. I couldn't find very much about her. She had worked as a medical transcriber.

That was my incomplete list. Of course Carla Reed would have to go to the top of it. Just because Bobbie thinks Carla might be getting railroaded doesn't mean she didn't kill Emily Fields. Carla Reed was a tough one to guess about. She was 48 with a muscular body. She had short hair and owned her own business - a 'by invitation only' women's body-building gym. She had very rich clientele. I was going to wait for her record, if she had one, but my guess was she had one all right, maybe only as a teen, but I was sure she had one. She had been partnered with Emily Fields for ten years.

It was amazing: nothing and no one jumped out from my notes and said, "I did it."

I stopped and checked the time. I had to cook tonight. Guess I needed to get started. I left my notes out, as I usually do, in case I remembered something or noticed something I missed earlier.

Chapter 7

Carla stood looking at herself in the full-length mirror. Her tight muscular body, short hair and brown eyes glistened in the dim light of the locker room. She stood there talking to herself. "No matter what Emily's family thinks, I'm still my own woman. I own my own business, a lucrative one at that, and it's the largest and most modern gym for women in the northeast. I'm in demand. Women come from all corners of the state while others travel long distances for weekend specials that they can't resist. I have the best equipment and trainers available."

She took a deep breath. "I deserve all this. I've worked hard and long to earn every penny I banked and no one, NO ONE, is going to shut me down or keep me from the money and the prestige that I've fought so hard for. I've built all this. Hell, I'm at the top of my game, and I'm staying on top no matter what. Okay, Emily was murdered and I'm their number one suspect, but they have no evidence. They have nothing…nothing on me! My teen records are sealed; my phony IDs worked before. Nothing can be found, to hell with everyone." She ran her fingers through her hair, shook her head and took several more deep breaths.

Turning sideways she took one last look, then, slapping her thigh, she headed out to the gym for her workout.

Carla inspected her gym. She was tense, lost, angry, and confused all at the same time. She walked past the mats and through the weight room to the bags. Her plan was to lift weights but the anger building in her was too much. She stopped at the punching bag. She studied the knots in it.

Finding and donning her old training gloves that she had used as a teen, she gave the bag a thump. She stepped back and began to pummel the bag, slowly at first, building a rhythm with each movement of her arms. Her punching became stronger and faster. Her heart beat and the blows were becoming one. The forced wind of her punches sent her mind into the past.

The neighborhood was poor and run-down; many of the houses had no windows and others were boarded with cardboard or plywood. Only the numbers on the door provided proof that the houses were different. Despite the looks of the neighborhood, it was a tight-knit family block. Everyone knew their next door neighbor and few, if any, secrets were kept hidden. Some talked about finding a better life and leaving the neighborhood, but few, if any, ever left the corner.

The boys believed playing pro sports or joining a gang was all that could save them. Obviously, school was not an option. Getting out of the neighborhood or moving uptown was a dream for most and would be difficult, if at all possible. When not congregating on the streets, some of the boys were allowed to work out in a small gym. It was owned by the local mob and was often called the 'alley of hope' by the boys. There, they boxed under the watchful eye of Geno, an old mob family member, when he wasn't passed out in his office. Every night Carla would sneak into the gym and watch. She wanted to be part of the gang; not a girlfriend, but one of the fighters.

One evening, she found the strength to ask the boys if she could fight. They huddled together and then called her into the ring. Her heart was beating so fast, and the butterflies in her stomach made her feel like she was going to heave. Carla thought she wouldn't make it to the ring but she found her inner strength and walked toward them. Holding her head high and filled with pride, she entered the ring.

Her dream was coming true…at last she was going to belong. She was going to be one of the gang, one of 'them'. The boys surrounded her, then, slowly circling her, they began to laugh. The biggest boy started calling her names and the rest followed. Then they began throwing their boxing gloves at her head, over and over, the name-calling never stopped. Then they jumped out of the ring, yelling "Slut, bitch," and ran out the door.

She stood in the middle of the ring for several minutes. Blood dripped from her nose. Carla picked up a pair of training gloves that were at her feet and ran home.

Rushing through the front door, she bumped into her father. He was a tall, strapping man, and she barely came up to his belt buckle. She stopped with a thud and looked up to see her father gazing down at her. He asked what happened and why the tears but he never asked about the blood from her nose that had stained her favorite sweater. Carla told her story through tears and sniffling, how she had found a way into the gym. Then she recounted how the boys teased and threw things at her while they kept her in the middle of the ring. Carla's father never interrupted and let her finish telling her story. When she was through with her story, she, for the first time in years, wrapped her arms around his waist. Her father took the gloves from her, pulled them on, and in an instant, hit her in the jaw, knocking her to the floor. He looked at her scornfully and laughed, calling her a cry-baby then telling her she would never be one of the boys. She was a girl and she'd better understand exactly what that meant. He returned to his chair at the kitchen table and continued drinking.

Carla's life changed forever that evening. She got up, went to her room, packed a few things in a pillow case, and crawled out the window, never looking back.

She moved onto the streets, hung out with the toughest she could find, and learned to survive from the strongest. Carla found out just how hard life could be. The cost of staying alive had almost been unbearable. But…Carla was tough. She lost herself on the streets, and she found a way to live with herself. She never asked for anything from anyone, she simply took what she wanted and gave nothing in return.

Over time, Carla grew. She became strong, both physically and mentally, and she threw all her emotions away knowing they only caused heartache and confusion. She learned to fight, to trust no one, and to use everyone. She started believing in herself and knew she would one day leave this neighborhood. One by one she tracked down the boys that had laughed at her in the ring and beat them mercilessly, always in an alley, and with any weapon she could find. After all, she could never be one of the boys, so fuck 'em.

She used men for one thing only -- survival. She learned how to compete and how to make money. She hated men, all men, and swore one day she would open her own gym, and no man would ever walk through her doors. Carla decided to focus on a career as a kick boxer, knowing one big win would give her the money she needed to get out of the slums.

Carla's mind came back to the present, but she kept hitting the bag as the tension slowly left her body. Straight shots to the bag a quick double shot and a kick to the bag, then a spin with a back fist, hitting the bag at a high speed. A left then a right, the rhythm and her memories returned.

Carla's dream of becoming the kick boxing champ ended in her first year of competition. She was scheduled to fight for the title when four men jumped her near the ring and shattered her knee. Her manager dropped her and took all her money, leaving her with broken dreams and nothing else. Then, to everyone's astonishment, two years later, Carla had the money to open her gym. She was determined to have the best equipment that money could buy, and only women were allowed to be members.

Carla missed a jab and the bag swung back and hit her

square in the chest. She gasped then laughed. Laughing reminded her of Emily. She recalled the first day she saw Emily walk through the doors of her gym. She was at the front desk talking to Roberta when this small woman in a flowered dress walked in. She had a round face, big blue eyes, and hippy braids that swayed as she walked. Carla took to her immediately and asked for a date that afternoon. Within a month Emily had moved in with Carla.

Carla returned to the bag, her punches coming harder and harder, her fists flying as the sweat began to pour. Her toned body was glistening as she continued to pound the bag.

"Damn!" Carla yelled out loud.

As if a bolt of lightning had struck her, Carla dredged up the day that Emily brought home a print by Salvador Dali. She was singing and smiling, something Carla knew she had done very little of lately. The print was titled *Meditative Rose*. And after its arrival Carla noticed a significant change in Emily. She became giddy, she seemed almost too happy. She had the picture framed and placed over their bed. A change in their relationship soon followed, but Carla wasn't ready to ask why, although she could tell Emily was acting colder toward her. Each night, however, Emily dusted the print, before she went to bed.

As Carla hit the bag, she began to think more and more about the print and wondered where it came from. She also wanted to know where the second red rose on Emily's casket had come from. Jackie had handed out all white roses and only had one red rose, which Jackie had given to her. The parents had had flowers delivered, as well as a large spray of spring flowers that lay on top of the casket. She couldn't remember seeing any other red roses or anyone who would have brought one.

Carla's thoughts began to run out of control. She realized that when the cops had arrived at the house, Emily had been found lying in the bedroom doorway, stretched out, blood dripping from her hand which was outstretched toward the bed. Or, was it the picture she had been pointing to? Carla shook her head. "Get a grip," she whispered to herself. "You're thinking too much. She couldn't be pointing."

Carla heard the front gym door open and flinched when she felt the cool breeze run through the openness of the room. She headed to the front desk.

"I'm not open for another half hour," she was yelling as she walked to the front entrance.

"It's just me, Carla," Beth said, as she walked toward her. Her arms were already outstretched looking for a hug. "How are you feeling?" she asked, as she wrapped her arms around Carla.

"Fine," Carla said, as she backed away from Beth. "I'm all sweaty from working out. What's up? Is something wrong?"

"No, nothing at all. I just wanted to check on you. I was showing a house not far from here and noticed your lights were on, so I checked and the door was unlocked. I thought I'd drop by and see how you were feeling."

"I'm feeling fine. I just want to open up, get back to work, and get all these asshole cops off my back."

Surprised, Beth asked, "Have they been bothering you?"

"Yes they're bothering me! It's been over a week, nearly two, and I still can't get into my own house."

"It's still a crime scene then," Beth whispered

"Well…it's still my house and I want it back. I have things in there I need, and I'm tired of sleeping here at the gym. I want my house back."

"You have a small apartment upstairs; you should be comfy." Beth waved her hands around the large space they were standing in.

"Is that so?" Carla roared. "This is my gym, my office, and my private apartment. I want my house back! My house! Not theirs, not Emily's, mine!" Wrenching off the gloves, she threw them onto the desk. "It's my damn house!" She turned. "And that's that. What do you want Beth?"

"Nothing, I just wanted to say hi and check on you."

"Well, as you can see, I'm fine. I'm going to take a shower. I'll see you later."

Beth stood silently at the desk, watching Carla walk away. Quietly, she reached for Carla's gloves. Pulling them close to her chest, she brought them toward her nose. Closing her eyes, she took a deep breath, and inhaled the smells of the leather and the sweat. Taking her scarf from her neck, she wiped the sweat off the gloves then laid them carefully back onto the desk. Rubbing her fingers across the gloves lightly, she turned and left the building.

Chapter 8

Jackie grew up in a place of safety, with people who accepted her for the person she was, and friends who would fight for her every right. She had grown into a woman; a lesbian woman. The neighborhood bar that was her home had survived the horrors of gay-bashing, name-calling, and threats upon women and those who were different. Jackie now owned the Gai Rendezvous, which, years ago, had been called 'the Neighborhood Bar.'

The locals were of all races and both genders, and had made this place their home-away-from-home. Now that Jackie owned the place everyone was still welcome as long as they followed her rule. There was only one: 'respect.'

Years ago, Joe had owned and operated the toughest back alley bar in the Boston area. Sarah was one of the local women who worked evenings from the bar. She was a regular, never missing a night. Joe took an interest in Sarah, as he did all the prostitutes, trying to keep them as safe as possible. Sarah was young and fearless and gave no consideration to Joe's warnings.

One evening, Sarah came back to the bar all battered and bruised. She refused to tell Joe who had done this to her, although Joe had a pretty good idea. He knew of a local detective who constantly harassed the women until he received the sexual favors he demanded. Sarah had been the only hold out. That night, Sarah was raped, and she soon found out that she was pregnant. For some unknown reason, she decided not to abort the baby. Joe feared it was a blackmail scheme and worried for Sarah's life.

While Joe was working one evening, Sarah went into labor. She refused to go to the hospital, so in the back of the bar, in a dark booth, she gave birth to a baby girl. They named her Jackie.

For the next five years, Sarah continued coming to the bar and continued to work. She would leave Jackie with Joe or with one of the other patrons. Jackie would run free, drinking cokes and eating chips while the local patrons watched over her. Each year on Jackie's birthday, Sarah had a standing appointment with the same detective. She always returned waving about extra money. On Jackie's fifth birthday, Sarah didn't return. Her body was found several days later with a bullet in her head.

Joe kept Jackie, and he gave her a home and became her father and caretaker. Everyone helped buy her school clothes and those who could, would sit in the back booth and help her with her homework. They all helped with what knowledge they had, some taught her math, others reading and writing, and still others how to survive each and every day. The men taught her how to play pool, cards, and the language of the streets. The women tried to teach her to dance, to dress up and wear makeup.

When Jackie turned eight, another little girl of almost the same age, began showing up at the bar. She called herself Carla; she was unkempt and living on the streets. Carla would sneak in to use the bathroom and would try to steal potato chips. After a while,

Jackie and Carla became best friends. Joe had his hands full as the kids grew. Carla was always getting into some dilemma and brought Jackie in with her each time. Joe spent many nights trying to talk to Jackie and explain how Carla was nothing but trouble. He said Carla would end up hurting Jackie in the future if Jackie didn't stay away from her. Jackie always told Joe that she would stay away, although she never did. And when she grew older, she finally told Joe she couldn't turn her back on her best friend. Where would she have been if Joe had turned his back on her?

Time passed and Joe stopped trying to keep the two girls apart. He asked an old friend if he would teach Carla how to defend herself when she was alone on the streets, and Joe tried to be a father to both of the girls and to teach them right from wrong. But he always left the final decisions up to them.

While she was in high school, the patrons all took turns going to Jackie's school functions. Upon her graduation, they put enough money together to let her start college. Jackie declined the college money and decided to stay where she grew up, where she felt cared for, and looked after…and where she felt safe.

As she grew older, she wanted to know about her mother's death and kept asking Joe questions. One day, he sat her down and gave her all the details he knew and what he believed had happened to her mother. Joe clarified the fact that no proof was ever found to bring the killer to justice, and that one day her mother's case simply disappeared.

One evening, when the two girls were in their teens, they were sitting at the bar consuming more beer than they could handle. Jackie confided in Carla about what happened to her mother and how everyone believed that a rogue detective had stalked her mother and raped her because she wouldn't do sexual favors for him.

Not long after their conversation, the detective stopped coming around. Later, the police department began coming by, and everyone soon learned that the detective had vanished. Word on the street was that this detective had been black-mailing so many women that the police couldn't keep up with the victims. The police were sure someone killed him, and after a month or so, no one came around and no more questions were asked. Everyone believed that the case had been solved, but the truth was that the case was still open. Jackie never asked or spoke about her mother again.

When Joe died, he left Jackie the bar. As far as Jackie was concerned, her life had begun here and it would end--here. She was content with the way her life was going

Today, when you step into the *Rendezvous,* it's like stepping into the past. Jackie changed very little in the twenty-something years she owned the bar. The same pictures hung on the walls, the pool tables were old, only the felt had been changed. The Tiffany lights still hung over the middle of the pool tables, the wooden racks that held the simple wooden pool sticks still were on the wall, stained and worn with huge half-used spools of chalk next to them.

The same chairs lined the walls, where men had sat watching

the likes of Fats play pool while money bets circled the room. The bar was made of oak, and the stools were still solid. The foot rail was flattened from the many shoes that had rested upon it.

The mirror radiated multi-colored lights through the different liquor bottles. The cracks in the mirror flowed from the time a stray bullet from a thirty-eight revolver, which was being waved by a drunk and went off and hit the corner. Pictures of baseball players surrounded the mirror, while a Louisville slugger proudly displayed itself over the cash register. The sign below it read *NO FIGHTING*.

There was a small dance floor in the far corner of the room, the floor warped with time. The juke box had music from the fifties and sixties. And, Jackie's favorite country song, number 226, *The Tennessee Waltz* was played so often that it needed to be replaced once a year.

Growing up at the neighborhood bar, she had become part of a family. She melted into the crowd and made *The Rendezvous* one of the best gay and straight bars in the area.

While checking out some local competition, Jackie met her partner of four years. Terri had worked at a local bar across town, waiting tables. Her dream was to teach dancing, a dream which was beginning to come together, for she was teaching part-time Sunday afternoons at the local dance studio. Terri was a scanty dresser, lean in body, and she had a sweet disposition. She had hair the color of chocolate, which matched her deep brown eyes. Jackie told her she had a face like an angel and the body to bring out the devil in everyone. Terri was forty-nine and looked underage. She had the reputation of never dating and never fooling around with the customers.

One day, she left with Jackie, and left everybody at her bar in total shock. No one knew how Jackie became Terri's partner or even how she persuaded Terri to go with her. Rumor had it that Terri made the first move, and Jackie knew a good thing when it slapped her in the face.

The one thing that seems to work for Jackie and Terri was that there was no jealousy between them, even with Jackie's flirting and Terri's dancing. When Jackie asked Terri to live with her, the gang at the bar threw a huge party and accepted Terri into the family as their own.

Chapter 9

It was a busy night and many of the regular customers didn't want to leave. Jackie had a tough time sending them on their way. She was tired, and while washing down the bar, she heard a knock at the door. She whispered, "Shit." She was sure it was Jerry. He was always forgetting something. He was a nice guy who had just lost his wife, and then his job. Drinking was all that was left for him; all he could do was sit on the stool, cry, and drink. Jackie felt bad for him and made sure he got a cab to get home okay.

Tonight, however, she was tired and hoped he had stayed in the cab that she had put him in, and that whoever was at the door would just go away if she ignored the knock. She kept wiping down the bar, but the knocking got louder.

"I'm coming, Jerry!" she yelled. "And I'm going to kill you." She threw the rag down and headed to the door. When she opened it, she stepped back, and her mouth dropped opened.

"Damn," she said.

"Can I come in?"

"Damn," Jackie repeated as she stepped aside to let her visitor in.

The visitor stepped inside and walked to the bar. "The place hasn't changed much."

Jackie closed the door and locked it. "I like it this way. Would you like a drink? I can't remember the last time you were down here to the old neighborhood. What's the occasion?"

"It's nice and cozy, homey."

"I see you're still just as sarcastic as always. So why are you down here? Slumming tonight, are we?"

"I'll have a Crown Royal, neat."

Jackie began laughing. "Damn, Carla, you always did have expensive taste even way back when, when you couldn't afford it. Royal it is."

Carla broke a smile. "Make it a double."

Jackie poured the drink and set the bottle down next to the glass. She then grabbed a couple of bottles of Mic Ultra. She set them on the bar and walked around, taking a seat next to Carla. Taking hold of the beer she twisted off the cap and took a healthy mouthful. She rolled the bottle between her palms and glanced over at Carla. "You know, it's been years since you've stepped inside this place. No matter how hard you try to get away from your past, it always seems to catch up and bite you in the ass. Something always draws you back to the beginning, even when you don't want to be home, home you come."

"I'm not back," said Carla as she tossed back the shot.

"Yes you are. You're sitting right on the same stool you sat on years ago. The only difference is you're drinking a whiskey that cost three times what you used to drink. And you know the sad thing about that? Both give you the same end result."

Carla slammed her glass down on the bar. "I'm out of here."

Jackie started laughing. "Who are you kidding? You came down here because you need something."

"Bullshit"

"Look, Carla, it's me. We've been friends since we were, what, eight years old? I know you. Remember? We're attached at the hip no matter how high you climb on that social ladder. So tell me what's wrong. Have another drink and spit it out."

Jackie pushed the bottle toward Carla. Carla poured a double, gulped it down, and poured a third. Jackie opened another beer and waited.

Carla took a deep breath. "I think I'm in big trouble."

"You think!" Jackie threw her arms up into the air.

"Emily's father is out to get me. He said he'd obliterate me one way or another. I think he has the connections to do it."

"Why? Have you given him cause to?"

"He believes everything Emily has told him about me. And now he thinks I killed her."

"Are you sure she told him everything? You think she told him that you've slapped her and lost your temper a time or two? Don't you think he'd have already come after you if he knew that?"

"Oh yeah, she told him everything. I'd bet the ranch on it. I wasn't the nicest partner. I never told her I trusted her, I never really gave her a chance. I certainly hadn't told her I loved her in years. God forbid I should say such a thing…fucking sign of weakness."

"Did she do something to make you distrust her? Or maybe

you just couldn't trust anyone. What?"

"I don't really know what happened. I just did what I always do; it was me being me, you know. It just didn't turn out to be the right thing."

"So she told her father you were an ass and that you hit her, right?"

"I'd say that and more," Carla reached for her glass

"And what else? This is no time to hold back."

"Like I said, now he thinks I killed her." Carla finished off the drink almost choking as she swallowed.

"Does he think he has any evidence or is this just assumption on his part? Maybe it's the fact that he just hates lesbians and assholes that steal his daughter away and then mistreat her and show no trust in her?"

"He thinks that for all those reasons…and probably more," Carla said calmly.

Jackie set her beer down and spun the stool around to face Carla. "You and I share a lot of secrets, my friend. So, I have to ask: Did you kill her?"

Chapter 10

The water was boiling and, as usual, I was still rummaging through the freezer looking for the raviolis. I never understood why someone couldn't come up with a better designed freezer. Why do things just get piled on top of other things, then it freezes, then you have to dig, shuffle, and pull them apart until you find what you're looking for, then you have to put everything back into the freezer that you moved out in the first place?

I hate to cook! Yes, I can do it, but it's such a hassle. You always have to have all the right spices, pots, and ingredients -- you know, all those things you never have around the kitchen. When you live alone, you find it's easier to bring something home or dine out. Yet Bobbie likes home cooking, so here I am trying to find the raviolis and hoping I have sauce in the cabinet.

I ended up adding more water to the pot after putting everything back into the freezer. I was about to warm the bread when I checked the time. It was 6:30 p.m., the time we agreed to have dinner. Well, Bobbie had never been on time in her life, and I am sure she will find a reason to be late to her own funeral. So I decided to wait another half hour. Sure enough, a little after 7:00 p.m. the door bell rang and I let Bobbie in.

"Am I late? Everything sure smells good."

I laughed. "Of course you're late, but I'm glad. I had trouble finding the raviolis. Damn freezers."

Bobbie went to the refrigerator and pulled out two beers, setting them on the table.

"Did you bring the files? I have a few questions that have been nagging at me."

"I have some of the files," said Bobbie. "Not everything has come in yet. I'm guessing not everyone was born and raised here, so it may take a few days to get everything. Computers are only as fast as the people who put the information into it. Speaking about computers, you remember Callie?"

"Is that the blonde with straight hair, about 5'5"? The one who is the movie trivia buff? I think she wears black rimmed glasses. She used to work for the department before she became a private investigator. What about her?"

"That's the one. The department won't use her for research or background checks anymore. She decided to help out her friend Suzanne with a problem, not department related, while she was on department time. Suzanne asked her to find some information about someone who she didn't care for and instead of checking Suzanne's reasoning and facts as to why she wanted this info, Callie just ran the name she was given and ended up running the wrong name. All the information that Suzanne received and used was destructive to that individual. The problem was that the information was completely unfounded and untrue even though the rumors were already spread about."

"Some friend Callie has there. Sounds like a few laws were

broken."

"Actually, what she did was border-line illegal, but even more, it was unethical. However, lucky for her, no charges were brought."

"Fine, then we won't use her. I have a friend who can get us the information we need quicker than waiting for some clerk to dig it up. Do you remember Annie?"

"You mean the cute one who drives the new Lexus?" Bobbie blushed.

"Yes. She's gone out on her own, doing technical writing and research. I talked to her the other day and she said she'd welcome any extra work I have, any typing or any computer research I might need. She has a good, ethical work code. And Bobbie…she's too young for you," I said as I smiled at Bobbie, who was still flushed.

"Great, let's eat. I'll set the table. You get the bread out of the oven. I'm hungry." Of course she was.

We sat and had what my friends always called comfort food. Our conversation was light and full of laughter. Just as we finished eating, Bobbie leaned on her forearms and tilted her head, staring at me.

"What?" I asked.

"So how are you doing?"

"I'm fine. I've just begun this case and it's a lot to think about. You know, getting back into the swing of things."

"That's not what I'm asking about and you know it. It's been nine months since you left Elizabeth. How're you handling it?"

Bobbie was always a great one to ask how I was doing. She had that sixth sense that psychics use.

I had left Elizabeth without ever giving her a reason. I just got up one morning and walked out. I never gave thought to how she would feel or how I would feel once I closed that front door.

She was the one I had intended to spend the rest of my life with, and I had never had any doubts about that. I wasn't ready to tell Bobbie why I left. I was still in too much pain. I wasn't ready to let my heart bleed on someone else. I avoided her questions by picking up my plate. "Come on, let's clean up the table and get some work done."

Bobbie was also very good at not pushing when she knew I wasn't about to be pushed into a conversation. We began clearing the table when Bobbie went to the sink and asked, "Hey, Paula, what is it about you? How come you never empty the drain basket? Is it something you're afraid of?"

It made me laugh, causing tears to well up. It was something I continuously forgot to do. "Just leave the dishes on the counter, I'll wash them later. Grab a couple of beers and the files. Let's get some work done before you need a nap."

"Hey, wait a minute. What about dessert?"

Chapter 11

Together we spread the files that were available to us on the kitchen table. We didn't speak for a while. I believe Bobbie was giving me the chance to get my head and feelings back into reality and into this case. I went to the fridge and retrieved two more beers. I twisted the caps from both and handed Bobbie hers.

"All right, let's get down to business. I need to make a plan and see if we can find a motive as to why Emily was murdered."

"Jealousy jumps out. It's always jealousy, just wait and see," Bobbie said. She reached for the folder on Carla Reed. "This woman has opportunity and I'm betting motive. Here's what I have so far, and this is probably why the department thinks she's the one who killed Emily."

Bobbie took a swig from the bottle of beer then went to the cabinet and retrieved a bag of chips. Sitting back down, she grabbed a handful of chips and shoved them into her mouth, spilling several pieces onto her sweatshirt. She unconsciously wiped them away. I sat back, lit a cigarette, and waited for her to stop chewing and tell me about Carla.

"I had a friend pull her Juvenile record. She certainly was a troubled kid; she spent most of her teens either in Juvie Hall or on the streets. We could take most of the night just going over this record."

"I want to know everything about her, right down to her shoe size. If she did kill Emily, I don't want her walking. And if she didn't, I want the proof to clear her. Otherwise, Mr. Fields will never believe she's innocent. So let's take this report apart and see what makes Carla Reed tick."

We began by separating the charges by her age. She was on the streets very young, according to the report that her father had filed. She ran away one evening and couldn't be found. He gave no reason, except that 'trouble was all she was' summed up his statement. When she was picked up, her father let Family and Children's Services take her. He stated he had washed his hands of her a long time ago. I wondered what kind of a father washed his hands of an eight year old. I made a note to see if Carla's father was still living. For my own knowledge, I wanted to see what type of man he was, and what had happened to Carla's mother.

Carla's record began at ten years of age; she was picked up several times for shop-lifting at a nearby grocery store. By the time she was twelve, she was running a shell game on the corner. She was picked up for truancy several times and quit school at sixteen.

From the age of sixteen, her record became more violent. I figured she must have had a tough time keeping drunks and other creeps off of her. The report claimed that she was known for brandishing a knife and had stabbed a man when she was seventeen. The charges were dropped by the victim. Reading between the lines here, I guessed it was a john and he didn't want his wife knowing what happened during his so-called business trips to the city.

Carla spent almost one year in Juvenile Hall for a credit card scam and was released on her eighteenth birthday. For the next few years she was in and out of the county jails, mostly for drunk, disorderly and assault.

In Florida, under the Baker Act, Carla had been placed into a hospital for psychiatric observation for seventy-two hours.

"Bobbie, is there any paper work on the hospital Carla was admitted to or why she was admitted?"

Bobbie looked through the folder and found nothing on her admittance to the psychiatric ward. I made a note to call the hospital and ask why she had been admitted. I assumed this was one of the reasons the department felt she was guilty of Emily's murder. They obviously knew something I didn't, and they were hiding it. I knew their next step would be to pick Carla up and charge her. I wondered why they hadn't done that already. I made a note to call my friend Kathy in the DA's office, to see if she could tell me what was going on and when they planned on charging Carla.

"You know, Bobbie, it seems that a lot of Carla's folder has been guardedly left out, and we're being sent on a wild goose chase." I threw the folder on the table. I hate it when the department chooses what to share. It's like working in the dark.

They used to do this when I worked with them. Politics, they would say, simply politics. They had already made up their minds about Carla and just like Bobbie said, they weren't looking for anyone else. The case might as well be closed.

"Bobbie, here's what I want you to do. Check on the whereabouts of the rest of Carla Reeds' folders."

Bobbie was smiling from ear to ear.

"Okay, now what?" I said, having a seat.

"Oh. Nothing I'm just glad to see you so interested in something again."

"Don't go there, Bobbie. Just find the rest of Carla's folders. I'll start my interviews tomorrow and we'll talk over the phone soon."

"What, no dinner tomorrow?"

"No! You're on your own for a while. I've got work to do."

Bobbie stood, stretched, and came over for a hug. Why everyone thinks they have to hug at every occasion, I'll never understand. I must be a little like Carla. What's with all the hugs? Yet I gave her a hug, patting her back at the same time. Then I thanked her for all the work she had already done.

She was right. I was on my way and I was a little excited to be working again. Bobbie grabbed the chips and went to the door. As I opened it, she turned to me.

"We should talk about Elizabeth soon."

"No we shouldn't. Good night, Bobbie!" I gave her a push and closed the door, leaning my head against the frame. I began gently tapping my forehead against the wooden frame, over and over.

Chapter 12

It had taken two days to get my appointments set up. I was in my office at the antique shop, trying to remember what to bring to my first interview, and even scarier, trying to decide what to wear.

The first person I would meet with was Jan Brown, and the only place she'd meet with me was at the dance held by a local women's group. She wanted her partner, Stacy Cordele, with her, claiming that this would be a good time for me to meet both of them.

Great! I didn't think it would be a good time for me, but I had no choice in the matter if I wanted to talk to either one of them. I grabbed my recorder, then put it back down and grabbed a small notebook. The noise at the dance would make it impossible to tape a conversation. I would have to rely on my note-taking and my own ears. Plus, I had forgotten to buy batteries.

My next step was to decide what to wear. A sweatshirt probably wouldn't work. I decided on black pants and a white shirt; I also threw on a vest. I wanted pockets for my pens. I hadn't been to a dance in almost a year and I was nervous.

I told myself to pull it together; it was business. Pay attention to why you are going. I reviewed what I knew about Jan Brown. She was fifty-five with dark brown shoulder length hair. She had a small build. I noticed at the funeral that she wore very sporty clothes. She worked for the phone company and had taken an early retirement. I didn't know why. Jan Brown has been with her partner for five years and they owned a condo together. They traveled extensively throughout the summer. I had a note in the margin 'Played poker in their home once a month.'

This is why I take notes. I have no idea how I knew this, which means I must have heard someone mention it on the day of the funeral. I tossed Jan Brown's folder and picked up Stacy Cordele's.

Stacy Cordele was fifty-six and had blondish hair with gray highlights. She had a medium build. She worked for a local college, helping anyone with disabilities get housing and class access, or anything else disabled students needed. The background history I had showed that she had been married, and that her husband had died after a lengthy illness.

I had made a note in the margin that she had been very attentive to her partner at the funeral. I could tell it was love, and being close seemed to come easy for her. It was nice. Their relationship was both open and confident.

On the drive to the dance, I played some of my favorite country music. Music always helped me relax.

The parking lot was full. Several women were standing near the door having their last cigarette before entering the dance hall. I thought maybe I should go back to the car and have one myself, which is exactly what I did. Several minutes later, I entered the dance. I was asked if I was a card carrying member of the group. I could have saved two bucks if I was. I wasn't and paid the twelve dollars it cost to enter.

The lights were low with a soft yellow glow that shadowed the dance floor. Several round tables with checkered table clothes and candle centerpieces filled half the room, while at the far end was the dance floor, and then past the floor stood the DJ behind her music set-up. To the left of the dance floor was a small bar.

The music was loud, and the dance floor full. I inspected the room and couldn't find Jan Brown or her partner, so I headed to the bar and ordered a double CC. While leaning against the bar, I spotted Jan and her partner dancing. I made the decision to wait until they sat down, then I'd find my way through the crowd and introduce myself.

I thought I recognized a couple of the women from my past, but made no move to bring any attention to myself. Before I was aware of it, the music had stopped and then started to play again. This time it was a waltz by Patsy Cline. I ordered another double and continued watching the women dancing.

I leaned back against the bar and recalled how it was when Elizabeth and I came to a dance. I could see Elizabeth waltzing across the floor. I remembered that when I watched her, I saw no one else. It was as if a spotlight followed her around the floor. Elizabeth moved with the elegance of a ballerina, her feet sliding with grace, her arms outstretched and her head held high. She had a smile that warmed your heart. She never danced the waltz with me, although it could have been because I couldn't dance the waltz, or maybe because I wouldn't let her lead. (Another ego thing I never grew out of, I guess.) But man, could she dance the waltz, and did I love watching her.

Suddenly, someone bumped my arm, and my drink spilled all over me. "Sorry," she said as she moved along.

I shook my head and wiped off my slacks. Grabbing a napkin, I wiped my forehead. The sweat kept building. I headed to the door. I was having trouble breathing. Outside, as I was taking in several deep breaths, a woman tapped my shoulder.

"Excuse me. Are you Paula?"

"Yes. Jan Brown, right? How are you?" I extended my hand.

She took my hand and gave it a solid shake. "We were on the dance floor trying to get your attention, but you seemed to be thinking about something else."

"No, no I was just watching everyone dance. I wanted to wait until you were finished dancing before I interrupted."

Jan started laughing and had trouble stopping. I gave her a strange look. "I'm sorry. You don't understand. When Stacey and I get on the dance floor we never get off until it's time to go home. You would have had a long wait. Why don't we go in and sit? We'll talk. Come on."

I followed her in, putting the dance out of my head and reminding myself once again that this was business. We sat next to the wall. The DJ was on break, so the music from the jukebox wasn't as loud, and I could actually hear the ladies speaking.

She introduced Stacey then asked what I needed to know. I explained how I became involved in the case and how I needed to know everything I could about Emily and Carla and any friends who were close to either of them. They both listened, nodding occasionally.

"Okay, are you ready for some questions?" I asked.

Stacey leaned across the table, so I would have no trouble hearing her. "I would like to see your ID before I'm ready to answer any questions, if you don't mind."

I admired that in her and was glad to show her proper identification.

"How did either of you know Carla and Emily?"

Jan scooted her chair closer. "This is a small community, as you well know, everyone knows a little about everyone else after awhile. It's hard not to, when we all usually go to the same dances and activities that go on in a lesbian group." She continued, "It's hard to go out to any regular activity without bringing attention to oneself, so, yes, we all get to know a little about everyone, as I said. Then we have a tendency to get into our own little cliques. It's not always fair, but that's pretty much what happens. Emily was well-liked, but Carla was strange and stand-offish."

"What do you mean by that?"

Stacy held Jan's hand as she spoke. "She wasn't really what you'd call shy; she just didn't say much and kept to herself. She was always around, more listening than joining in on the conversations. I think she wasn't sure how anyone would take the things she said. Maybe she just wasn't real sure of herself. Or maybe she was the type who liked to take everything in before she decided to be friendly."

"And this caused problems?" I asked.

Stacy thought a moment then said, "Not really. We have this one woman who just can't seem to find anything positive to say about anyone, and after a while, listening to all the negative stuff, some of the other women just didn't have a lot to do with Carla. It's like they were all being safe instead of sorry - that kind of thing. Foolish, yes, but some women don't like change or taking chances. She was an outcast in some ways. It was harder on Emily than Carla. Carla didn't seem to really care. But, then again, I'm not sure if that's really true."

I broke in. "Did something happen to make you think that?"

Stacy replied, "No, nothing specific. It was just a feeling I got when I was around Carla."

Jan leaned forward, and resting her elbows on the table, she said, "I think that's when Carla became extremely jealous of Emily and that began to cause problems among the women. You know, like they wanted Emily to come somewhere with them, but not Carla. After awhile it made it hard for the two of them to socialize. I'm sure it made things difficult between them. Emily liked going out and visiting friends."

I thought about that for awhile. I know how negative talk can affect people when they hear it enough. It never turns out good, not for anyone.

"Do you think Carla had reason to keep Emily on a tight leash?"

Jan thought long and hard before she answered. I began to think she wanted to say something but wasn't sure how to word it, or maybe she didn't want Stacy to know.

She took a drink, then said, "I don't think Emily would have gone through so much loneliness if the group hadn't been so inflexible, and if everyone had at least put on a front when they were together. Carla was controlling. But who knows if things would have been different. Maybe Emily was able to find some other group or outlet. I'm not really sure, and I'd rather not speculate. But, truthfully, I think Emily really loved Carla once."

"I heard Emily had started to go to the museums and art shows, but always alone as far I knew," Stacy said.

Jan raised her hand and pointed her index finger up, as if to make a point. "I thought she went to the museums with Darcie."

"Darcie?"

Stacey was shaking her head. "Darcie and Emily went together years ago, remember? When Emily first came out, she and Darcie were friends, and then Emily brought Darcie out. I think they had gone to school together. They were both just babies and it didn't last long. I recall Emily giving Darcie a locket, remember

Jan? And Darcie never took it off, still wears it today as far as I know. They both went their separate ways, but stayed friends. I think Darcie just happened to be at the museums at the same time Emily was. I think Darcie was either into painting or liked art, also. I can't really remember which."

My little notebook was getting full, and my head was spinning. How can so much go on in such a small group? It's hard to keep track of what's what. I could see they wanted to get back onto the dance floor, and I had had enough of the music for one evening. I asked if we could continue this at another time, or if they thought of anything else that pertained to the case to please call me. I gave them my card and watched them return to the dance floor.

I walked to the door, stopped, and turned to look at the dance floor one more time. I imagined Elizabeth and myself waltzing across the floor. After a few moments, I shook it off and headed to my car. The drive home was quiet. I had enough information to process without thinking about music, dancing, and Elizabeth.

Chapter 13

Bobbie grabbed the bag of Snickers, looking at it several times. Something was different with this bag. Finally, she realized that they were the miniature bars. "Damn," she whispered.

She ripped the bag open, causing the bars to fly all over the floor. She had to laugh at the sight of tiny chocolate bars flying through the air. Sitting in her chair and pushing it with her feet, she began rolling the chair around the floor, stopping occasionally to pick up a Snickers bar. She spotted several under her desk, and rolled to the opening of the desk. Bending over, she moved the chair into the desk, and there, half under the desk, she remained out of sight, picking up Snicker bars. She started to laugh again, thinking about what anyone would say who happened to enter her office at that moment. Maybe they'd think I was folded over in my chair dead, or after all these years on the force, I finally cracked under the pressure. She couldn't reach the last bar, and, stretching, almost fell out of the chair.

"Detective," an eager voice came from the door.

Bam! Bobbie hit her head trying to get out from under the desk. "Son of a …." She looked up, rubbing the top of her head. "This better be good. You scared the …"

"They just arrested Carla Reed, and she didn't come in easy. She put up one hell of a fight. One of the guys has an abrasion on his neck and the other guy has a scratch down his cheek. She's cussing up a storm, and it took four of our guys to get her into a holding tank."

An hour earlier, Carla Reed had been leaving her gym for the day. Two Detectives and two officers came up to her, identified themselves, and told her they had a warrant for her arrest. They announced that she was under arrest for the murder of Emily Fields.

Carla stared at them and turned to see if any of her clients were watching through the window. She wanted to be as far away from the gym as possible. She started walking away and yelled, "Fuck off!"

One of the detectives ran at Carla and pushed her against the building, while the others surrounded her, to keep her from being a flight risk. Carla's face was pushed against the wall. She began yelling and kept trying to get her balance. She took a deep breath and spun her arm around, fist balled, and struck the detective who was holding her by the neck. She swung on the other detective hitting him square in the jaw. Using her foot, she kicked one of the officers.

The second officer was reaching for his weapon when Carla landed a punch to the side of his head. He fell back against the parked cars; his weapon went sliding to the edge of the sidewalk. By then, the two detectives had her by her arms and wrestled her to the ground. Carla's feet came out from under her and she was dragged, kicking and screaming. They pushed her to the ground, forcing her face into the sidewalk, and slammed her head into a parked car. Two of the officers were sitting on her legs, while the other two detectives cuffed her.

A crowd from the gym had gathered outside, and several were snapping pictures on their cell phones. When one of the officers saw this, he immediately began to push the crowd back, yelling there was nothing to see. Carla started yelling to the crowd that the bastards were trying to kill her and to call the press. After another small scuffle, they picked Carla up, put her back on her feet, and pushed her into the cruiser. As the car door closed, the crowd could hear the officer telling Carla her right to remain silent.

The crowd was yelling about police brutality as they drove Carla away. She kicked and screamed cuss words all the way to the station.

Bobbie got up and headed to the door. Upon arriving in booking, she noticed Carla was still yelling. She was cuffed to a bench in the holding tank. Her hair was untidy and her clothes were torn. Hanging from her arm was her jacket sleeve. Blood flowed from her nose, and her knees were scraped.

Bobbie pulled out her cell phone from her pocket and called for medical help. The officer at the desk looked at Bobbie and shrugged his shoulders. Bobbie turned her back while calling. She returned the phone to her pocket, turned and faced the officer at the desk.

"Why didn't you call for medical help?" she asked

He rolled his eyes. "She refused any kind of help," he said

casually, then returning to his work.

Bobbie retrieved the key and opened the cell. She walked to Carla and pulled a Kleenex from her pocket. She wiped the blood from under Carla's nose.

"You all right?" she asked, throwing the Kleenex away.

Carla took a deep breath. "Do I look okay to you? Those bastards shoved me against the wall right in front of my business…in front of all my clients. My clients! Who the hell do they think they are! I'll kill 'em!"

Bobbie stepped in front of her. "That's enough," she said. "You'll never get out of here talking trash like that."

Carla's eyes darkened. "I'll never get out of here anyway, so who gives a shit? I've already been convicted as far as you people are concerned. So fuck off!"

Bobbie turned and walked away, leaving Carla still ranting and raving. As she was walking down the hall, she bumped into the District Attorney. She thought of talking to him but kept walking, giving only a nod.

Bobbie reached for her cell phone again, thinking there was one more important call that needed to be made.

Chapter 14

Down a flight of stairs from my loft was my antique shop, reaching the landing I stopped. I swiped my fingers across the back of one of the ladder chairs that sat at the bottom of the steps.

Rubbing my fingers across my thumb, I could see the dust that had built up from my neglect. I began to see what a waste this was. I should open the antique shop full time or sell it. It was time to make some hard decisions. The dust had collected on every piece of furniture and art in the store, making the place look dull and gray.

I had opened the shop after Georgia died to give myself something to do rather than sitting and thinking of all the things I didn't do for her, or things I should have done. Our time together had become so easy that I often think we may have missed something important, where we didn't do things together, thinking we had more time.

I sat with her the last twelve hours as she struggled for every breath she took. My hand rested on her heart while I sat helpless next to her. I had no reaction that last night as her last breath slipped across the top of my palm. I sat still, watching the life drain from her body as she fought for that last little bit. Life had come to an end. I didn't know why, and I'm not sure I am supposed to know even today, but it does cross my mind.

I walked slowly through the shop, looking at all the furniture piled in corners and so many paintings leaning against one another next to the wall. I walked to a nicely framed print by Picasso. The dust gave the distorted face a moustache. I couldn't help but smile; it essentially improved the print.

I inhaled as much air as I possibly could, and moved to the far corner of the shop. I opened the closet, fumbling around all the cleaning bottles and cans; I found the can that guaranteed to pick up all the dust. Using one of my old tee shirts, I began dusting everything in sight. I started high on the walls with all the paintings and prints by the great masters. I had to remind myself to keep working, for after each climb down the step stool I would stop and admire the great works.

I could never really draw or paint like I would have liked, so my hobby became collecting art, and over time I had enough stored to start a small shop. I liked the old masters the best. It always appeared to me that they felt their art, and I believed personally that all art should pull some kind of emotion out of people. Picking the paintings I would sell took weeks.

The antique part of the shop came from my past. My great-grandparents were antique dealers. They had had a shop at the North Station in Boston and they traveled extensively across the states, buying antiques. Some summers I traveled with them.

I was day dreaming again, looking at a Monet, when someone knocked on the glass by the door. I turned, startled, and noticed a small woman waving at me. As I walked to the door, I tried to check my memory bank to see if I knew her or recognized her face. Nothing came to mind. As I opened the door to greet her, I secretly hoped she was a stranger.

"Hello, can I help you?" I asked.

"I've been coming by here often, hoping to find you open. I'm looking for a job and I saw your sign in the window weeks ago, but you're never opened. So I was hoping you still needed help. I saw your light on in the back, so I knew someone was around."

"So you think I need help?" I stepped back to let her inside. She walked over to the window and removed the sign 'help wanted' holding it in her hand.

"I see all this beautiful art," she said, pointing to the walls. "All these paintings are just leaning up against the wall. They need care or the paint will turn darker and the work will be ruined."

She walked over to the can of cleaner and picked it up. She held it high and pointed out to me the number of chemicals inside the can and proceeded to tell me the damage it could do to the antique furniture. I actually knew that but hadn't thought about it. All I was thinking about was that the dust bunnies were overtaking the shop.

"Follow me. We'll fill out an application in my office. That is, if I even have applications in my office. What hours can you work? Personally, I'm not always here. I'm a private investigator and sometimes I'm unavailable to whoever works at the shop. I'd need someone who could work on their own with little to no supervision, be on time and maybe work late some nights. They would know how to handle money and keep records. Also when inventory comes in, they would have to make sure everything that comes in is what it says it is."

"Are you trying to scare me away? If you keep talking, it might work." She began to laugh.

"If I re-open the shop, I need to be sure I hire the right person. This shop means a lot to me."

"I have good references. You're welcome to check all of them if you want to." She reached into her pocket book and pulled out a resume and handed it to me.

"I like your style. By the way, what's your name?"

"Oh, sorry, I'm Sheila. It's nice to meet you." She had a smile on her face.

"Okay, we'll give it a try and see how you work out. You can start right away if you're ready."

"I'm hired?" she asked, excitedly.

We settled on an hourly wage she could live with and I could afford to pay. She picked up a clean rag to begin cleaning, when the phone rang. She smiled brightly and answered it.

"Paula's Antiques, may I help you?" She listened intently. Then, as she passed the phone to me, she told me it was a Detective Bobbie Kerry. I took the phone, and as she left the office, she closed the door behind her.

"Who in God's name was that?" said Bobbie.

"It's the new woman I just h….."

"Never mind that now. Have you got your TV on?"

"I don't even have a TV in this office, you know that. What's happening?"

"They arrested Carla Reed in front of her gym and it didn't go well. It's all over the news. A bunch of bystanders took pictures with their cell phones and sent them to channel four. Hell, one of them took a video. It isn't a pretty sight. She's officially been charged with the murder of Emily Fields. Then the DA attached assaulting an officer, resisting arrest, assault and battery, and carrying a concealed weapon, which was a pocket knife. Believe me, they didn't tell the public what it was, just that it was a concealed weapon."

"You've got to be kidding me."

I was shocked. I didn't think the DA would move on Carla Reed with the flimsy evidence they had. I was sure they needed more time to build a better case. "What made them decide to arrest her now? Have they more evidence?"

"I heard through the grapevine that the pressure was on from way up the ladder. That means Mr. Fields got to the Mayor. And he got to the Chief of Police, who moved it on down the ladder to the Captain of Investigations. From him it went to Homicide, then right down to the lowly arresting officers. I went to booking to see Carla. She was pretty beaten up." She let out a sigh into the phone. "So were the four guys who went to pick her up."

"Did she have anything to say?" I wanted to know if she

confessed.

"Oh yeah, plenty of cussing and a lot of name calling, but nothing else."

"Where did they take her?"

"Last place I saw her was in booking. I'll have to check if you're really interested."

"I'll call you later. I'm hiring a woman to work in the store and I want to get her settled and put to work right away." I hung up before Bobbie could ask too many questions that I couldn't answer.

I sat down, making notes. Things were moving faster than I expected. I needed to find out more about the Fields' family and their daughter Emily. Nothing made me more nervous than politics.

I called the morgue and asked if I could drop by for a copy of the autopsy. I had spent many off-duty hours at the morgue, trying to learn what I could about human nature. Nothing teaches you more than learning how and why people kill one another. 'A dead body always tells an interesting story' was the medical examiner's famous line, and Frank Nelson was one of the best medical examiners I knew.

Chapter 15

No matter how many times I've walked down this corridor, I always remember my first time. I was a police academy rookie, and our class was visiting the morgue to watch an autopsy. We had all made jokes about who would pass out first or lose their breakfast. Secretly, though, we were all nervous.

It was a silent walk down the corridor, and upon arriving at the doors, they opened automatically. The stench of raw flesh stopped us in our tracks. The smell was worse than entering a butcher shop in the summer. There were no windows, and half a dozen people were working in the quiet and eerie room. There were several stainless steel tables with bottles of formalin sitting on top. The florescent lights made the floor look dull. There were cabinets to the back of the room with glass doors exposing the cutting tools. They looked like tools used by carpenters. The sinks were polished stainless steel. We had to be told to enter. We were all frozen between the door frame, half inside, half outside, all hoping the door would close with us on the outside.

As we moved to stand around the stainless steel table I noticed it was tilted at an angle and had several round holes in it. This, we were told, was so the fluids would run off. The body had a block under its back to raise it several degrees, also for drainage. As we began observing the autopsy, many of us tried holding our breath or our noses. We were told that putting Vicks under our nose would help a little, but we were not allowed to do this that day. The Medical Examiner wanted us to remember the smell of death. Believe me, once you smell death you never forget it.

The first thing they did was look for trace evidence. This included cutting the body's fingernails and gathering anything on the victim's clothing. His hair was combed in all areas, and his mouth swabbed. A sample of all bodily fluid was taken.

They have several colored vials for each kind of fluid. Each vial was marked and signed. The body was then measured, stripped naked, if any clothing was left after trace was collected, then the technician washed the body. Several of us felt sick and began walking toward the door.

The Medical Examiner laughed, but didn't allow us to leave. He told us this was only the beginning. A couple of the guys sat down putting their heads between their legs. I wanted to, but I was too stubborn for that.

The Medical Examiner waited until the body was clean, then stepped to the table, reminding us to gather closely so we could understand what was happening. I had a front row seat. A "Y" incision was made into the body trunk, and then the skin was peeled back exposing the ribcage and abdomen muscles. The odor was, without a doubt, horrifying, and the stench traveled up through my nose, and I felt the presence of the blood in my head. It was sickening. A couple of my classmates fainted. The technicians waved smelling salts under their noses to revive them so they wouldn't miss anything else.

The bone saw was used to cut and remove the ribcage, and the abdominal muscle was removed, exposing all the remaining organs. Each organ was removed, weighed, and a slice cut out and bagged for future testing. The brain was the last thing to be removed. The scalp was cut at the hairline and pulled back. Then the cranial bone was cut. As the saw cut into the skull, the bone began to singe, leaving a burning smell that was hot and putrid. The brain was placed into a brain bucket with formalin covering it. This, we were told, helped harden the brain in order to be able to handle it more easily because it is generally soft and tears easily. This hardening process could take several days.

The organs were then placed inside the body cavity, sometimes in a garbage bag. The technician then sewed the "Y" incision using a zigzag stitch. Then the body was cleaned once again and placed in a thin paper bag for transport to the funeral parlor.

The Medical Examiner then told us after all the testing was done that a formal report is compiled and then issued with the cause of death.

It took days for the sight of all those organs to leave my head. The smell has never really left. I can smell a dead body within several feet before I ever find it. This never leaves an officer after he has found a body, and some have never been able to work in the field after catching one dead body. They either quit, move to desk duty, or take on traffic control.

I was nearing the door when it opened and Roger Spence came out. I knew him from the time I had been on the force. He was the newest autopsy technician hired by the Chief Examiner. I was pleasantly surprised to see he was still working here.

"Roger, how are you?"

"Detective Graham, it's been a long time since you've been down here. What's up? Working a case?"

"I'm retired from the force and now I'm a private investigator working on the Emily Fields case. Is the Chief in?"

"He is, just go right in. Good to see you again." He took off down the hall. I could tell he had matured in the past year. He was much more confident, and moved around with ease.

But then, I was no longer that same rookie, so I took the jar off the shelf outside the door and put a small amount of Vicks under my nose and entered. The smell was still strong, and the reflex to hold my breath was automatic. I tried to swallow before the bile reached my mouth, knowing it couldn't be done. The chief was standing at the back of the room pulling out the bone saw from the cabinet. I was surely hoping to get out of there before he plugged in that saw. He spotted me crossing the room.

"Paula!" Frank was genuinely glad to see me. He replaced the saw in the cabinet (to my relief) and headed to me, arms open. The hug I received was sincere.

"How are you? I heard you're a detective now. Where are

you living, still over the shop? Is the shop opened? Is…"

I was laughing too hard to try and slow him down. I pushed away from him gently and held up my hand, palm outward. "Whoa! How are you? I'm fine and I am, as you already know, a private investigator. Yes, I still live over the shop and yes, the shop is open for business. I managed to hire a nice woman to work the shop when I'm not available," I answered.

He looked confused as he processed it all, then a huge smile crossed his face. "It's really good to see you. I've been lonesome down here without you popping in and out asking all your questions."

"Well, I'm back and I'm full of questions."

"Great! Let's go to my office and see if I can't answer a few of them for you. Follow me." He took my arm in his and together we headed to his office.

Chapter 16

Chief Frank Nelson's office was just the opposite of Bobbie's. He had shelves that started on the floor and reached to the ceiling on every wall except the one behind his desk. There he had hung his credentials. Each shelf contained hundreds of files arranged by date of death. The files were color-coded to help identify means of death, and another color told him if the case was closed or pending.

Chief Nelson stood straight and tall with a full head of gray hair. His face was worn with heavy bags under his eyes from the long hours he put in. He always wore a freshly starched white shirt with a tie under an equally fresh lab coat. His smile was always genuine, which astonished me because of all the death and human misery he dealt with every day.

"Would you like some coffee?" He was already pouring a second cup.

"Is it still so strong you can stand a spoon in the cup?"

He handed me the coffee and returned to his desk, sitting in one of those new ergo-dynamic chairs.

"It's good to see you," he said.

I took the chair nearest to him. "You said that already, Frank. But it's good to see you, too." I took a sip of coffee and grit my teeth, making a face as the hair stood up on the back of my neck. "Wow! It's stronger than I remembered."

Frank got up and walked to one of the refrigerators and brought me back a diet Pepsi. "I thought maybe you grew up and could handle good coffee by now."

I set the cup on his desk and reached for the Pepsi. "I'm glad you're still here Frank. I know you're a stickler for details. Is there anything you can tell me about the Emily Fields' case?" I popped the top of my Pepsi.

Frank opened the middle drawer of his desk and removed a thick file. He tossed it onto the desk. "Take a look for yourself and tell me what you see. You were always good at spotting abnormalities."

He leaned back in his chair and folded his arms across his chest. This was the way he always sat when I first learned to read his reports as a rookie. He spent hours teaching me what to look for and what to expect from an autopsy report. We became good friends, and I give credit to his teaching, which I believed helped make me a good detective. He always pointed out the oddities in a case, but constantly reminded me to never overlook the obvious as well.

I picked up the file and began reading. It starts with the end. It's an outlined report of what is usually between three to any number of pages. Following the outline, each category was then described in full detail. Emily's murder was brutal. She was bludgeoned to death with an unusually marked, heavy object that had not been found or identified as yet. I began reading the autopsy, which included her name, date of birth, age, sex, the pathologist's name and the title of the doctor (coroner), which was in the upper left hand corner. The right hand corner identified the autopsy number, the date and time of death, the autopsy date and time, and an ID number assigned to the deceased. Then, the final diagnosis was outlined.

1. Craniocerebral injuries
    A. Scalp contusions
    B. Fractures to the right side of the skull
    C. Abrasions to the left side of the skull
    D. Subdural hemorrhage
    E. Five contusions to the temporal lobes
    F. Mark on back of skull (a round circular mark with stone shapes)
2. Broken right cheek
3. Abrasions to the left cheek
4. Bruised left shoulder
5. Broken right shoulder
6. Abrasions to lower back and posterior
7. Shattered right leg

I had to stop. It had been a long time since I had read a report so filled with cruelty. I leaned my head back and closed my eyes. How could anyone do this kind of damage to a living person? This was definitely someone out of control.

I understood why the department believed it was Carla Reeds' work. It had rage and passion written all over it, probably the result of significant jealousy. This kind of crime is usually committed by someone very close to the victim. I closed the file and replaced it on the desk. I picked up my Pepsi and looked at

Frank.

"It never gets any easier. No matter how many of these reports I read or how many dead bodies I see, it just never ends. The brutality that one person can do to another just blows me away. Why and how do they do it?"

Frank leaned forward resting his folded hands on the desk. "If we knew the answer to that, we'd both be out of jobs." He picked up the folder and opened it, passing it back to me and said, "Read the toxicology study."

I read on. The blood alcohol level was negative, but, interestingly, the blood drug screen showed a high level of antidepressants. I flipped through the pages to the blood work. She had high levels of the drug Prozac in her system.

"Was there a prescription for Prozac in her house?" I asked.

Frank shook his head "There's no information that Emily was seeing any doctor or had any prescription. Interesting, isn't it?"

"Very! What else can you tell me?"

"In a nutshell, I'd say someone went into a rage and beat this poor woman to death. She suffered a lot before she died. The first hit knocked her down, then, following the path of these contusions, I'd say she was hit several times above and below the waist. See here?" He pointed to a picture on the autopsy report. "You can tell by the blows that she was on the floor. She must have turned over and began crawling, trying to get away from her assailant. She didn't die until the final crack to the head, and I bet she felt every strike until then. This woman really suffered."

He pushed his chair back, got up, and refilled his coffee cup. I couldn't say anything. I just kept imagining Emily trying to get away. I wondered how she must have suffered knowing that she was going to die, in all probability, at the hands of someone she knew.

Frank walked me to the door. "Thanks Frank," was all I could say.

As I walked down the hall, the stench of the room faded, but I couldn't get rid of the bile that kept creeping up my throat. I used my cell phone to call Bobbie, and we set the time to go through Emily's house for tomorrow at ten sharp.

I had to get home. I longed for the evenings when I could cuddle on the couch and watch TV with my love wrapped safely in my arms. Those days were gone, and I was feeling lonely and cold.

Chapter 17

I woke early after having a restless night. It had been a while since I had worked a case that took so much out of me. On top of that, I was having trouble concentrating on the case. Police officers and detectives die everyday when they are not paying attention. An innocent person could spend a lifetime in prison -- or worse -- a guilty person could walk free. I had to get my head into the case and be sure this is what I wanted to do, or turn it over to someone else and return to selling antiques.

Carla had been arrested and charged. The case was done as far as the department was concerned. Unless she made a confession, it would eventually be up to a jury. In my opinion, Carla had no chance with a jury. She was brash, hotheaded, and would not be easily liked. She had a history of violence, ever since she was twelve, and had spent time in a mental ward when she was younger and had run away to Florida. I thought of taking a trip to Florida but nixed it; too much time had passed and all records would have been destroyed by now.

The other question on my mind was where Carla Reed came up with the money to open her business. The building and everything in it was deeded in Carla's name, and I couldn't find documentation for any loan or debt. I couldn't imagine anyone with her background coming up with the cash she would have needed for the business.

I had Annie run a financial on Carla, and she found almost nothing. I also found out she owned the house that she had lived in with Emily. I kept wondering what I was missing. I couldn't believe the district attorney would file charges without a solid case. I hoped Annie would use her genius with the computer and dig up more info on Carla for me. I made several notes: call the DA's office, and the Registry of Deeds. I kept telling myself notes are good. I just hoped I could remember where I put them after the day was done.

I made an English muffin and grabbed my usual diet Pepsi. I took a long shower and was ready (I hoped) for the day. I called Bobbie around 9:00 a.m., confirming where we were to meet. She told me we would have to hurry. Carla had made bail, and the court released the house as a crime scene, and we would have to beat the police to the house before they remove the crime scene tape. Once it was down, we wouldn't be able to enter without Carla's permission and that, we knew, wasn't going to happen.

I was there exactly at 10:00 a.m., and Bobbie hadn't arrived yet. I stood in the driveway taking in the beauty of the yard. It was immaculate. The shrubs were trimmed, and the edging along the driveway had been done to perfection. I saw no weeds anywhere. There was a two car garage with a breezeway leading to the house. The house was a one story, built in a ranch style. I guessed it had three bedrooms.

Bobbie pulled up to the curb and got out carrying a Dunkin Donut's bag and coffee. I shook my head, and she put the bag back into the car.

I stood in front of the sidewalk and tried to imagine the killer walking up to the door. As I got to the door I noticed the opaque stain-glass panels along the frame. There was a brass knocker and a doorbell. Bobbie waited, sipping her coffee, as I ran a few more theories through my mind.

She then opened the door and waited for me to enter. Facing the door on the wall hung a Monet. It was entitled *Woman with a Parasol*. Its colors were woven together so well that where the color of the grass blended in with her skirt, you were unable to tell where one began and the other ended. It's believed to be a painting of Monet's wife and son.

To the right, sitting in the corner, was an old bamboo umbrella stand filled with antique walking canes. I picked one up and rolled it through my palms. It was a pique cane. At the top was a large ivory knob with silver inlay. Returning it, I moved the canes around. There was an antique Russian cane, 'Cloisonne Enamel', which I recognized, and a scrimshaw cane, both unequaled in beauty and style. There was also a gold quartz cane. I knew of one that had sold for almost fifty thousand dollars at an antique cane auction where they had only expected to get two thousand dollars.

One of my hobbies, besides my antique shop, was traveling to auctions and taking classes about old European art objects and glass. I noticed another cane, often called the 'Black Man' cane. It had a caricature-like face and was often called the working man's cane in its day. There were several others. I made a mental note to check the canes for blood or damage, although I was sure that trace had checked every inch of them or they would never have returned them to the house. There was a short hall leading into the living room.

I had to step back and survey the room. I couldn't believe it; it was like stepping into a museum. Nothing here fit the character of Carla Reed. Nothing like one would have expected from the Carla Reed who was the girl from the streets.

I was curious if these things had belonged to Emily. After all, between the two, she was the art lover. The furniture was modern: a Pablo Hutch entertainment center, a leather convertible sofa and two lounge chaises, one a Solway and the other an Artek. What impressed me the most were all the antique glass statuettes in the cases, and the art that was neatly hung through out the rooms.

Over the fireplace was an incredible Dali. It was called *The Persistence of Memory,* and is one of my favorites. It was painted in 1931. A surrealistic painting, it showed multiple timepieces like watches and clocks bent over different objects and flowed into the earth. I always felt like it was telling me how much time we waste and lose when we get stuck and can't move on, or have unfinished business, or some emotional block that we unwittingly suffer. Other pictures on the walls were by Mondrian, Hals, and Braque. Bobbie gave me a shove and reminded me our time was limited.

I wanted to follow the crime, step by step, using the crime

scene photos, to see if I could picture Emily's last moments. I backed up to the front door. I pulled out the autopsy and crime scene pictures. I asked Bobbie to go through the crime scene report pages as I followed throughout the house. I pictured the door being opened by Emily, since evidently it had not been forced. I assumed it was someone she knew. Maybe she had a smile that slowly changed to fear as she was pushed against the wall. I looked. There was still a blood stain was on the wall.

    A crime scene picture showed the phone had been knocked to the floor in the living room. She must have been hit again when she went for it. A blood stain had expanded in the carpet. If it had been me, and I was able, I would have headed to the bedroom for the second phone and possibly locked the bedroom door.

    According to the pictures, the hall leading to Emily's bedroom was covered with blood spray. I re-read the autopsy report. It showed Emily was hit on the back of her legs and her back and several more times on her shoulders. I assumed she fell here, at the start of the hall, where she was repeatedly hit with some object that was swung by the assailant. She put up a good effort to escape her attacker. Looking back at the pictures, I could follow her efforts down the hallway.

    She had fallen in a few places; the bloody handprints on the wall showed where she tried to get up. The blood splatter leading down the wall showed where she fell or had been knocked down, over and over. Nearing the end of the hall, she had tried to drag herself into the bedroom. One last blow to the head had killed her, but not before she suffered.

I noticed something in the autopsy report that I had missed. On Emily's head was a small round dent with unknown particles that had embedded in her skull.

The last picture showed Emily covered in blood, half of her body over the bedroom threshold. Her arm was stretched out inside the bedroom, her hand reaching toward the bed. This could have been her last ditch effort to pull herself into the bedroom, but I wanted to read more into it. I gazed into the bedroom. I noticed a large print by Dali hanging over the bed. *Meditative Rose.* I knew this picture; it was a red rose floating in midair. I was just stepping into the bedroom when we heard the front door being unlocked.

Before we could turn around to see who was there, Carla stood behind us. "What the fuck are you doing in my house?" Her face was bright red; her fists were clenched.

Bobbie reached for her badge. "This is a crime scene and we're investigating the…"

"Bullshit! You're snooping in my house and you're probably planting evidence against me. Get out!"

I stepped forward and introduced myself. "I'm Paula Graham, and I'm a private investigator trying to find out who killed Emily. If I can I have a few minutes, I have some questions."

Walking past us, Carla grabbed the door knob on the bedroom and slammed the door shut. "Get the fuck out! You probably work for Fields! Get out!" She pointed toward the front door.

I had to get some information, so I didn't move. Bobbie was already headed down the hall.

"Look, I don't work for the Fields family. I want to find the killer. I..."

Carla slammed me into the wall. Her teeth grinding as her strong hands wrapped around my neck. I started to choke.

Just as fast as Carla pushed me into the wall, Bobbie had her gun barrel to the side of Carla's head. "Let her go, now!"

After a few tense moments, Carla dropped her hands. Spinning Carla around, Bobbie put her face into the wall and handcuffed her.

"You must really like jail," Bobbie said. She swung Carla around to face us.

I was still rubbing my neck and trying to swallow without hurting. "I'd like to ask you a few questions," I said.

"Fuck you! Arrest me or let me go! Either way, get the hell out of my house!"

Bobbie asked if I wanted to see the rest of the house before we took Carla in for assault. I did want to see the rest of the house, but decided if I found any evidence it could be considered a result of an illegal search and thrown out. The house had been released to Carla and was no longer a crime scene. I shook my head and told Bobbie to release Carla. I wasn't going to bring charges against her.

Carla was true to her colors and cussed us all the way to the front door. Obviously, jail didn't scare her as much as someone being in her house. I turned to her to make one more plea, as the door slammed in my face.

We walked to Bobbie's car. "Wow! That's one uptight woman," I said to Bobbie.

"Uptight! She damn near killed you! I think the DA's got the right killer." She reached for the Dunkin Donut bag.

"I think she's scared; scared she's going to lose everything."

Bobbie walked over to me and placed a hand on my shoulder. "Paula, she would have killed you if I hadn't been there. She's dangerous! You've seen people like her many times. I think she's guilty, and if you think about it, you'll agree."

She was right. Most people with that temperament can't find a way out without using violence when they're backed into a corner. So, they end up in jail. I hadn't expected her to flip out. I wasn't prepared. Thinking about it, I knew Bobbie was right. She would have killed me.

Bobbie took the last bite of the doughnut and she pointed her finger at me, "She's guilty Paula; stay away from her."

An hour later, while standing in the shower, I kept rubbing my hands over my neck. The soap didn't take away the ugly feel of Carla's hands.

When I had first arrived at home, I tried watching TV to take my mind off things. It didn't work. My throat hurt, and the vision of Carla, grinding her teeth, her wide, black eyes staring at me, and her strong hands around my neck, wouldn't go away. I wanted to talk about it to someone, but no one was here. I paced the loft, then jumped into the shower.

I put on my favorite sweats and made a cup of hot chocolate. I found my yellow legal pad and decided I needed to put things down on paper. It made things easier for me to sort through when I could see it in print.

I then proceeded to list the glassware and other objects I could identify having seen in Carla's house. There were several glass and ceramic pieces and statues in the hutch. I wrote down the ones I could remember. A Staffordshire salt-glazed female figure probably made around 1750. I noticed a Staffordshire model of Britannia, woman with lion, a nineteenth century piece. I closed my eyes and leaned my head back.

"What else," I whispered.

On the end table sat a Wedgewood black basalt figure of Venus on a rock. There was a grandfather clock at the beginning of the hallway leading to the bedroom. It had a flame-mahogany eight-day long case, but I couldn't remember the brand name.

I was in awe when I checked my antique books and totaled up the value of the few things I could remember that were in Carla's house. I was beginning to think Carla was doing more than exercising at her gym. Maybe she was selling drugs. Maybe Emily asked too many questions and Carla flew off the handle, not meaning to kill her. I saw her rage earlier and…I hadn't provoked her.

I was tired and looked around the house. I noticed the clutter of dishes that I hadn't taken to the sink, and how much dust had accumulated. I had let the place go for too long. Because of my mess, it dawned on me, Carla must have a housekeeper. Her house was clean. "Damn," I said, thinking who came in and cleaned for Carla.

I went to pick up the phone and realized it was after eleven. The dishes and dust could wait another day. I decided to take a couple of aspirin and go to bed. Tomorrow I'd get answers if I had to personally knock on doors.

I sat down on my bed. Stretching across, I grabbed the pillow that Elizabeth used to lay her head on, and I snuggled the pillow close to my chest. Closing my eyes, I tried to sleep.

Chapter 18

The Prudential Center in Boston held one of the offices owned by Fields and Fields. A man wearing a brown leather bomber jacket stood at the main entrance. He looked at his watch every few seconds. The cigarette he held between the first knuckles of his middle and index fingers was closing in on the filter. He paced to the edge of the sidewalk and back to the door, checking his watch. Nodding to himself, he threw the cigarette butt to the road and entered the building.

He walked through the alcove, directly past the security desk, to the elevators. He pushed the button for the elevators, waiting for one car to arrive and the doors to open. Once in the elevator, he pushed the button to the fifteenth floor. He stood with his head bent forward never looking toward the surveillance camera.

Stepping into the hallway, he noticed the name Fields on the wall with an arrow below the name, pointing the way to the receptionist. The man in the jacket pushed the huge glass doors open with ease. He was greeted by a woman who walked over to him, her hand outstretched in a friendly gesture. She was wearing a Brooks Brothers black suit with a white blouse. She had a pearl necklace and wore two inch black leather heels.

He did not shake her hand. He whispered that he had an appointment with Mr. Fields. She asked his name politely but he simply shook his head. She pointed to a chair, where he sat, checking his watch. The woman went to her desk and picked up the phone. He could see her shaking her head. He moved his head in a slight half turn toward her and grinned. He knew he wouldn't be kept waiting long; he was much too important to Mr. Fields. He made sure he came in exactly when he was told, not one minute earlier or later. In his mind, he was finally going to become an important man.

Twenty minutes later, he was still waiting. He had become hot in his bomber jacket, but he didn't dare take it off. He didn't want Mr. Fields to see that his shirt was stained and his cuffs worn. He tried not to get angry as he watched the clock over the reception desk. At last, the woman in the black suit walked over and told him to follow her; he was relieved. He was beginning to think Mr. Fields had forgotten their phone call.

As they entered Mr. Fields' office, she asked if anyone would like some coffee. Mr. Fields raised his hand, palm down, and waved her out of the office. She closed the door behind her.

"Sit down, Mr. Smith -- if that's your name."

"You can call me Mr. Smith. I like that name," he said.

Mr. Fields was flipping a pen through his fingers and tapping the desk with his other hand. "What do you know about Carla Reed?"

"I can prove she killed your daughter," Mr. Smith said.

"What do you know and what do you want? I'm guessing it's money, seeing you didn't go to the police. I'm a busy man, so get to it." Mr. Fields was leaning forward on his elbows looking at Mr. Smith. "What do you want?"

The sweat built on Mr. Smith's forehead. "For five hundred thousand dollars I can get Carla Reed to admit she killed your daughter, sir."

Mr. Fields stood and walked over to the corner of the desk and sat down. He leaned into Mr. Smith's face, and Mr. Smith swallowed loudly. "And you guarantee Reed will confess?"

"I'll make it look like she did it, and when they find her body, they'll find a confession."

Mr. Fields went and opened the door calling for Mr. James. Mr. Smith was sure he was calling for the money. He began smiling. Mr. Fields held the door for Mr. James as he entered carrying a folder. He walked over to the desk and sat next to Mr. Smith.

"Mr. James, would you please tell us what you have in the folder."

"Yes sir," he said as he opened the folder and placed a picture of Mr. Smith on the desk. He read the report, "Jake O'Rouke born in South Boston of immigrant parents. Father worked on the docks, mother worked in a shoe factory as a leather cutter before a fire took her life. Father was an alcoholic and died in an alley near where he worked. You were then fostered out for several years, changing homes every six months because you couldn't stay out of trouble. Eventually, you landed in juvenile hall until you were eighteen. You knew Carla Reed when you were both children; you were one of the boys she attacked in an alley, and she broke one of your legs. You haven't kept a job more than a year, and you have a reputation of bilking old ladies out of their social security checks. You've been in jail thirty-five percent of your adult life. He closed the folder and stood.

Mr. Smith, or should I say Mr. O'Rouke, was extremely nervous; he was looking for a way to get out of this mess.

Mr. Fields went to the door and opened it. "Mr. James, would you escort this gentleman out to the sidewalk? The police should be waiting for him. Thank you!"

Mr. James grabbed the shoulder of Mr. O'Rouke and hauled him out.

The receptionist appeared at the office door. "Did you buzz me, sir?"

"Yes, Becky, would you get the DA on the phone and tell him I need to see him immediately?" Becky turned, closing the door behind her again. Mr. Fields went to his desk and opened the drawer, pulling out a bottle of Scotch. He poured a drink then reached for his private line, asking for an overseas operator.

Chapter 19

I awoke to the sound of rain on the roof. I wanted to stay wrapped in my quilt where I felt warm and safe, but I knew I had to get moving. I had made an early appointment with Beth Winslow to meet me at the diner. I was running a little late and was glad I didn't have to eat before I left. That gave me just enough time to review my notes.

The rain wasn't heavy, so I decided to walk. The diner was old-fashioned, like the ones you see when you're watching a fifties movie on TV. In those days, they had long white counters with little round stools, and you'd always see a bunch of old men sitting there, drinking coffee and having scrambled eggs with toast. Inside, they had booths with little juke boxes that hung on the walls that played those great oldies you grew up with.

I wanted a booth; I didn't want Beth to feel uncomfortable answering my questions with people sitting next to her. I found one far away from the door and took it.

A waitress came over and asked me if I'd like coffee. I couldn't take my eyes off the string that held her glasses as they dangled over my table. I shook my head. "No thank you. But would you bring me a diet Pepsi?" She looked at me strangely then walked away.

I folded my hands under my chin and placed my elbows on

the table leaning my lips on the tops of my fingers.

As I watched the waitress walk away, I began to recall the first day I met Elizabeth. I entered a diner one morning and picked a booth. I noticed the waitress immediately; she was wearing black jeans, black shoes and a red shirt. She was leaning over a table with her right leg lifted from the floor. I knew she had to be short because she couldn't reach across the table without raising her leg.

Meanwhile her glasses dangled over the table from a string around her neck. She had dark hair, and when she turned, I noticed huge brown eyes. She smiled and told me she'd be right with me. I just sat there staring, and all that went through my mind was *Wow!*

I never took my eyes off her as she hustled across the room pouring coffee for each person she passed, always with a smile. I was surprised at the way I felt. She brightened up my day and made my insides tingle. *"Wow!"* was all I could say as she walked toward me carrying a fresh pot of coffee. I turned my cup over and let her pour before I remembered I didn't even drink coffee. "Hey," was all I could say to her as she poured.

The pair of glasses that dangled from the string was covered in grease, flakes of food, and what looked like glue. I had to ask her about them. She told me that without them she couldn't read the words on the computer and would push the wrong food selections. She also told me they got caught all the time on the tables when she wiped them down, and in the plates as she carried them to the kitchen. They broke so often she decided to glue them together.

She laughed and when she did, I felt like I had to laugh with her… hopefully for the rest of my life. I felt we made a connection instantly. When she put her glasses on, I laughed so loud it brought attention to my table. The glasses were crooked and twisted from catching the end of the tables. Elizabeth looked so silly. Her eyes went one way, the glasses another, and oh, yeah, let's not forget her head. It looked like it went another way altogether. It was hilarious. What was so great was she was laughing with me.

She told me she'd be off in an hour and would sit with me for awhile if I had time. I told her I'd have all the time in the world -- for her! She laughed again and walked away pouring coffee into each empty cup she passed. My body filled with warmth. I couldn't believe that I was going to have a second chance at happiness with another woman. I knew in my heart this woman and I would be together the rest of our lives.

"Excuse me, are you Paula Graham? Excuse me. Hello!" She said, as she tapped her cane on the floor.

I jumped and noticed Beth Winslow standing next to my booth. "I'm sorry. I was thinking about something."

"I could tell you were in deep thought. I tried to get your attention several times. May I sit?"

I waved my open hand to the seat across from me. Beth sat down, turned her coffee cup over, and the waitress poured her coffee. I cleared my throat, and took a drink of my Pepsi. I reached across the table and shook Beth Winslow's hand; she asked me to call her Beth. We made small talk for a while. She talked about her animal rescue group and told me she has had up to seven dogs and five cats at her house at one time. Then she informed me that she had arthritis. It was intermittent, but when it flared up, she needed to use a cane. She was excited about her causes and all her medical history and would have talked for hours if I hadn't stopped her.

The waitress came and went, filling Beth's coffee cup each time it was close to empty. I watched her walk away each time, wanting her to be that short woman in black jeans, black shoes and red shirt. Beth was still talking when I became conscious that I hadn't been paying attention. I shivered as I picked up my pen and opened my notebook.

"Do you think you might answer a few questions for me?" I asked as she drank her coffee.

"I'll try. What is it you want to know?"

"What can you tell me about Emily Fields and her relationship with Carla Reed?"

Beth became quiet and wiggled a little in her seat. I waited patently, holding my pen to my notebook.

"Emily should never have been with Carla," she quietly exclaimed.

I was surprised by the way she came out with her statement. "Why do you say that, Beth?" I asked, not trying to stop her momentum.

"She was all wrong for Carla. I kept telling her that. I talked to Emily everyday, and everyday, I told her how she shouldn't be with Carla. How Carla wasn't the right one for her. I told her over and over she'd never be happy with Carla." Beth's face was flushed as she took another breath and continued. "Emily could never be happy with Carla, and Carla was just all wrong for Emily. I told Emily to leave her. Repeatedly! She never listened."

I had to interrupt; I couldn't believe what I was hearing. "Weren't they together for ten years? They must have been happy at some time in their relationship." I just looked at Beth, but she paid me no mind and went on talking.

"I was Emily's best friend, and we talked every single day. And let me tell you, I told her everyday to get rid of Carla, she would never be the right one." She picked up her coffee to take a sip.

I took this moment to ask her another question that was nagging at me. "If you were Emily's best friend, why didn't you support her in her choice of partner? She must have seen something in Carla if she was with her all that time."

Beth continued, "Years ago, I told Emily how awful Darcie was when they were going out, and finally Emily got rid of Darcie and then she told me that I had been right. As her friend, I thought it was my duty to tell Emily how I felt about the women she picked."

By this time, I had had enough of Beth and her so called best-friend theory. I couldn't figure out what Beth got for herself from all this negative talk.

I always believed that if your best friend found happiness with someone, you should be happy and supportive, no matter what you thought or felt about her choice. Anyone who heard nothing but negative talk, day in and day out, would start to believe that maybe they had made a mistake.

That kind of pessimistic talk could make a good relationship go bad without either person knowing why. Beth was still talking, her face turning a deeper red. I never saw a woman talk so much for so long and say nothing. I needed specific answers to specific questions, and I wasn't sure Beth was capable of answering any of them honestly. I decided to interrupt her again.

"What can you tell me about Carla Reed?" I asked, expecting her to go on another disapproving rampage. But, to my astonishment, the opposite happened,

"Oh, I think Carla is great! She's a hard worker and worked hard to get to where she is today. She's a little cold, but I think that's because she hasn't found the right woman yet."

"So, you actually like Carla?" I asked, surprised.

"Of course I do. Who wouldn't? She's got a prosperous business, a beautiful house, and an incredible collection of art and antiques that anyone would like, even though she doesn't appreciate any of it."

I muttered, "What, do you have a thing for Carla?"

Beth was surprised and looked around for the waitress holding onto her empty cup. Once again, she started twisting around in her seat. "Of course not." She waved at the waitress. "I just think she's having a tough time right now and needs my support. She's accused of murder, you know?"

"Yes I do. And she's accused of killing your best friend. Do you think she killed Emily?" I was gripping my pen to the point where I almost snapped it in half.

Suddenly, Beth placed her cup on the table and stood up. She grabbed her cane and walked to my side of the table and held out her hand.

"I forgot I had another appointment on the other side of town. Call me if I can help you again. It was nice meeting you, Ms. Graham. Goodbye." She turned and walked away.

The waitress returned with the bill. Placing it on the table she said, "She certainly can talk."

"And is one miserable person," I murmured.

Chapter 20

Carla stood facing the closed front door, her hand outstretched, holding on to the door knob. Her body was shaking, the sweat beading on her brow. She couldn't let go of the door knob; the bile began creeping up her throat. She tried holding it back until her stomach wrenched with pain, then, bending over, she heaved. The spew splattered the door, and the dribble oozed to the floor from her mouth. Carla fell to her knees, the tears rolling down her cheek. She wrapped her arms around her stomach and began to rock. She raised her head and leaned it all the way back letting out a silent scream until she fell on her side, her body trembling uncontrollably. Carla lay on the floor in anguish wrapped in her grief and her thoughts.

Finding the strength, she pulled herself to her feet and went to the kitchen sink to run water. Filling her, hands she placed her face into them. Shaking her head, the water flew everywhere. She grabbed a towel and wiped her face.

She headed back to the front door. All at once, Carla thought she heard something moving in the house. She stood silent, turning her head from one side to another listening. She heard nothing. Holding her hand straight out in front of her, she saw it no longer shook, although her insides still trembled. She took another deep breath, slowly letting it out. Shrugging her shoulders, she looked at the mess and decided to leave it there. No one's here, she thought. Who cares if you leave the floor a mess? Pull yourself together. Get strong, she thought to herself. Show no weakness.

She started to walk through the house. She was convinced the private investigator and the cop had been there to plant evidence for Emily's father. She wasn't taking any chances. She would look everywhere and find what they had planted and get rid of it. She'd beat them at their own game. She knew about hiding places and hiding things; that was something she was good at doing.

Carla spent several hours in the living room and worked her way into the kitchen before moving to the bedroom, where she stood at the foot of the bed. All the sheets, pillows, and the bedspread were pulled off the bed and tossed into the corner. Next, Carla went to the dresser and opened the drawers. She picked up Emily's tee shirt and, taking a moment, she rubbed her thumb and finger along its sides. Then she reached into the drawers and pulled everything out and threw the clothes on the floor. She turned the drawers over and checked the bottoms.

She returned to the living room, taking the pictures off the wall and checking behind them. She knew that cops bugged houses and often hid things behind something. The couch cushions and chairs were turned inside out and thrown on the floor. All of her cabinets were opened, and the drawers emptied and turned upside down. Carla was so sure that evidence was planted she didn't want to give up without finding something. She stood in the hall near the front door, slowly looking over the space and trying to remember everything that she had had in the house.

Suddenly she ran to the living room and grabbed the phone. She had speed dial and pressed number one. Jackie answered. Carla sounded worried.

"Jackie, I have to see you tonight. Something's missing in my house and I'm worried it might implicate me in Emily's murder." They agreed she would go to see Jackie within the hour.

Now looking at the mess, she wanted it cleaned as soon as possible. She called her housekeeper and told her the police had returned to her house and turned everything upside down and she needed the place cleaned immediately.

The housekeeper knew that if she said no, Carla would have her fired and replaced instantly. The housekeeper told her she could come the following morning. Carla felt satisfied with her rampage through the house. She was finally convinced that nothing was hidden. They left nothing or she would have found it.

The phone rang; Carla went to answer it. Picking it up, she gave a gruff, "hello."

"Carla, this is Mark James."

Carla was immobile; her eyes widened as she held her breath. The bile started returning to her throat. She cleared her throat. "Mark! How are you? What's going on?"

Mark James was Carla's financial advisor, the man who took care of her money. They only met once a year at tax time…unless something was seriously wrong.

"Carla I think we should meet and discuss what's happening with you and this case." In response Carla felt her blood pressure rising.

"What are you talking about? This case has nothing to do with my finances."

"I'm afraid that's not true, Carla. Your manager at the gym has already called me with notice that over half of your clients have cancelled their membership, and most of them are asking for the return of their dues. And Mr. Fields has called the IRS. They, in turn, called me and they want to see all of your books for an audit by next week."

Carla was speechless. She heard the words Fields and audit. "Can he do that?"

"He told them that you used Emily's money, and since her father gave Emily her inheritance early, he believes he has the right to know where it went."

Carla's voice rose. "Can he do that?"

"No, of course not, you two were partners, and if Emily gave you money or didn't give you money it's none of his business. He had to give the IRS a reason to suspect you were cooking the books or they wouldn't have agreed to an audit. He wants to know where you got all this money to buy the gym, the equipment, and your house. He's harassing you Carla, that's all. He's just throwing his weight around. It's Fields way of letting you know he's coming after you. The books are fine; let them look."

All at once, the phone went sailing across the room, breaking into several pieces when it hit the wall. "That bastard!"

* * * *

The housekeeper reached for her key, but noticed the door was ajar. She pushed it open slowly, stepped inside, and gasped at the mess that lay throughout the house. She knew Carla wouldn't be home. Carla was never home when the housekeeper worked.

The housekeeper began gathering the clothes that were lying on the floor throughout the house. As she stepped into the bedroom gathering laundry, she looked at the wall over the bed. She noticed the wall was discolored. A picture used to hang there; she hoped the wall would easily wash clean.

Chapter 21

I was finishing breakfast when I heard some noise coming from downstairs. My newly hired assistant (Sheila) was opening the shop. She was a hard worker, never complaining about the hours or that I was hardly ever around to answer any of her questions.

I quickly showered and put on clean jeans and a long sleeve shirt. I checked the mirror and saw how shaggy my hair was getting. I ran my hands through it, hoping that would help to keep it behind my ears, something even gel wasn't going to do. I told myself this might be a good opportunity to get in an interview with Joanne Adler. She was a hairdresser, and I certainly needed a haircut. My usual hairdresser would be disappointed but, hey, business before pleasure, right?

As I reached the bottom of the stairs, I could smell the coffee brewing. I wasn't even aware I owned a coffee pot. The place looked and smelled great. Things were clean and the place was well-organized. Pictures were hung, tables and chairs were together; a different section looked like you walked into an 18th century sitting room. She had matched everything for that period. I was impressed. She might need a raise, I thought to myself.

Sheila smiled at me when she saw me entering the room; I was glad she couldn't read my mind about the raise. It was only a thought. I waved and headed to my office.

Before I could take a seat, Sheila was at the door asking if I would like a cup of coffee. I said no thanks and turned to look for my notes on Lori Fields. We had set an appointment and were to meet at the new café in the Boston Museum of Fine Arts called *Bravo*.

Its new, stylish bar served light lunches of eclectic and contemporary food. *Bravo* is located on the upper level Galleria in the west wing. They have a rotating selection of some of the Museum's masterpieces hanging on the walls. I was looking forward to going.

I also wanted to go early to check out the exhibit in the Gund Gallery: *Napoleon and the Art of the Empire Style 1800-1815*. It was the grandest and most opulent collection in the history of decorative arts. I knew the designs had been inspired by Greco-Roman antiquity with its bold colors, elaborate materials, and massive scales of size. The theme was "Symbols of Power" and had over a hundred and ninety objects; furniture, silver, porcelain, bronzes and more that could be seen.

I thought about all the art and antiques that were in Carla's home. Power and money! I was beginning to understand that Carla was a woman from the streets trying to use art and antiques of astronomical prices to fit in and be one of the 'elite'.

Time was getting short, so I called to make an appointment to have my haircut. Damn, a busy signal! I couldn't wait; I'd try later.

I didn't have time to see the exhibit, so I rushed up to the west wing and entered the *Bravo*. Lori was nowhere to be seen. I found a table in the back, ordered a drink, and waited. I was just looking for the waitress to order another when I spotted a woman standing in the doorway. She looked scrawny and ashen with hardly any neck showing, and by her stooped stance, she appeared depressed. She gazed across the room looking for me. I waved, and she walked over to me. She stopped at the table, her shoulders tucked close to her neck and her hands clasped together in front of her dress. She tried to speak but her voice was hardly a murmur. "Ms. Graham?"

I stood and offered her my hand. As she seized mine, a small smile came across her face. I motioned to the chair, and she sat. Looking at her casually, I noticed she had no make-up on, and her hair was dull and lackluster. Her eyes were blue and almost lifeless. She had creases on her forehead and crow's feet around her eyes, all of which made her look older than she was.

The waitress came by and left the menus; I ordered another drink. Lori looked toward me with caution. When I nodded to her, she asked for a Coke. I could see how shy she was and I knew I'd have to be exceptionally careful when I asked her any questions or she might shut down and I'd get nothing from her.

"So what kind of food do you eat?" I asked. "Please order anything you'd like. I'll put it on my card as a business expense." I laughed lightly to ease the mood.

Lori sat back slightly, shaking her head. I wasn't sure what that meant or what my next move should be. "I'm having a roast beef sandwich with fries. I hear it's very good here. Maybe you should try one."

I looked her straight in the eye. She dropped her head and nodded, saying, "Okay".

I ordered for both of us. Before the sandwiches came, I made light talk with Lori, mostly about the art on the wall. To my surprise, she was very knowledgeable about most of the art work. I could see she was relaxing as our conversation continued.

"I like art," she said. "My sister loved it. She went to every museum she could. Once, she even went to Paris with my father. He said she spent the whole time in the Louve, looking at the pictures, and missed everything else going on in town. She loved going to the movies, too, but..." Lori began to tear up. "... but Carla wouldn't let her go unless she went with her, and Carla was always busy. Emily hated to be home all the time; she used to be such a free spirit."

Lori took a sip of her water and closed her eyes.

I wanted to ask a question, but I didn't want to lose her if she got scared. I started slowly, "Did your sister enjoy traveling with your father?"

Lori's eyes opened. "She did, a long time ago. Until my father found out about Emily being ... being, you know gay and all."

"How did he find out about her being a lesbian, if you don't mind me asking?"

"She went out with this girl named Darcie Chambers when she was real young. Darcie was her first girl friend, you know? Em even gave her a very expensive locket that Darcie still wears today. They were school friends and one thing led to another and they ended up having an affair. Emily told me that Darcie was fun, but had times when she was way too moody, and Em was always so happy-go-lucky. She said Darcie wasn't the right girl for her, but that she knew then she definitely liked being with women. They didn't last long. Emily saw a few other women, but nothing was ever serious, until Carla."

Lori seemed to be totally relaxed now, almost like she had been waiting to unload everything she had had pent up inside.

"Anyway, when they broke up, Darcie really got pissed. And Darcie kept calling Emily everyday, but Emily wouldn't take her calls, so Darcie called my father and told him everything. He went berserk. He called Emily every name he could think of and some I'd never heard. He said if she continued with this perversion, he would disown her and leave her on the street. He tried to take back her trust fund, but couldn't."

"Did Emily and your father ever make amends?" I asked.

"They spoke a few times, like when Emily tried to get away from Carla once."

I looked at Lori. "What happened?"

"My father told her she had made her bed, so lie in it. Emily left the house crying and they never spoke again." Lori began to cry.

She picked up her napkin, her hands were shaking, and she tried to hide her eyes. I wasn't sure what to say. Lori was distraught, and I was afraid she couldn't answer any more questions without falling apart emotionally.

"Did you spend a lot of time with Carla and your sister?" I caught the waitress' eye, and she nodded, heading toward the table.

"Would you like more Coke?" I asked Lori.

She took a breath, wiped away the tears, and seemed pleasantly relieved. "Yes, please." Then she continued, "I tried to spend time with Emily, but my father found out, and he wouldn't allow it. I had to do what he said or I wouldn't get any kind of allowance, and I don't work."

"Why is that, Lori? You seem intelligent and personable and you have a really nice way about you."

Lorie smiled. "Thanks. I did go to college, but my father won't let me move out on my own, so I just hang around the house with my mother and do what he says."

I didn't want to push the father issue, so I went back to asking about Carla. "Do you know if Carla ever hurt Emily or can you tell me what happened to their relationship?"

Lori was quiet for some time then raised her head and said, "They were fine for a long time. Then, it seemed like overnight, everything changed. Emily became cold toward Carla, and Carla got more and more suspicious that Emily was seeing someone. Emily went to the museum every chance she could and submerged herself into the various art shows when they were in town."

I could understand that. I also liked to go to art shows when I could get myself out of the loft. "Did she go alone, or did Carla go with her?"

Lori actually started to giggle. It was a nervous laugh, but a laugh nevertheless. "Carla didn't care about seeing the art; she only wanted to own it - the more expensive the better. Carla wouldn't know a Stuben glass from…," she picked up her water glass, "from this glass. Emily told me once that Carla wouldn't go, but that Darcie had caught up with her a few times at the museum, but that's all I know."

I had more questions, but I could see Lori was getting nervous again. She began fidgeting with her watch and looking around. "Is there something wrong?"

"My father will be looking for me. If I'm not home helping my mother when he calls, he'll get mad. He always calls around four. I should get going."

"I understand. Just a few more questions if you don't mind. Do you know anyone who might want to harm your sister?" Lori shook her head no. "And I hate to ask this, but do you think Carla might have murdered your sister?" I picked up my pen again and turned the page in my notebook. Then, I sat silent and waited. Lori rearranged her dress several times then exhaled.

"I'm not sure. Maybe, I don't really know. Listen, I have to go." Lori got to her feet and brushed off the front of her dress. "I hope I was able to help, Ms. Graham. It was nice meeting you. Goodbye." She turned and walked away.

I had the distinct impression that she knew more than she was saying. As to why she wouldn't tell me, I guess I'd have to figure it out. I thought maybe she was protecting her father, or maybe she was just afraid of what he would do if she did know anything and said something about it. I glanced at my notes, moving my pen from top to bottom, looking for that one clue to jump out at me. I thought about how Lori was so unlike her father.

I was sitting there figuring out the tip before I signed the receipt when I heard a voice calling my name.

"Paula! It's so good to see you again. I was going to call you. I've found the most incredible sketch by Pissarro and I know you'll love it."

There in front of me stood my friend, Darla DeVito. She was the owner of one of the largest and most prestigious art galleries in town. She was roughly one hundred twenty-five pounds, with an hour glass figure. Darla wore a black business suit with three inch heels. She found many of my art pieces and knew what I liked. She was always on the lookout for something special.

I gave her a full-sized smile and stood up, giving her a hug. "Pissarro is one of my favorite artists. So, how are you?"

She sat and told me that her business was booming, and that

we needed to see each other more. I agreed. Darla had to get to a meeting, so she kissed me on the cheek and started to walk away. Suddenly, she stopped and turned.

"By the way, how did Elizabeth like her antique painted pewter tray? You certainly went without a great deal of lunches to buy it."

"I'm not sure. We're not together anymore. Someone told me it went out in Monday's trash as soon as I was gone."

"That's a shame; it was a great piece. I'm sorry for your loss…and hers." She waved and disappeared through the crowd.

Chapter 22

The courtroom was buzzing with people who were rushing in to find a seat. The lawyers were finding their chairs at the front table and emptying their case files onto the same table. The guards led in the prisoners, their legs in irons and their hands cuffed in front of their waists. They quietly and slowly moved to their assigned seats.

Carla's lawyer was pacing and checking outside the double doors of the courthouse every ten minutes. He knew the Judge would go through the mundane drunk-driving and trespassing cases quickly. Carla's case would be called up within fifteen minutes after they removed the prisoners.

The prosecutor was gathering his files on Carla and placing them in numerical order. He kept watching Carla's lawyer become more and more nervous. The prosecutor knew if Carla didn't show, the Judge would immediately have a bench warrant issued for her to be arrested and picked up. His case would only get easier from there.

The Judge, drawn from the pool, was old fashioned and hated homosexuality. Those facts alone made the prosecutor smile.

"All rise. Hear ye hear ye, hear ye. The General District Court of the County is now in session. The Honorable Judge Thomas Lendman..."

Carla's lawyer went out to the hall again and pulled out his cell phone. First, he called his office asking if they had heard from Carla Reed. They had not. He tried calling her house, but there was no answer there, either. On a hunch, he called the gym, and got the receptionist. She told him that no one had heard from Carla in two days, which was unusual. He snapped his cell phone closed, then put it on vibrate, and replaced it in his pocket. He went back into court and sat at the table facing the judge.

The prisoners were called one at a time, the charges were read and a plea entered for each. Those who wanted a trial were given a date and those who pleaded out were given their fate. Judge Lendman was a tough judge, and most of the prisoners got hefty sentences. They called for a ten minute break while the guards removed the prisoners and the lawyers wrapped up their paperwork.

Carla Reeds' case was called, and the Judge asked the DA if he was prepared and then he asked Carla's lawyer.

"Your Honor, I'd like to request a …"

The Judge stopped him. "Where is your client? I see here…" the Judge looked at the papers in front of him, "that she is required to be here."

"Yes, your Honor, she's been delayed. I'm sure she'll be here."

"Delayed? Do you know where Ms. Reed is or not?"

"No sir, but I'm sure I…"

The Judge tossed the papers on his desk. He looked at the DA.

"Your Honor, we were against the release of Ms. Reed from the beginning. We felt she was a flight risk. With her assets, we felt she could and would abscond, but Judge Mercedes ruled she could post bail. The DA's office would like a bench warrant on Ms. Reed."

"Granted," The Judge pounded his gavel.

"Your Honor," said Carla's lawyer, "I'd like…"

"Next case," said the Judge as he hit his gavel.

Carla's lawyer called Bobbie as soon as he left the court room. "Detective Kerry, this is Joe Persico, Ms. Reed's attorney."

Bobbie remembered Joe from other cases. He was an average attorney who did what he had to, but no more. He never got involved with his clients beyond the attorney-client level and never put any extra effort into a case.

"How was court today?" Bobbie asked.

"Listen, Bobbie, I owe you, so I'm letting you know my client didn't show. I'm just reporting to give you a heads up. The Judge issued a bench warrant for Carla Reed, and I'm officially giving the case back to the court. I don't waste time on clients who can't make their appointments with me and don't show in court." He hung up before Bobbie could have the last word. Bobbie turned around and called Paula.

"Hello! This is Paula's Antiques. May I help you?"

"Where's Paula?" Bobbie asked.

"She's in her office. Can I ask whose calling?"

"Just tell her it's Bobbie."

"I'll transfer you. One moment please."

Bobbie was laughing when Paula picked up the phone. "What's so funny?" she asked.

"I'm just not used to you having a secretary and everything sounding so formal."

"Me either. She runs to the phone when it rings and makes me think the place is on fire and I should grab my coat and head for the door. I'll have to talk to her and let her know that I'm able to answer the phone myself. She's a very good worker. Even wants to bring me coffee when I'm here in my office."

"You don't drink coffee."

"Exactly. But I might have to start. I don't want her to quit. What's up?"

"You're going to have to start earning your money. Carla didn't show up at court, and a bench warrant's been issued. The DA's office thinks she ran. I do, too."

"Has anyone checked on her whereabouts this morning?"

"Her lawyer, Joe Persico, called me to let me know she didn't appear in court and that he quit. Guy has no guts, only wants the winnable cases. Joe said he checked her home phone and the gym, and no one has seen her for a couple of days. Carla pulled Judge Lendman and you know this guy likes to close his cases. So, pal, get to work and see if you can find out where Carla is and whether or not she left the country. I have a dozen cases on my desk this morning, but I'll do what I can from this end. I'll call you tonight and we'll compare notes. Talk to you later, bye."

Bobbie was gone. She left me with little information and a missing Carla. I was beginning to believe everyone was right. Carla Reed killed Emily Fields and all I had to do now was prove she'd left town -- or the country -- and the case would be closed. It was time for me to find Carla, and my best bet was to head to her house.

There were two cars in the driveway. I recognized Carla's, but not the other. I checked the front of the building and walked around to the back. There was nothing that looked out of place or unusual.

I returned to the front and rang the bell. A woman with a mop in her hand answered. She had a gray and white uniform on and looked every bit the part of a housekeeper. I knew she worked for an agency here in town that called themselves *The Gray and White Ladies*. Their motto: 'Nothing too Gray to Wipe Away.'

"Hi, is Ms. Reed in today?" I asked.

"No, she never here when I come," she answered.

I smiled and pulled out my ID, holding it up in front of her. She seemed confused.

"I need to speak to Ms. Reed. Do you have any idea where she might be?" I took one step into the house. She backed up, but held onto the door.

"She no here when I come. She not like when I here and she

here too." She tried to explain in her broken English.

I nodded and took another step in. She closed the door behind me, looking nervous. I told her my name and asked her what her name was. She told me 'Garcia'.

I shook her hand and said, "Hi! So, you have no idea where Ms. Reed is?"

"No." She bent her head forward, looking at the floor. "I need go back work now or Ms. Reed make a complain' to my boss."

"May I look around?"

Garcia shrugged and went back to the kitchen with her mop. I took the shrug as an okay to snoop. It may not hold up in a court of law, but it worked for me at the present time. Everything was spotless; no dust or blood remained anywhere. I could see the housekeeper was very good at her job.

I walked through the living room once again admiring the glassware, the art on the walls, and the statues that were in the hutch. Carla had some beautiful pieces. I wondered if she knew what she had, or even cared about the beautiful objects she was displaying throughout the house. I didn't think she did. But maybe Emily did, and maybe she had gotten some happiness from the items that were in the house.

I walked into the master bedroom and looked around. It didn't look like anyone slept here; no clothes were on the chair in the corner, nothing on top of the dressers. My room always had clothes in a corner and on top of the dresser, and sometimes in the middle of the floor. My loft had what I called that *lived-in* look.

This room looked like it was waiting for a picture to be taken for one of those magazines like *Home and Garden*. It was just too clean, not even a wrinkle in the bedspread.

I walked to the dresser and opened the drawers. They were empty. I went to the chest of drawers and opened them. They held clothes, tee shirts in one drawer with jeans in the others. The jeans were folded in three and placed carefully in the drawer. These had to be Carla's things; everything was placed in a precise manner. Her sock drawer had each set placed in a perfect line, side-by-side, with the colors matching. Nothing was just tossed or placed randomly.

I walked over and opened the closet. All of Carla's clothes were still hanging. Each long sleeve shirt hung in a line, all facing to the right, then short sleeved shirts, pants (all color coded), and then sweaters. My closet never looked like this. I couldn't believe Carla would leave and not take her clothes with her. I also wondered where all Emily's clothes were. Maybe the housekeeper would know.

I closed the closet door and walked into the kitchen. The housekeeper was washing the cabinet doors. I tried asking her about Emily's clothes. All I could understand was the word 'wash'.

I noticed the mail was sitting on the table. I walked over to it and started to move the envelopes around, allowing me to see where the mail had been sent from. I knew I couldn't open it. That was a no-no for everyone; the federal government was real clear on mail tampering. I noticed the usual utility bills, credit card bills, and a bank statement. The bank statement was open, and since it was in clear sight, I couldn't resist looking. I checked to see if Garcia was watching me; she was still washing cabinets and paying me no mind. I picked up the statement and looked it over. Carla had a handsome sum of money in her checking account, and all the checks that were written were to the usual bills. Nothing big or unusual popped off the paper and hit me.

    I put all the mail back into a pile and started looking around the kitchen. I noticed another pile of mail on the counter by the back door. I went over and picked it up. Everything in this pile was addressed to Emily Fields. As I went through it, I saw several announcements from museums and art shows, as well as credit card bills, and a bank statement. So, Emily had her own bank account, I said to myself. I called Mrs. Garcia, and she turned and slowly walked toward me. I held the envelopes up and asked her, "Did you put these over here on the counter?"

    "Ms. Carla say, mail for Ms. Emily, put on counter here."

    "I see. Mrs. Garcia, when you were working, was Ms. Emily ever here with you?" Mrs. Garcia looked anxious and stepped back. I grabbed her hand, "It's okay, don't worry. I won't tell anyone. This is very important. I'm trying to find the person who killed Ms. Emily."

    "No one is here when I work. Ms. Carla say she fire me if someone is here."

I understood and nodded. "I promise no one will ever know what you tell me. Was Ms. Emily ever here with you?"

Garcia nodded, her hands fumbling around her neck and face.

"Good, good," I said. "Now, this is important…did Ms. Emily ever have company, anyone who came over to the house when Ms. Carla was not home?"

Mrs. Garcia's eyes got big and she shook her head, saying almost in a whisper, "No, never."

"Did she ever call anyone that you know of, on the telephone?" I said, miming holding a telephone receiver.

"One time, she on phone for long time. She talking to Ms. Carla, I think."

"Why did you think it was Ms. Carla? Did you hear her say Carla's name?' I stepped toward Garcia. "This is very important," I told her.

She tilted her head again then smiled. "She laughing long time when she talk on phone."

I couldn't imagine after all the things I had heard were going on between Carla and Emily that they would be laughing on the phone for any length of time. "Mrs. Garcia, do you remember what day this happened? Again, this is very important!"

"No. I come clean house Tuesday and Friday. I work ten o'clock in morning and five o'clock I go home."

"Thank you, Mrs. Garcia. You were a big help. I have to go

now and don't worry; no one will know I talked to you, I promise."

Mrs. Garcia smiled and went back to washing the cabinets. I took one last look through the house, when I suddenly remembered this was Monday. Mrs. Garcia had just told me she only worked Tuesday and Friday. I yelled for Mrs. Garcia; she came running.

"I thought you only worked Tuesday and Friday?" She nodded. "Today is Monday, why are you here? Did she call you to come clean up?"

Garcia said, "Yes, yesterday…she say police come back and make big mess. She say, come clean soon. I come today. I no want get fired."

"This room was a mess?" I waved my arm around, indicating the whole bedroom.

"Yes, all the house, big mess. I clean all day. I clean everything good: walls, floors, everything." She said, mimicking my arm movement and indicating the whole house.

I thought about what Garcia had said. The police had returned? We don't do that. Once the crime scene has been gone over and the tape removed, we rarely go back and tear it up again.

I decided I'd check out Carla's car. Garcia stayed on my heels as I went to leave. She smiled at me as she opened the front door and nodded. I took one last glance at the Monet that hung across from the door when I thought I noticed something on the painting. I moved to the picture, peering at it.

"Mrs. Garcia, what is this dry spot on the corner of the

painting here?" I was pointing to a dry but sticky-like substance that covered the corner of the painting, dulling the colors.

She squinted and then jumped back. "I clean! Ms. Carla be mad if not clean." She started to leave.

"Wait, Mrs. Garcia. You don't want to touch this. This could be blood or something." Her eyes opened wide again, as she mouthed the word 'blood'. "I'm going to take this picture to the lab and have it checked."

I handed her my business card and removed the picture from the wall. She looked confused, so I took the card back. "Its okay, Mrs. Garcia," I said, nodding.

I didn't believe Mrs. Garcia had to worry about Carla coming home. I was beginning to think that Carla was in trouble…and might have even skipped town.

Chapter 23

I hadn't been to the lab in over a year, but I hoped Gail Watkins was still working. Gail was the most knowledgeable woman I knew when it came to possible unknown fluids. She couldn't be rushed or persuaded to guess about anything. I liked her a lot.

The lab was a series of rooms, one room had a number of microscopes, another looked like a regular kitchen with at least one or two (sometimes more) refrigerators. You see blenders just like the one you may have in your own kitchen. You would see many sample jars filled and labeled and several cups filled with what looks like a milkshake. Not to be drunk. Testing toxins is done only in the liquid state. It's a consuming process of illumination.

In the lab, there are two types of machines used: the gas chromatograph and the mass spectrometer. You would be surprised to know there are few anatomical changes in the body that point to poison.

The problem facing people like my friend Gail is that you need to have an idea of what you might be looking for. Gail keeps coming up with ideas. Another thing people believe is that science can prove anything. That's false; it can't.

I was standing in the doorway holding the Monet, looking for Gail when I spotted her at the same time she noticed me. She waved and headed toward me.

"What! You think it's a forgery and I'm going to prove it?"

I started laughing and was pleased to see she was still here. "I need your help with this case I'm working on."

Gail smiled. She always had a beautiful large smile. "I was told you got your investigator's license and you would try to use this lab when you needed something checked out. The captain said to tell you to go to a private lab and pay to get whatever it is done."

I was still giggling and I reminded her I was working for the captain. She nodded, grabbed my arm and the picture, and started to pull me into the lab.

"Doesn't matter to me; I'll always help you. You know that. I'd be upset if you went to anyone else."

I stopped. "Is there anyone else?"

I followed her in, and we went to a long table where she placed the picture. "So what's up?"

"I'm working on the Emily Fields case. Her partner, Carla Reed, was arrested and charged with her murder. Bobbie brought me the case. She thought Carla might not get a fair chance because ...well one, she's a lesbian, and some of the old-timers still don't work as hard on these type of cases. Two, they think she really looks good for it and aren't looking any further. I'm actually beginning to think she's guilty myself."

"And now you're not so sure. Didn't she try to strangle you? That would make me think twice about looking any further."

Gail went to grab some hospital gloves and handed me a pair. As she was putting them on she asked, "So what makes you think she might be innocent now?"

"She didn't show up for her court date. Her lawyer couldn't track her down at home or work, and no one has seen her in two days." I began putting on my gloves.

"Sounds like she took off. Pretty much says she's guilty. Not many run if they're innocent."

"True, but I went to her house, and she took nothing with her. Her bank statements were on the table, and she hadn't emptied them. I called the bank, and she hasn't had any action on her account in over three days. No use of the card at all over the weekend. That's unusual, according to the bank. Apparently, she's like a lot of us and carries no cash and always uses her debit card for transactions. That tells me something's happened. Not only that, she didn't take any of her belongings with her. Believe me, money is very important to this woman."

Gail moved the picture around looking at every inch of the canvas. She picked up a magnifying glass and held it over the frame corners. "I'm finding some kind of stain that is recent in this corner, see, look, right here." Gail pointed to the canvas and handed me the magnifying glass. I adjusted the glass so I could see clearly. "Right here it looks like something was sprayed from a distance and hit some of the canvas. About three feet or so, I'd say. See this void? It looks like something blocked part of the spray."

"Will you be able to tell what kind of spray it was?"

Gail patted my back. "By the time I'm done, I'll tell you what made the void. Are you sure the housekeeper didn't use any household chemicals to clean it?"

"I'm sure. I talked to her personally, and she would never touch the canvas. She knows better. Carla Reed is not someone you would screw with. Besides, the housekeeper was very good at her job."

Gail took the picture and put it near her desk. "Ok, give me about a week and I'll let you know something."

I held my arms out with my palms facing her. "What? I need this sooner than that! I don't have a week. If Carla didn't run, and I'm not convinced she has, she might be in trouble."

"I understand, but if she is guilty, she's gone, and I bet no one will find her. If she's clever, she probably has money stashed for a time she might have to run. And this chemical might have nothing to do with Carla and actually prove she used it on Emily. You know you can't rush this process. It's not like Law and Order on TV. These things can take weeks, not an hour; especially when you're not sure what to look for."

I gave her the pleading eye look, and she began to laugh.

"I'll do my best as fast as I can, but no faster. Now get out of here and let me do my work. It's not like I don't have dozens of cases going on at one time."

I thanked her and promised to call her for a dinner date soon.

She waved a hand at me shooing me out of the lab. As I was leaving the lab she hollered at me.

"It's great seeing you out and around again. I'm glad for you."

Gail was already checking one of her milkshakes before I could say anything. I watched her work for a moment. I knew nothing was going to be solved in just a few minutes. I wanted to know if the chemical had anything to do with the case or if I was looking at nothing.

I thought about the threats the Fields family had made, and I was sure Mr. Fields had heard Carla didn't show for court. If he had decided that the DA couldn't win their case against Carla, he might have taken things into his own hands. And if that happened, we might never find Carla. Proving Mr. Fields had done anything to her was unlikely. He wasn't the type to make mistakes.

I decided not to call, but just drop in unexpectedly on Carla's best friend Jackie Steiner. Maybe, if I caught her off guard, she couldn't hide anything, and I'd be able to tell if she was lying to me. As a detective, I had met with some of the best liars on the streets. Everyone has a 'tell' and once you find it, they can never lie to you again, at least not without you knowing it.

Chapter 24

Traveling the back streets of Boston to the Gai Rendezvous was considered a dangerous thing to do. I could still remember all the calls Bobbie and I had had in this part of town. Fights, domestic disputes, and shootings were everyday occurrences. My guess from the sight of things was that this part of town hadn't changed much since then.

There was no designated parking for the Rendezvous, so I had to circle the block a couple of times until I found a space I could squeeze into. Walking into the Rendezvous was a step back in time. The place had little light; the front windows were covered with flyers and cardboard signs telling you about the different beers available. The bar and woodwork were all dark. The light in the back of the bar came from the old Tiffany that hung over the pool table.

I had only seen Jackie Steiner in person once before. I didn't think the woman behind the bar was Jackie, but the light in here gave off a shadow and I wasn't sure.

I decided to take the direct approach. I walked to the bar and pulled up a stool and made myself comfortable. The bartender was rinsing glasses and nodded to me. She wiped her hands on the bar rag and carried it to wipe the bar off in front of me. While doing that she asked, "What'll it be?"

I could see she wasn't Jackie. She was much older, and if I

didn't know better, I would have seriously mistaken her for a man.

"Hi, I'm Paula Graham." I was fumbling for my ID.

"What'll it be? I can see you're old enough to drink," she said with a slight smile.

I laid my ID on the bar. "I'm a private investigator working on the Emily Fields' murder case. I was hoping to talk with Ms. Jackie Steiner. Do you know when she'll be in?"

She looked at her watch. "In about fifteen minutes; she's always here by four sharp. You could set your watch by her... always on time. So what'll it be?"

I ordered a CC on the rocks. She poured an honest drink and brought a bowl of peanuts over with it. She went back to rinsing glasses. I sipped my drink and tried to imagine this place in the old days. I bet it was hopping all the time.

Local bars and pubs were like a second home to many: those who lost their job, had no family members, or had no home and needed a place to get warm on a cold wintry night.

Just then the bartender called: "Hey Jackie, some broad wants to talk to you about the Fields' case."

I couldn't remember the last time I was called a broad. Jackie walked over with a smile and took a seat next to me. The bartender brought her a Mic Ultra.

"You'll have to forgive Sandy. She never came out of the late fifties. Still thinks women are broads and complains all the time about living alone."

Jackie's smile was genuine, and she was not visibly shaken about Sandy mentioning Emily Fields.

I reached over and shook her hand. She had a good, grounded grip. "I'm Paula Graham. I'm investigating the murder of Emily Fields. Can I ask you a few questions?"

"Sure, grab your drink and we'll sit in the back booth. That way we won't be bothered; come on." Jackie picked up her beer bottle and headed to the back of the room. I followed.

Sandy followed behind us carrying two more drinks and another bowl of peanuts.

Thank God for peanuts. I was hungry, and didn't think to eat before I came. Jackie pushed all the way into the booth and leaned against the wall, putting her feet up on the cushion. I slid in across from her. I wasn't sure how close Jackie and Carla still were. Just because they had been friends as kids doesn't mean they were still friends today.

"How long have you known Carla?" I asked.

Jackie closed her eyes and tipped her head back, lightly hitting the wall. "All our lives," she said.

"Are you still friends?"

Jackie moved her head from the wall. "Best friends," she answered.

"Okay, I get it. She's your best friend and you're willing to co-operate but you're not volunteering anything. Fine, but Carla missed her court date today and a bench warrant was issued for her.

The DA's convinced she ran because she's guilty, so if you know where she is, you need to tell me."

"What do you mean she ran? Have you checked her house, the gym, her friends?" The concern on her face was real. "It's not like Carla…she called me a couple of days ago. Told me something was missing from her house and she needed to talk to me. I was expecting her to show up that night. When she didn't show, I figured she found whatever was missing."

I was trying to get a time-line of when Carla may have gone missing. "Was it yesterday she called you?"

"No, this would be the third day since she called me."

I was thinking about the housekeeper. So that was three days ago, the same time Mrs. Garcia was called to clean up.

"Is it like Carla to just disappear without telling anyone?" I was looking directly at Jackie, but she showed no sign of being anything but concerned.

"She would never take off and leave that gym. That was her whole life; she put everything into that place. It was her pride and joy, her way of showing every high powered man that she was as good, if not better, than them. She did that by keeping the male population out of her place and having a gym that topped any male gym in the northeast. Top of the line for Carla, nothing less. I'm telling you she would not have left without telling me. That, I'm sure of! You think something has happened to her, don't you? That's why you came here. Am I right?"

I was nodding my head. "Her place was tossed, and she told the housekeeper that the police came back and made the mess. I know for a fact no one from the department went back to her house. I hoped you were hiding her or at least knew where she would go if she took off. Are you sure she would call you even if she was in deep trouble?"

Jackie was flashing back to the time they had sat at the bar as teens and Jackie had confided in her about her mother. "She knew she could trust me with anything she said or did. We're best friends and nothing or no one could ever come between us or separate us, nothing!"

I believed every word Jackie said. I still wasn't sure Jackie wasn't hiding her. "Did she talk to you about Emily's father?"

"She told me she was convinced he was out to get her whether she was guilty or not."

"I heard the same thing. Was there a reason for Carla to believe Emily was cheating on her? Or maybe just seeing someone that she told Carla about, as only a friend, but Carla thought different?"

"Carla was a jealous bitch and didn't treat Emily the best. Sure, she lost her temper a time or two and might have hit Emily a few times. I was against any kind of abuse and I told her so, but she was always sorry about it later. She tried to make up for it by buying Emily all kinds of things. Course it was really for herself. After a period of time, things seemed to calm down. If Carla thought Emily was seeing someone, she'd go after that person. She hated to lose anything."

"Sounds like motive for murder. Did you tell the DA the same thing?"

"I told them Carla didn't do it."

I still had one big question to ask: "Jackie, did Carla tell you she killed Emily?"

Jackie leaned back against the wall. I wasn't sure, but now I felt she was holding something back. I debated if I should try and push her into talking more. Jackie slid to the end of the cushion and got up.

"Look, Ms. Graham, I know Carla wouldn't leave without telling me. She hasn't called since that night and she hasn't come by. Now if you'll excuse me, I need to let Sandy go home. Nice meeting you. Good bye."

Well, that certainly let me know I wasn't getting anything more from her. I walked out of the Rendezvous with the cold evening air attacking me. I was glad I didn't have far to walk to my car. The night had brought the neighborhood to life; women gathered on each corner wearing short skirts and fishnet stockings, standing in high heel shoes with short faux fur coats wrapped around their shoulders.

The doorways were crowded with men sharing the whiskey bottles they bought with their day wages or managed to steal from the local liquor store. The alleys contained barrels full of trash and broken down chair parts and thrown out skids being readied to be burned later that evening when the cold turned frigid.

While waiting for the car to warm, I tried to review all the things Jackie told me. What I realized was that Jackie was a true friend, and what a wonderful thing it must be to know someone cares enough for you to trust. What was she hiding?

Suddenly, there was a tap on the passenger window. I nearly jumped out of my seat. I leaned over, looked out the window, and saw a face pressed against the glass. He had a bushy beard and a dirty face. He was winking, and began to lick the window.

I placed the car into gear and slammed the gas pedal down. The car tires spun and then, to my glee, I was heading down the street. I checked my rear view mirror to make sure I didn't run over anyone; the bearded man was standing in the middle of the road swinging his arms and giving me the finger.

I felt dirty, and the first thing I wanted to do when I got home was jump into the shower. When I entered my place, I stood in the doorway and took everything in. I didn't want the silence around me; I wanted someone to be here when I came home. I forgot about the shower and grabbed the quilt from the couch. I wrapped myself in it and curled up, pulling the quilt tight.

I heard many things from Jackie except the answer I was looking for…did Carla kill Emily? Did she run? Would she hide her? Jackie wouldn't answer the most important question. Why?

Did that mean Carla admitted she had killed Emily or that Jackie just believed that Carla killed Emily?

I was so tired and empty that I could feel my strength dwindling. But my mind wouldn't stop running every kind of scenario, so I pulled the quilt closer and tried imagining a warm fireplace with the flames dancing throughout the night.

Chapter 25

Jackie rinsed the last glass of the night then walked to the front to lock the door. She turned off all but one light. She went behind the bar and pulled a bottle of rye off the shelf. Grabbing a glass, she moved to the bar stool where she filled her glass. The first shot went down easy, the heat rising in her throat, the second shot went down a little slower, but gave her the same warming effect.

Putting the glass down, she placed her elbows on the bar then placed her forehead into her palms. She unconsciously rubbed her eyes. She couldn't imagine Carla leaving, not without talking to her first. Taking another sip, she closed her eyes, and running her fingers through her hair, she pushed it behind her ears. She remembered the night that Carla and she had sat on these same bar stools and talked until dawn. They were only in their late teens. They told each other their dreams, their problems, and hashed over their childhood.

On that night, their friendship became unbreakable. The friendship they formed would be tested many times over as they grew older and became independent women. The times Carla was arrested on assault charges, the times she was beaten and called for help in the middle of the night. When Carla was in juvenile hall and needed someone to visit, Jackie was there. Over and over, Carla needed a friend and Jackie never questioned a thing, just went to help her in her time of need. Then again, Carla never failed to help Jackie when she was in a financial bind. At the beginning, Carla gave her what money she needed, never asking for it to be returned and always arguing with Jackie when she tried to return it.

Jackie was feeling guilty about their last meeting. She poured another drink.

Carla had showed up after closing one evening, upset about Fields coming after her. She needed to talk to someone she could trust. This was the first time that Jackie had ever questioned Carla to whether or not she had done anything wrong. Before, it had never mattered. For some unknown reason, though, Jackie asked Carla the question: had she, in fact, killed Emily? Carla walked out disappointed and hurt by her friend; she felt betrayed by their friendship. Jackie felt she should have believed in Carla and given her the support she was looking for and never asked that question.

Jackie just couldn't get the look out of her mind, that indecipherable look that Carla had on her face when she asked if Carla had killed Emily. Regardless, Carla still would have called her if she was running away. Jackie slammed her fists on the bar then brushed her arms across the top; the bottle of rye tipped over, and her glass crashed to the floor.

"Damn!" she yelled. "Why didn't I believe in her? Why?"

She grabbed a bar stool and threw it into one of the tables; she then turned and kicked the other bar stools over as she walked to the front door. She threw it open and walked into the chilly night.

She began to walk east, then started to walk faster. Soon she was running as fast as she could. Several blocks away, she stopped, bent over, huffing and puffing, holding her ribs in pain as she tried to breathe.

Jackie stepped to the curb and hailed a cab. She gave the cabby Carla's address and leaned back, resting her head against the seat. Her hands were shaking, and her chest was still heaving from the cold air while her body shook uncontrollably. The sound of her beating heart grew louder and louder.

"That'll be twelve fifty," said the cabbie.

Jackie looked through the window. The house was dark, but a small light shone through the windows on the side of the front door. "The light in the hall," Jackie whispered to herself. She handed the cabby fifteen dollars and told him to keep the change. The cabby pulled away mumbling to himself.

Jackie went to the side of the building and found the fake electrical box where she removed the key to the front door. She passed through the door, feeling the emptiness of the house. Nothing was stirring, but the silence was deafening. Jackie flipped on each light as she moved through the house. Everything was clean and in its proper place. She entered the kitchen, the hallway, the bedroom, looking around and searching for something -- anything. She stood at the doorway of the master bedroom and looked around.

She remembered Carla saying that something was missing. She went to the drawers and opened them. Emily's things were all neatly folded and in their place. She opened Carla's chest of drawers and then the closet. All of Carla's clothes were still folded or hung in the closet.

Jackie moved to the end tables and pulled out a small box from the drawer. She held it out looking at it from side to side, then ran her fingers across the top. Jackie knew inside this box was a seashell that she gave Carla when they were kids. They both had one and they both kept it in identical boxes that they handmade one summer. She knew if Carla left, she would have taken this box. No matter where she went, Carla always kept the box with her. Jackie didn't open the box because she knew the seashell was inside. She replaced it and closed the drawer.

Now Jackie began to worry that something had happened to Carla. She took one more look around the room. She thought she remembered some kind of picture hanging on the wall, but wasn't sure. Besides, who would steal only one picture when there were so many more in the living room worth thousands of dollars?

Jackie wanted to check one more thing before she became convinced that something had happened to Carla. She went into the bathroom and removed the medicine chest from the wall. Behind it was a built-in panel that slid open and contained a locked box. Jackie reached around, feeling for the money she knew Carla kept hidden for emergencies. The money was gone.

"Damn," Jackie said as she re-hung the medicine chest. She was no longer sure Carla hadn't taken off to avoid going to trial.

She sighed and walked out of the house, closing the door as she left.

As she stepped off the porch, she stopped, looked up at the stars and started chuckling. "It's three in the morning, Jackie girl. Did you think to tell the cab to wait?"

She returned to the house and called a cab. While waiting by the curb, she thought about Carla and wondered if she was so angry that maybe she had left without telling her. I let her down, and I was the last one she would have believed would do that…yes, she might have left without telling me. She prayed that Carla was pissed and just took off. At least that way she was still alive.

Chapter 26

"Can't you close for just one day? You never go anywhere with me!" Darcie threw a hair brush across the floor.

"Stop acting like a baby and pick that brush up before my customers get here! What's wrong with you? You've been moody all week. You know I can't close. I have appointments, and this is how I make a living. I told you I can't go with you today. I'll go Sunday if you really want."

Darcie dragged herself off the chair and picked up the brush, defiantly tossing it on the counter.

"Damn it, Darcie! You can't just throw things around! It's dirty now and has to go into the jar to be cleaned. Jesus, Darce!" Joanne moved over to the counter and picked up the brush. "And look at you. You're a mess. Your clothes look like you slept in them and your hands are filthy. You need to pull yourself together. Go home. I'll call you later." She was waving the brush at Darcie.

"Go home? You can't take a day off, you won't have lunch with me and you can't go to the museum with me. Are you sure we're partners or what? I don't want to go home. I want to be with you and go to the museum. Ever since Emily died, I don't have anyone to go with me to the museums. I want company." She grabbed Joanne's hand. "Please, please go with me."

"Stop acting like an idiot. Emily didn't go with you to the

museums. You met her there on occasion. You followed her sometimes. Did you forget how mad she used to be when you chased her down and stayed by her side all day? Are you taking your meds? I think you're losing it and forgot to take your meds."

"You know they make me feel funny. And sometimes I ..."

"How long?" Joanne took Darcie's arm. "How long has it been since you took your medicine? Tell me."

Darcie pulled away. "You know I don't really need it. I'm fine, see?" She jumped back and twirled around.

"Shit! You only think you're fine, but when you take the medicine, you are. When you come off them, you aren't fine. Remember the doctor explained this, and he explains it every time you get off your meds. He told you the medicines keep you in balance and you have to take them! Damn! I better call him and let him know you haven't been taking them."

Darcie leaped up and put her arms around Joanne. "No! Please! He'll make me go back into that hospital, and I hate it there! You promised me you'd take care of me. You promised!" She held on tight. "You said I would never have to go back there!"

Joanne took Darcie's arms and pushed her away. "I said as long as you took your meds you wouldn't have to go to the hospital, remember? I never said you couldn't take your meds. Go home, take your medicine, and leave me alone."

Darcie drew a deep breath and backed away. "I knew you never loved me! I'm going to pack my things and get away from you and your oh-so-high-and-mighty self. You're the one who needs medicine, not me! Everyone is against me! Everyone wants to control me! That's why I have to take the medicine, so everyone can tell me what to do and how to live and where to go and when to pee. Everyone is after me! I can tell!"

Darcie started to leave when Joanne suddenly grabbed her wrists. "You have to take the meds. It's what keeps you from making all these wild accusations, and you're so paranoid all the time. Believe me, no one is after you, and no one is watching you, honest! And you know how I feel about you."

Darcie pulled away and headed for the door, but before she left, she turned her face askew and yelled back to Joanne. "See! I'm right! You said 'how you feel' not that you loved me! You hate me! I know you do! I'm leaving. You'll never see me again. I'm going to run away and kill myself. You'll see; you'll be sorry…you'll take back all those things you said to me or I'll, I'll…" She ran out the door.

Joanne stood looking in that direction. Shaking her head, she grabbed the broom and began sweeping. The room seemed large and empty as she began talking to herself. "Yes, I don't love you. You're crazy! I feel bad for you. I kind of feel responsible for you, but you're right; I don't love you, and I wish you would run away get out of my life so I can be happy again. Maybe you could find another woman to fall in love with, but you're wrong. I don't want you to hurt yourself or kill yourself or hurt anyone else."

The phone had been ringing, but Joanne didn't hear it or even see the customer come into the store. The customer stood there watching Joanne as she swept the middle of the room. The customer waited as Joanne's mind raced through all the things she should do before Darcie made a mess of her house again.

The woman moved toward her. "Are you all right Joanne?" she asked. "You look pale as a ghost."

"Helen! I'm sorry. I just had a little altercation with Darcie…again."

"Is she alright? The poor dear was so out of it after her friend died. She had to quit work and moped around for days and days. She is all right, isn't she?"

"She's off her meds again, Helen, and you know how she is when that happens. I'm not sure how much longer I can put up with all this. I have a business to take care of and I'm planning on expanding into health and beauty. I've been working on a program that will make women look younger and live longer. Maybe they'll all look like me."

She laughed with Helen. "Maybe you could make a deal with your plastic surgeon and get kickbacks from all your referrals."

They both laughed more as Helen sat in the chair. Joanne put the cape around her and reached for her scissors. She wet Helen's hair, combed it through, then pulled lightly and began to cut.

She stopped short and rubbed her eyes. "Helen, give me a

minute will you? I need to make a phone call. I'll be right back."

"Certainly, dear, are you planning on calling Darcie's doctor? He should know she's off balance and feeling like everyone's after her again. Remember the last time she did this? She had to be hospitalized. Go make the call."

"I'll try the house first. Just give me a minute." Joanne went to the front desk and picked up the phone.

Darcie answered. "I'm sorry. I came straight home and took my medicine. I promise I'll take it every day."

"I think I should call the doctor to…."

"No!" Darcie cried. "I'll go everyday to the out-patient clinic; everyday, then you'll see I'm taking them, okay? Please? I was only off a few days. You'll see I can take them, and I'll be okay in no time. I knew you weren't really after me. I was just saying that…okay? Please don't call. I can do it."

Joanne sighed. "You promise you'll go to the clinic everyday and take your meds in front of them?"

"I will, honey, I'm sorry. You know I love you; I never planned on running away. You knew that."

"All right, Darcie, but if I think you're not taking the pills, I'll call the doctor and you'll have to go into the hospital."

"Okay. I'll call the clinic right now and set up a time to go, so you can stop worrying. Now go back to work, and I'll make us a nice supper tonight. You'll see; everything will be fine. Bye now, I'll see you tonight." Darcie hung up the phone before Joanne could say anything else.

"Is everything all right, dear?" Helen asked as Joanne returned to her station, picking up the scissors.

"I think so. She promised to go to the outpatient clinic and take her meds. I'm so tired of her bullshit. I just don't know how to break away from her without her going over the edge. You know what I mean, Helen? I want to have a good, happy life, not always worried if my partner is going to make a scene in front of all my friends."

"Everything will be okay, dear. She'll go to the clinic and get her meds then she'll level off and be her sweet self again. Don't take too much off the side, dear, I don't want my hair too short." She reached up and patted Joanne's hand.

Darcie still had the phone in her hand as she began twirling around and talking to herself. "Who does she think I am? I know when someone's following me, watching me, talking about me. Sure I slipped up a little. I'll become the perfect partner and go back to work. I can fool anyone," Darcie twirled, laughing out loud.

Chapter 27

I heard the buzzer go off in the plant as the steel door opened and the people began exiting. People started running to their cars while others shuffled along. They laughed and hollered at each other. If it wasn't hearing about the pub across the river, I would have thought I was watching high school students being dismissed for the day. The only thing missing was the school bus. I kept a close watch for Nancy Hargraves. I'd seen her at the funeral and I had a copy of her driver's license picture in my hand. I also parked next to her Toyota Tundra in case I couldn't recognize her, or simply missed her in the crowd.

Walking toward the truck was a large, big boned woman wearing a baseball cap, jeans, and a sweatshirt that said *Utah* on the right hand breast pocket. She was pulling out a small plastic bag that had some kind of little red package of rolling papers, and what I knew was grass. She walked right by me and unlocked her truck. I watched her jump in behind the wheel and take out the rolling papers. She pinched some of the grass into the papers and began rolling a joint. She was obviously adept and rolled the joint with one hand.

I walked over to her truck and knocked on her passenger window. The knock startled Nancy, and the plastic bag and the grass flew all over the truck seat. The look on her face was worth millions. One I had seen many times, just before the suspect was arrested.

I opened her door. "Hi, I'm Paula Graham. I appreciate the fact you agreed to meet with me today after your shift."

Nancy was busy trying to gather what she could of her mishap with her weed. "You scared me," she said, still scrambling to gather everything up.

I slid into the truck. "I'm not the police and I'm not here to bust you, so relax. I just want to talk to you about Emily Fields' death and what, if anything, you know about Carla Reed."

Nancy finished sealing her baggy and placed it in her ashtray. Why people think the law doesn't know that -- and that's the first place to look for weed in a car -- I'll never understand. They all think it's their first time and no one would look in the ashtray. Wrong! Everyone forgets that even police officers were young at one time or another, not that Nancy was still a teenager.

"Sorry about that," she pointed towards her ashtray.

I shook my head, and she realized it was okay.

"What can I do for you?" she asked.

"I'm curious if you know where Carla is?"

Nancy looked at me strangely. "Why would you think I'd know where she is? I'm guessing at the gym or home."

"I think she might have skipped town. You didn't know she was missing?"

"Missing? No." Nancy was staring at me.

"She didn't show up for her court date and the DA believes

she ran away because she was guilty of murdering Emily. Do you think she would run away?"

I watched Nancy as she unconsciously reached to the ashtray and drew her arm back, grabbing the steering wheel. "I didn't even know Carla was going to court. I knew she was charged, but I didn't know when the court date was, nothing like that. You said she might have skipped? I know I'd be long gone if I was accused of murder."

"I know she didn't show for court, and a bench warrant was issued for her. The DA's convinced she's guilty, and every law enforcement agency in the state is looking for her. I talked to her best friend, Jackie Steiner, the other day, and she said Carla wouldn't have run off without telling her first. What do you think?"

Nancy was still staring out the front window, her face pale. "I didn't even know Carla had a best friend. She was never friendly with anyone in particular; she didn't seem close to anyone. I certainly didn't know Jackie was her best friend. I thought she was just one of the women in the group. Carla was mean to Emily, everyone knew that she was jealous all the time, and Emily hardly went out alone because of Carla. We thought things were getting better these last few months."

I looked over at Nancy. "Why these last few months?" I hate to interrupt someone when they're talking, but I wanted to get an answer, and I was afraid I'd forget the question. I forgot both my notebook and recorder today.

Nancy continued, "Emily was much happier these last few months. We had a women's get-together at Joanne's house one evening, and everyone who was on the board of directors and a lot of the other members of the Women's Club were there. Emily came early, which was unusual, because she always came and left with Carla. Emily was happy, mixing with everyone, mingling with all of us. When Carla showed up much later, she wasn't upset with Emily. They seemed to be getting along just fine."

"Would you know if Carla was upset with Emily?" I asked. I was curious if Carla showed her rage in public.

"Believe me, when Carla was mad, she had her way of showing it. Emily always seemed scared, and then she would get quiet and moody. This time, she and Carla both stayed upbeat. Everyone had a great time, and even after Carla and Emily left, we all talked about how well they seemed to be getting along."

Nancy made another move to her ashtray. I knew by the way she kept going to her weed that she must be a heavy user. I wondered how she kept her job when they had their random drug testing. Nancy was checking her watch, and I saw she was ready to go.

"Is there anything you can think of that might help me know where Carla might have gone, or anything about anyone that may help me with the case?"

Nancy shook her head. "I wouldn't even want to go there. She never really blended in with this group, kind of stayed in the background. But I just can't see it. As unpleasant as Carla was, I can't see her as a murderer."

I knew Nancy was impatient, but I had a few more questions to ask before I was going to get out of the truck. "Let me just ask you this: Do you think Emily was seeing someone else? Maybe when she went to her art exhibits or the museums? Could she have met someone?"

Nancy looked up at the roof. She noticed a small tear in the foam and started repositioning the torn cloth. "I don't know that much about where Emily went. I wasn't privy to that portion of her life. Some of these women think working in a factory makes you…well, you know, not the type who would be interested in art and museums. No one ever asked me to attend those functions with them. It's okay. I'm not all that interested anyway."

Nancy's fidgeting told me that she did care. Another assumption made by many women. "I heard Emily met Darcie several times at the museums. Do you think they might have started seeing each other again? I know they went together before."

Nancy laughed, "They went together years ago, and Emily couldn't take all the mood swings that Darcie had. She used to say it was like living with Dr. Jekyll and Ms. Hyde. Emily went to school with Darcie and was Darcie's first love. They didn't last long. I think when Darcie went off to college, Emily was relieved. Darcie came back after school and had had a few relationships, but none that have lasted any length of time."

"I didn't know Darcie went to college. What did she study?"

"She has a couple of degrees; one is a Masters in something, I can't remember what. She's really smart, but she has such mood swings, she can't keep a job. She argues all the time with the boss."

"How long was she gone before she came back?"

"You mean from college?" Nancy asked, looking confused about the questions.

"Why, was she gone somewhere else?" I gazed at Nancy.

"I don't like talking bad about the women in my group."

"Listen, Nancy, this is about a murder and anything you tell me might help me find the truth. That's all I'm looking for. I don't want to hurt anyone. I'm not going to tell anyone where I heard anything. I just want to find the truth. If Carla is guilty, I want to prove it and the same holds true if she isn't. Sometimes we don't know what helps until we have all the information and put the pieces together. It takes all kinds of information to do that and sometimes the littlest thing helps. So please, I know you're not talking out of turn."

"Well, Emily told me once that Darcie was put into a hospital for a year to help her with all those mood swings. I think she was suicidal or something along those lines. Right after she came out of the hospital, she went off to college. So she was gone about seven years. When she returned, she connected with Emily again, but only as friends. I don't think they socialized any other place. I really don't know anything else. Our group has its own little clique, and not everyone is open, or even willing to find out the truth. I hope Carla is innocent. I hate to think anyone would kill someone they loved."

I knew from my years as a detective that it happens. Love turns sour and people do kill the ones they love. This happens more than the average person would want to know. I reached for my card and slipped it into Nancy's hand. I held her hand for a second. "Thank you for talking to me. If you think of anything, anything at all, please give me a call."

I slid out of the truck and returned to my car. The temperature had dropped several degrees, and it was getting dark earlier each day. I knew winter would be arriving soon. I turned on the heat in my car and waited for the chill to leave.

I looked over toward Nancy as she sat in her truck. She took several drags off her hand-rolled joint. I thought of the impression she had left on me - a lonely woman. Pot had taken over as her only friend. I hoped that wasn't her future.

I put my car in gear and headed home where I knew I would have to write everything down as soon as possible before I forgot what Nancy had told me. I thought about Emily and how she was happy toward the end of her life, and the museums and art galleries she visited so often. I was beginning to think that maybe she and Darcie had been rekindling their relationship, and I was speculating that maybe Carla found out about it, bringing trouble back to the Reed household. I needed to find a time that Darcie was free to meet with me. I also needed more information about Darcie, as I didn't want to go into an interview without knowing more about their relationship--and Darcie's past.

As I pulled into my parking space, I noticed the light over my back door was out. The walk from my car to my door is a short one, and as I exited my car, the hair on the back of my neck stood straight up, and a shiver went up my spine. I pulled my sidearm from its holster and held it close to my side as I walked to my door. As I unlocked the door, I felt someone was watching me. Holding the door open, I looked over my shoulder to the right and then the left. I couldn't see a thing in the dark. But I could feel something. I turned on all the lights and walked around the loft before I put my weapon away. When the phone rang, I left the floor with a start.

"Graham here."

"Hi, it's me Bobbie. I hadn't heard from you in a couple of days and thought I'd check on you. So how are you doing? Got any news on the case?"

"I just got back from an interesting meeting with Nancy Hargraves. She really likes her pot."

"Great, you're looking for a murder suspect and you find a drug dealer."

"Nope, she only uses for recreational reasons. I think she's a little depressed. I don't believe she knows anything about Carla. She wasn't even aware that Carla had a court date, never mind that she didn't show."

"Do you have any idea what happened to Carla? The DA is convinced she ran off. I'm beginning to think the same thing."

"It's hard to say. I can't find anyone with a reason to kill her, except maybe Fields."

"If it was Fields, then you'll never find her, and you can be sure she's dead."

"Bobbie, it's like she just vanished off the face of the earth and not a soul seems to know a thing -- or care. It's sad."

"Tell you what; tomorrow I'll go talk to Mr. Fields and see what kind of a reaction I get from him. What's your next step?"

"I think I'll see if I can talk to Darcie Chambers. She seems to be the one who saw Emily the most before she died. I'm hoping she can help me, maybe with who Emily might have seen last. Maybe they were still friends and Emily confided in her. Something I need to check on, anyway."

"Okay, I'll call you tomorrow and let you know what happened with Fields…unless you want to cook dinner tomorrow night. I could go for..."

"Good night Bobbie."

Chapter 28

I hit the snooze button three times already and I was thinking I should just turn the alarm off, pull up my quilt, and stay in bed for the day. I had had a terrible time sleeping; I couldn't get the feeling of being watched out of my head, even when the rain started. I was sure someone was outside, waiting for me to exit my door, whereupon I would be jumped, mugged, or worse.

I called the department and arranged to have a car drive by as often as possible. If they had seen anything out of place, they would have called me. We are very good at taking care of our own, and I knew they were out there. Once, years ago, Bobbie and I were on a stake-out, and I had the same feelings, and sure enough, when Bobbie got out of the car to go for coffee, someone came out of a doorway and tried to rob her. The fool didn't know she was a detective until he ended up face down on the pavement. From that day on, I've listened to my intuition.

The day was gray, the rain was still falling, and I tried to get up, but couldn't muster enough energy. I pulled the quilt up around my neck and fell back to sleep.

I wasn't sure how long the phone had been ringing before I heard it. "Hello," I said, still groggy.

"What's this I hear? You requested a car to drive by and check your place last night?"

"Good morning, Bobbie." I sat up, throwing my feet over the

side of the bed. "I got one of those feelings last night and just felt someone was out there."

"You didn't tell me that last night."

"I didn't want you to worry, and I didn't want you to haul your ass over here and sit outside all night. A drive-by was good enough. If anyone was out there, the…"

"You know better! We were partners for a long time; you don't keep things like that from me. It's wrong! Understand?"

Bobbie was angry, but I didn't think she needed to know or worry. After all, it was only a feeling.

"It was nothing. I was just a little spooked. What time is it?"

"It's after one in the afternoon. Why are you still in bed?"

"I had trouble sleeping; this case is keeping me awake. First, I thought Carla was innocent. Then, she almost choked me to death and I thought she was guilty. Then she disappears, and everyone thinks she's guilty. This case just keeps getting weirder everyday. Did you get a chance to see Mr. Fields?" I was up and walking to the fridge to get a diet Pepsi. Not sleeping is like waking around with a hangover.

"He damn near threw me out of his office. He's convinced Carla skipped and he's putting up a twenty-five thousand dollar reward for anyone who turns her in. It'll be on the news all day. We'll have every crack-pot in town calling with sightings. The captain has already called in all off-duty officers, and everyone works until they run every call down or Carla is found. He doesn't even care how she's found, just found! So, I'll be working until one of us solves the case. So wake up, get up, and get to work. I'll call you later and don't ever leave me out of the loop again when you think something is wrong." Bobbie hung up.

I couldn't worry about her feelings right now. I had to get moving and make some calls. I was in the shower when I heard the phone ringing again. They can wait, I thought. The water running over my face was comforting; much more than the heavy winds blowing the rain against the building.

I pulled out my notebook and trailed my index finger down the page, looking for Joanne Adler's phone number. The busy signal I kept hearing became annoying, so I decided to try my friend Darla DeVito at her gallery. I reached her on the second ring, and she reminded me she had found the Pissarro sketch I had been looking for. She told me it would be the perfect size for my stairway leading down to my shop. She was holding it until I found time to see her. I agreed that today was a good day to be inside a gallery. I was excited about the Pissarro, and the thoughts of staying home in bed disappeared.

Camille Pissarro was born in the Dutch West Indies and moved to Paris in 1855 where he entered the Academy Suisse. He joined the Impressionist painters of the time, but he avoided painting rivers and seascapes, unlike many of them, and liked painting land and cityscapes instead. Like Monet, he could capture a scene at a particular moment. I was looking for his 1872 LeVerger also known as *The Orchard*. It was done in oil on linen. It always reminded me of the apple orchards of New England. Like all my art, it has to talk to me, and this picture did.

Thinking about the picture had taken my mind off the 'feeling' and the case. I needed the break. I drove through the rain with ease and arrived at Darla's gallery without incident. A slim but curvaceous woman, not much taller than a ten year old, was headed toward me. Her smile was as large as the breasts she carried. She always wore black outfits with three inch heels. Darla DeVito had worked two shifts and still found time to attend college. She studied art and when she graduated, she opened *The Gaelar*. She has been here in Boston for over twenty years.

We met at a gallery opening on the south side of Boston more than fifteen years ago. She was quick and always up-beat, a very likeable character.

"Paula!" She was coming toward me with open arms. "Like I said at the museum, it's been way too long. How have you been? Just wait until you see this sketch. It's just what you wanted, and I think the price is right. Well, actually, it's a bit high, but it's worth every penny. Come look!" She took my arm by the bicep and walked me to her office. Her enthusiasm brightened the day.

"Slow down Darla! I'll see it, and I'm sure it's beautiful."

She paid me no mind and pulled me into her office. She went into a vault she had installed in her office and brought out the Pissarro. She was right. It was magnificent - the details captured the moment.

"I love it," I said as I took it in. "You're right, it's the perfect size, but I'm not thinking the stairwell, more like my kitchen area."

Darla began laughing. "Not the kitchen area! It would be bad for the painting to be around all the smells and grease spatter."

I laughed. "You think I actually cook enough to hurt it?"

"Not the kitchen, but not the stairwell either. You'll find the right spot. I'll have Tom wrap and crate it and it will be delivered to your door next week." She replaced the sketch into the vault. She sat and pointed to a chair near her then she called and ordered a coffee and a diet Pepsi. "So tell me about the case. How is it going? Tell me everything." She leaned back and locked her hands behind her head.

"I'm working on a case where everyone believes this woman, Carla Reed, killed her partner Emily Fields."

"Hummm," Darla leaned forward, "…a very powerful family," she said.

"You know the Fields?"

"I put all the art in the Fields' offices throughout town. His daughter Ellen Kipfer comes down here and either picks out what she wants or puts an order in. I send them out, get them hung in the right place, and cash a huge check."

"I haven't been able to get an appointment with her. What's she like?"

"She's very sure of herself. She makes quick and sound decisions. She knows what she wants and doesn't leave the room until she gets it. She is very cool, almost cold. She's a lot like her father. She gives very few interviews, and sees no one -- unless *she* calls *them*."

"Do you know her sister, Lori?"

"No. I only know Ellen, her father, and of course, I did know Emily. Does any of this help?"

"How well did you know Emily?"

"She was a regular here, a benefactor. She was on the list to notify when new shows were being held. She never missed an opening, and sometimes came more than once."

"Did you also know her fricnd, Darcie Chambers?"

"I know Darcie, but I wouldn't call her Emily's friend. Darcie came almost as many times as Emily did, and hung over Emily's shoulder constantly. Emily put up with it for a while, then one afternoon, they had a big blow out, and Emily told her to back off and stop following her around like a puppy dog. Darcie got all hysterical and ran out the door. After that, Darcie stayed in the background, but she was still around whenever Emily was. They never had any more contact that I saw, so I didn't think I needed to ban Darcie from the gallery. Emily didn't seem to care or she just didn't see her. Either way, I never saw them speak again."

"Damn, no one else knew they had a fight. Everyone I talked to thought they were still friends, good friends. Well, that puts a spin on things."

It was getting late and I knew Darla liked to mingle with her clients, always treating them as if they were the only client she had. "I should get going. I can't wait to get my picture. I love it already. I know I'll be giving up a lot of lunches, as you say, but it will be worth it."

I was almost out the door, when Darla yelled to me, "You know about the woman Emily had been seeing, right?"

I turned with a questioning look. I was shocked. All this time I kept thinking maybe Emily was seeing someone and Carla found out. I thought it was Darcie. "What woman?"

"I don't know her name, but a couple of months ago, this woman started coming to the openings and she would stand next to Emily. It looked up-and-up, just casual. But then I would see them touching hands occasionally. Before long, they held hands throughout the gallery. Once I even saw her kiss this other woman. It looked like love to me. This woman handed Emily a long stemmed red rose every time they were here. Emily never took it out of the gallery. I always found the rose by the front door, lying on the coat counter. The only thing that I know she took out of the gallery was a print that the woman bought her. The one by Dali called *Meditative Rose*. You know the print. The one where a red rose is floating in thin air."

"Thanks, Darla! That helps a lot. I'll call you soon. Dinner on me, I promise."

"After you pay for the sketch, I'd better pay for dinner. I wouldn't want you fading away from starvation."

As I walked through the gallery, it came to me. I hadn't seen the print *Meditative Rose* or any rose in Carla's house.

Chapter 29

I watched out my loft window at the wind blowing the leaves off the few trees that lined the sidewalks. The leaves swirled as they landed on the street and the street sweeper scooped them up into a vast vacuum.

Staring out the window I was flooded with memories. I was standing in our bedroom looking out across the yard. The trees were dropping their leaves and the wind was causing the pond to send ripples across the water's top.

I could see Elizabeth riding her lawn mower, chasing down the leaves. It made me laugh as I watched. She was so determined to get every leaf. I, on the other hand, would be raking the leaves from the hedges and filling barrels to carry into the woods to dump. Then, after trimming the hedges, and making sure every tool was cleaned and returned to its proper place, we would walk around the yard admiring the plants and planning our next project. We always had a new project in mind, maybe new plants to be planted, or changing a grassy hill into a garden of flowers and succulents. We were always planning an easier route, preparing for our older years.

She would reach out and take my hand as we walked. It was a small thing that warmed my insides and meant so much to me. We watched the reeds that sat on the edge of the pond swaying as the surrounding trees began to lose their color.

I gazed over to the stack of wood that had been piled high by her grown children every spring. The logs were carried to the splitter, split, and then stacked, waiting for the winter winds and cold to arrive. Part of the wood would soon to be lugged to the porch. Later we would use that same wood to warm the house as we lay on the couch at the end of a long wintry day. There we would cuddle and pretend to be watching TV when really, we were napping between episodes of Law and Order.

    With winter coming, the yard work was done, the mower would be cleaned and placed into the shed upon the hill. The snow blower would be brought down and take the lawnmowers' place in the second shed near the back door. There it would sit through the winter. Elizabeth was too short to handle the machine and worried anyone else would break it. So it sat in the shed as we used shovels to clear away the snow blown driveway. We would trip over the snow blower many times throughout the winter. Then in the spring, we would take the snow blower out of the second shed and move it back to the shed on the hill. There it would stay until the following winter, where once again the switch would be made. I laughed as I thought about our routines as the seasons changed.

    I missed the raking and carrying of the leaves, but mostly the walks through the yard, and the feel of her hand in mine. The wind whipped, causing the leaves to hit my window. I tried to forget the memories that were suspended in my mind. The day was dry, barren, and gray, and I felt as empty.

    I could hear the phone ringing. As I walked to answer it, I

hoped I would be too late and the person on the other end would give up and hang up. No such luck.

"Hello," I said as I plunked myself down on the couch.

"Hi, it's me, Annie. I have all the information you asked me to check on last week. It's not real interesting about Fields, but it's interesting when you check on Carla Reed."

My head and thoughts were still with the weather and Elizabeth's back yard. I shivered and ran my hand through my hair, rubbing the back of my head.

"What? Annie, is that you? I'm sorry, I'm in another world. What was it you said about Fields?"

Annie was laughing. "Wake up Paula. I've got those reports you asked for."

I returned to the present and was back paying attention to Annie and working on the case. I got my notebook and pen, which is never far from my phone, and began to listen.

"I didn't find anything out of the ordinary with Fields' finances. He has the best financial brains working for him, and if he's hiding anything, it will take more than me to find it. But what I could find and see is, he's above board and could pass any IRS audit. I found no huge unexplained withdrawals from any of the bank accounts that I could find. I'm sure he keeps petty cash around. A man in his position will always have cash on hand. He's set each of his daughters up with a very nice endowment. They're set for life and their children's children. He's very wealthy. Started with a small business and turned it into a multitude of businesses. Each business builds off the one before it. Fields is a very smart man. I wouldn't say he didn't have the right connections, but he definitely knew how to use what he had. He brought in his daughter, Ellen, as the new CEO, while he still dabbles in the business."

I wasn't really expecting anything out of the ordinary to be found, but I was hoping Annie might have found something interesting that I could have used if and when I got to talk to Ellen Kipfer.

"Not much there we didn't expect," I said. "What did you find on Carla Reed?"

"Now that's a different story. Her father was a welder who drank most of his check every Friday. His wife left him and Carla when she was just a baby. No one knows where she went. I couldn't find any Social Security number being used by her, and no employment records. My guess is she got married and never worked a day in her life. So we know Carla didn't get any money from her family."

"Is this leading up to anything good, Annie?" I was beginning to get interested again.

"Well, fifteen years ago, Carla Reed bought her gym and all the equipment. Then turned around, the day after, and bought her house. Every bit of it was bought and paid for in cash. She told everyone it was an inheritance. She's done very well ever since.

Her business was booming until she was arrested and her customers began walking away."

"What did you find out about all the art and antiques she has in her house?"

"She has insurance on over two million dollars worth of art and antiques in her house, and in the office at the gym. She has an agent who buys for her. I made a call to her agent and found out that Carla doesn't care what it is or even what it looks like, as long as it's expensive. Her agent just sits back and collects his percentage. He told me Carla believes the more money she spends, the more the rich will be willing to accept her into their circle. His words not mine."

"Were you able to track down this so called inheritance?" I couldn't believe Carla had any family that would have left her that type of money.

"No. All I could find out was that fifteen years ago she came into a bundle of cash. She didn't have to explain where she got the money to open up her business, just where the money went after she was opened and began bringing in the cash. She has a financial advisor, and he does everything by the book. Her advisor files every year on time. I couldn't find anyplace where she might have gotten the money, at least not on paper. Not yet, anyway. I'd like to keep looking, if you don't mind"

"Good work I'll send you a check tomorrow."

"Anything else I can do for you, Paula?"

"I'm not sure, but if I think of anything, I'll call. Thanks again." I hung up and made a note to check on any large criminal activities fifteen years ago.

I was hungry, and the refrigerator was keeping some freshly cut roast beef waiting for me. A sandwich was at the top of my list at the moment. I sat at the table with my sandwich and began separating the things that Annie had told me. Where could Carla have gotten the money for her business and home? Blackmail came to mind; robbery was another thought. I made a note to get on the computer that night and see if I could dig up anything unusual from way back then. It would have to be something that happened near here, probably in Boston. The sandwich was good and a second was about to be made, when the phone rang again.

"Hello."

"Paula, this is Gail. I found out what the liquid was on the painting that you brought in the other day. It was unusual and very interesting. The spray on the picture was Nitroglycerin from an aerosol spray."

I was shocked. "Aerosol spray, I can't believe it. Why would anyone…."

Gail continued, "When it's sprayed, it dilates the blood vessels. Enough of the spray can cause an effect on the muscles, causing collapse, or even respiratory paralysis, or sometimes even a coma. Are you thinking that Emily was sprayed when she opened the door?" Gail asked, then continued before I could answer.

"Someone had to know exactly what and how much to spray in order to subdue a grown woman. Too much could result in coma and then death; not enough could just give someone a headache the size of Montana. The thing about this toxin is, it's not hard to get a hold of, but not just anyone would be knowledgeable of its use, especially in a liquid spray form. I'd say someone wanted your suspect unable to run too far away from the house, and this was the way it was done. When this toxin is used, the conversion of hemoglobin to methemoglobins, and the build up of fluids in a multitude of organs disappears, in standing blood, and if the test isn't done quickly, all your evidence is gone. My guess is if you check Emily's toxic level, you wouldn't be able to prove that she was poisoned. All the evidence will already have disappeared."

Gail was trying to remember the report. "I thought Emily was stopped at the door then chased through the house."

"Maybe it was used to slow her down so she couldn't get away from her attacker. Who would know how to use this toxin?" My case just kept getting weirder.

The nitroglycerin spray must have been used when Emily was killed. But, why? Maybe someone had just wanted to restrain Emily and it was never supposed to be a murder. Maybe something went wrong. Emily might have fought, and the killer lost control. Maybe the dose was wrong. But that makes no sense if it was Carla. She wouldn't have to subdue her or surprise her at the door. She'd just walk in and kill her. No. Something didn't make sense.

"Paula, is there anything else I can do? I'd like a chance to see the crime scene. I may be able to tell if Emily was attacked first at the door with this toxin."

"Everything is just supposition at the moment," I said. "This may have nothing to do with the crime."

"Oh, I'd say it has plenty to do with this crime, all right. The 'who' we may not be sure about, but the 'how' is becoming more obvious."

"I'll see if the DA will give me a search warrant. With Carla gone, he might agree to let me back into her house. I don't know if he'll agree with my theory, but I'll try. I'll call him tomorrow and let you know. Thanks for getting this done so quickly for me."

"Any time. Call me as soon as you know if we can get in Carla Reeds' house."

I needed to know if Carla killed Emily and then, if someone, maybe Fields killed Carla or if she took off.

I walked back to the window and looked out at the last leaf falling. As my eyes welled up, I closed them.

Chapter 30

I was sitting in Mr. Fields' office, waiting for him to return from a meeting. His secretary told me the meeting would only run another ten minutes. It was already thirty minutes past the appointment time. I got up and walked along the wall, reading all the business awards Mr. Fields had hanging. He had been awarded *Man of the Year* several times. As I walked around, I took in all of the pictures in the office; pictures of statesman, several governors, and senators, all of whom were shaking hands with Mr. Fields. He also had one with Bill Clinton at the White House.

"Busy man," I whispered.

The secretary returned to the room and asked me if I'd like any coffee. I asked for water and she left, returning two minutes later with a bottle of Poland's and a glass on a sterling silver tray. Just as she was about to leave the room, she turned.

"Mr. Fields doesn't like people wandering around his office. Please, have a seat at the table."

She closed the door. I finished walking around the office before I took a seat. I had just poured my water when Mr. Fields walked in. He looked taller in person, and his eyes appeared to looked through you. His presence in and of itself was impressive. I could imagine how he got where he was; he looked all the part of a big, powerful man.

"What is it you want, Ms. Graham?" He asked as he walked

to his desk.

On the way over here, I had gone through a dozen scenarios in my head and decided to use the one that he wouldn't expect from anyone. Straight out attack, full force ahead.

"I want to know what you did with Carla Reed."

I watched his eyes come up from the paperwork that sat in front of him. He dropped the pen from his hand and stood. "You'll have to leave, Ms. Graham." He called for his secretary.

She came immediately, "Sir.'"

"Please show Ms. Graham out, and make sure that she doesn't return."

"Yes sir. Right this way, Madame." She pointed to the door and expected me to get up and follow her.

"I'm not finished here," I said quietly.

Mr. Fields' secretary didn't know what to do, which is exactly what I was hoping for. I hoped to throw everyone off and maybe get some answers. She stood in the middle of the office floor with her arm still extended toward the door. Mr. Fields walked around his desk to the door, where he stood for what felt like a lifetime.

"It's okay Becky. I'll handle it from here. You can go."

Becky left and Mr. Fields closed the door behind her, returned to his desk, and sat. "I have no idea where Carla Reed is."

"I don't believe you." I walked to his desk and sat in the chair nearest to him.

He picked up his pen and leaned way back in his overstuffed office chair. He began tapping his pen against his wrist. "I had no idea Carla was missing until a Detective Kerry stopped in and asked if I knew anything about her disappearance. I'll repeat to you what I told her: I have no idea where she is. She ran away because she was guilty and you people let her out of jail. She never should have been allowed bail. She murdered my daughter and now she's gone. She's probably sitting on some island in the sun, laughing at all of us, freezing our butts off here. My daughter is dead and Carla is gone. If you don't find her, I will. There is no island where she can hide from me, no place in this world. She killed my daughter and she will pay. Pay big." He threw his pen down and leaned forward, looking at me with his penetrating eyes. "Now, get out of my office and never return." He called for Becky again.

This time, I got up and walked out with her.

The wind was blowing, and snow was on the horizon. I turned my car on and waited for it to heat up. I grabbed my cell phone and called Bobbie.

"I just left Fields' office and I confronted him about Carla. I asked him straight out where Carla was and…"

"I bet he flipped out. You're telling me that you just spit it out?"

"I asked him the big question: 'Where is Carla Reed?' He told me he has no idea where she is. I told him I didn't believe him and then he kicked me out."

"I already told you that. Did you get any kind of feeling? Do you think he had her killed?"

"You know, Bobbie, I don't think he did anything. I think he will if he can find her. He certainly doesn't believe the law will find and prosecute her - that much he said straight out. But, I just don't think he was involved in her disappearance. He seemed too sure, not worried about anything or anyone. I'm beginning to think Carla did run off. As much as I hate to say it, it's looking more and more like she's guilty and I'm wrong. You know how I hate being wrong."

"It's not the end of the world if you're wrong. So Carla runs off…prove it, and we can close the case. All these extra hours are killing me. The captain has us chasing down every lead that comes in, and I'm getting tired of listening to every weirdo in town. You wouldn't believe how many there are. They call and tell me they're having coffee with her. I chase it down and I end up in some bar with some guy asking me to buy him a drink, and then he'll tell me what kind of sex they had, and where she went. It's bizarre."

I was chuckling to myself. The car was warming, and I wanted to see if I could stop in at Joanne's and get a hair cut. I never connected by phone; maybe walk-ins are welcome.

"I have to go, Bobbie. I'll call you later.

"Do me a favor and solve the case. I'm going crazy over here." I could hear her laughing as she hung up.

I put the car in drive and headed across town to Joanne's.

Maybe she would know something about Carla or Emily that I haven't already heard.

    The days were getting shorter, and dusk was catching up with me. I turned on the headlights and prayed it wouldn't snow today. I thought about the hair cut I was going to get. She was new to me, and my usual hairdresser would not be happy if I went to someone else. I'd have to hope for the best. I knew this was the fastest way to get my questions asked and answered.

Chapter 31

It took me a little longer to reach the hairdresser's. Traffic and not paying attention got me lost three times. There was a time Elizabeth and I were traveling the highway heading out to pick up something at a Home Depot. But as we were traveling on the highway, talking and laughing, we missed our exit. At the next exit, we turned around and, too busy yakking, missed the exit again. This happened once again, and we decided we wouldn't speak until we were on the exit. Today I had no excuse, I was just lost. I would have loved it if Elizabeth was the reason I missed the exit, but the lack of knowing how to use the navigation system was the cause.

It was quiet here with only a small Toyota and an old van in the lot. The van was a Chevy. The lights were on in Joanne's place, and I could see a woman sweeping the floor. I headed in, holding my coat closed from the cold.

"Are walk-ins welcome?" I asked as I entered. "I'd like to get a haircut, if you have time."

"You're a lucky woman. I just had a cancellation. Do you want a wash, too?"

I was trying to decide how to approach the subject when Joanne spoke.

"Aren't you the private investigator whose been snooping around and asking all those questions?"

I was stumped. I didn't think about all the women talking

about me. I should have. I'd been asking all kinds of questions over the last couple of weeks, and it would make sense that word spread around. I didn't consider myself a snoop.

Joanne began talking again. "Jan and Stacy called me and told me about all the questions you asked at the dance. You didn't think we wouldn't find out you were investigating Carla, did you?"

She sprayed water on my hair with a spray bottle and began combing my hair back.

"I was wondering how to start the conversation with you while you had scissors in your hand."

She began laughing and then pulled up some hair and held the scissors over the comb. "How would you like this cut?" She asked not moving her hand.

"Just a trim. If I have too much cut off, my regular hairdresser will have a fit and my next haircut might be to the scalp," I said jokingly.

"Well, I won't take off that much,"

"Mind if I ask you a few questions while you work?'

"Ask away," she said. "I'll tell you what I know."

"How long have you been friends with Emily Fields?"

Joanne was clipping away. I knew this because I was watching her in this mirror that took the entire wall in front of me. I watched her hesitate just for a moment.

"I wouldn't say we were really friends. More like acquaintances. We hung out with the same crowd, went to the same dances, things like that. We didn't go out unless it was a group thing. Not like two friends would."

I was nodding my head subconsciously when she pulled it slightly. "Ouch!"

"Hold still or you'll need the buzz cut for sure." I saw her smiling as I looked into the mirror.

"Your partners' name is Darcie Chambers? Does she know Emily?"

Joanne had no hesitation to her answer. "Oh yeah, they went to school together as kids and when they were teens they experimented with each other. Later they had a short relationship. Darcie always liked Emily. They met a few times at the museum. They always seemed to be okay."

"As far as you know, was Carla jealous of Darcie?"

"I don't even know if Carla cared one way or the other about Darcie. She was always polite enough to her," Joanne said.

"Did Carla and Emily spend any unusual time with any one person that you can think of?" I was trying to get a fix on someone that either one of them might have spent a lot of time with.

"I think Emily was seeing some woman over the last few months," Joanne said.

"Really? Why do you say that? Do you know who she was?" I was curious as to how she knew.

"I'm a hairdresser and lots of people come through here. I'm like a bartender. People love to talk while there hair is being cut.

This place is like the Grand Central of gossip. They don't know who I know, so they just talk away, and I just listen. I don't let them know that I know who they're talking about. Sometimes it's interesting and most of the time it's boring, and once in awhile, I hear about someone I know." She kept clipping away.

"So you're saying someone was in here talking about Emily having an affair with someone? Did you tell Carla?" I asked.

"Course not. I'm a listener not a talker." She was pulling out the trimming shears to shave my neck and trim around my ears.

Most couples tell each other many things and they know it's to be kept between them. I wanted to ask Joanne if she told Darcie, but my guess was she had, and I didn't want to impose on their private life.

"Do you know the woman who was seeing Emily? Did you hear a name?" I wanted to connect with this woman if I could, or at least have Annie run a background check on her.

"Not that I can remember. It was several months ago," she said.

"Who was the woman who told you? Is she a regular customer?"

"No. She was a walk-in, like you, and I think she had a wash and cut, but I didn't know her personally."

"Can you describe her?"

"Black straight hair, no dye, and her hair was cut short." She was pleased with her ID.

I was amazed. I was expecting height, weight, and an actual description of a person, not a description of her hair. "Is that all you have?"

"I'm a hairdresser, not a cop. I see the hair, not the face, and I'm not trained in all the stuff you cops are trained in." She began to get defensive.

"You're absolutely right. I'm sorry. Thank you for all the information you gave me; it's more than I had before. What do I owe you for the trim?" I turned and checked it in the mirror and ran my fingers through the sides of my hair. "I like it."

"Forty dollars," she said.

I almost choked when I heard that. I handed her fifty. I would be counting pennies after that one for awhile. My regular hairdresser cuts mine for fifteen bucks, I give her a twenty, and we're both happy. I can even have lunch after. I thanked Joanne again and left my card in case she remembered anything else about the mystery woman, or the woman that gave her all the gossip in the first place.

The day had ended, and the cold came in with the darkness. The wind had picked up and all the signs were telling me that it was going to be a cold winter. I looked up toward the sky, squinting to see the stars. Most were covered by thin scattered clouds. I pulled my collar up around my neck, and placing my hands in my pockets, walked away.

Chapter 32

"Hello," said Darcie

"Hi Darcie, It's me, Beth. What are you doing? Got any plans today for lunch?"

"Phew…I thought you were Joanne. She just left for work and she was bitching again about the house being a mess and me not doing anything. You know, all the same crap I get every day. She's nagging me again about my meds, too."

"I don't understand why everyone wants to run your life. Always on your case, it's awful. You're too smart for that woman, I keep telling you that. You don't need those meds. You know what's best for you, not everyone else. You should listen to me. Wasn't I right about Emily? And you know I was right about that other woman you went with. You gotta listen to me. They were all wrong for you. How many times do I have to call and tell you how wrong she is for you before you start to listen to me?"

"Sometimes, I don't know what I'd do without you, Beth. You're a real friend. You always try to warn me. I just don't listen until it's too late. I can't have lunch today. I've got to clean the house and wash clothes today or Joanne will throw a fit again. I have to be the perfect partner for a while, or she'll start again on the medicine crap," Darcie said.

"Doesn't mean we can't talk for a few hours, does it?"

"We talk everyday and we always will. You keep me in the

know. I'd be lost without you calling me every day."

"You should have been with me on this last sale I just made. This couple wanted this house so bad they could taste it. The problem was they weren't sure how to pay for it. You know me, Darcie. I made a few changes here and a few there and I convinced them they could swing it."

"Will they?" Darcie asked.

"Sure, until they get in there, and then the bills will bury them. But not until I collect my commission." She began laughing.

"You sure are a clever one, Beth. I wish I was there to hear you spin that yarn."

"I know how to get anyone to believe anything. You just have to keep drilling it into their thick heads. It doesn't matter if it's true or not. After a while, they begin to believe it themselves. I tell you, Darcie, I can play anyone."

"Joanne told me a secret last night," Darcie whispered.

"Tell me, tell me! Is it like the other one you told me?" Beth was giddy, waiting for the new secret.

"Well, yesterday, that private investigator whose been asking all the questions about Emily and Carla, well, she walked right into Joanne's salon and asked her all kinds of questions. And, Joanne told her about the 'other' woman."

"She didn't know about the other woman?" Beth asked inquisitively.

"No, and she asked about me and Emily. Course my sweetie

told her nothing."

"So the P.I. didn't know about the other woman? Didn't I tell you that when she interviewed me I told her squat?"

"That's right, you knew all about the other woman. You were the one who told me. How come you didn't tell her that you showed the woman a house?"

"Remember, Darcie, I told you Emily was no good for you, and that she was a cheater. I only tell my best friends the important things. It was none of that P.I.'s business, and I didn't want her investigating my business. Don't forgot, this is between us. Don't tell Joanne our secret. Bear in mind, she can put you in the hospital if she wants, and I know she's not good for you."

"Don't worry," Darcie said, "I'm good at keeping things from everyone but you. I'm so glad you're my best friend. You know what's best for me. I'd be lost without your friendship."

"You better go clean the house. I'll call you later this afternoon. Remember, if you hear anything else about this P.I., let me know right away."

"Don't worry, I will. Bye." Darcie hung up feeling better, knowing that her friend was always looking out for her.

Chapter 33

"What do you mean you can't find her? I don't care how much it costs, find her and find her now! Fly in anyone you need just do it!" Fields slammed down the phone.

Becky knocked lightly on the door, then opened it, and walked in. "Your daughter is here, sir."

"Ellen? Send her in. She…"

"No, sir, Lori," she said.

"Lori? She should be home with her mother! What does she want?"

"She said she wanted to see you. She says it's important."

"Fine, send her in. And Becky, hold all my calls while she's in here with me.

"Yes sir." She walked out, leaving the door partly ajar.

Lori stuck her head inside. "Daddy?" She walked in and sat in the chair next to his desk.

"Why aren't you with your mother?"

"She knows I'm here. She said to tell you she went to the garden club and would be home at four."

He shifted in his chair. "Why are you here?"

"Daddy," she said quietly. "I don't think Carla would have killed Emily and I don't…"

He jumped up, startling Lori, who leaned further back in her chair.

"What are you talking about? That queer bitch killed your sister! She went into a rage and hit her over and over, and now she's run off to avoid going to jail for the rest of her life!"

Lori was shaking her head, "Daddy, I know Carla was a hot head, but she wasn't crazy."

"Not crazy? She's a lesbian! And you know she hit Emily! Hell, Emily told you that herself."

"Yes, but Emily said they talked about it and Carla promised never to hit her again."

"And you believe that? You should go home and not worry about this. I'll handle the family affairs. And don't ever bring up Carla Reed's name ever again! Do you understand that, Lori?" He wagged his index finger at her.

Lori was nervous. "Daddy, I'm thirty-six, and I should be able to say what's on my mind. And I saw that private investigator the other day and..."

"What?" He reached over the desk and pulled Lori up out of the chair by her collar.

"You're hurting me!" she yelled.

"What did I tell you? Didn't I tell you not to talk to anyone about your sister? Do you want people saying she was a lesbian and died because of it? What did I tell you?"

Tears welled up in Lori's eyes as she tried to pull herself away from her father. "She was a lesbian, but that wasn't the reason she died."

She jerked away from her father's grip and fell back into the chair. He sat down and became quiet. Both said nothing for a short time.

Lori looked over at her father. "I loved her, Daddy, and now she's gone and is never coming back. I want to find the killer, too. I just don't believe it was Carla. Daddy, I need to tell you something."

His face softened as he glanced toward his daughter. His eyes watched her hands as they clenched together. He shook his head and reached for her hand. "Look, Lori, I've always taken care of the family affairs, and I don't want you talking to anyone about Emily. What did that investigator ask you about?"

"She was very nice. She met me at the BFA and treated me to lunch. She said if Carla did kill Emily, she wanted to prove it. But if she didn't, she wanted to find the one who did."

"Hmm," her father leaned forward. "I think Carla killed Emily because Emily wanted a different lifestyle. I think she was ready to leave and start a new life. She finally woke up and realized how wrong she was living with that woman."

"She was, but not in the way you think," Lori said.

Her father went to the bar and made himself a drink. Then, carrying a soda back to Lori, he stopped in front of her. "What do you mean, Lori? Do you know something that you're not telling me?" Lori was sipping her soda. "Lori?" He stood in front of her. She began to tremble. "What is it Lori? Tell me."

"I didn't tell the private investigator," Lori mumbled.

"Didn't tell her what?" His voice rising.

"Emily was leaving Carla, but not because she was changing her lifestyle, but because she fell in love with another woman. Daddy, she was going to move in with another woman. She told me the last time I saw her. She was so happy, daddy, she…"

"Shut up, just shut up! I won't hear anymore of that! Go home and we'll talk about this when I get there. Don't say a thing about this to your mother. Not a thing." He went over to refill his drink.

Lori finished her soda in one quick swallow and headed to the door. She turned to say something to her father, saw he was filling up his glass, and quietly left the room. He drank the shot and refilled his drink again. Walking over to his desk, he buzzed for Becky.

The door opened immediately, and Becky entered with a notepad in hand. "Yes sir?"

"I need to talk with the DA in ten minutes, and get me a private overseas line, now." He tipped his glass back and finished off his drink. "One more thing, cancel the rest of my appointments for today. Oh, and Becky, after you get the DA, take the rest of the day off. I'll see you tomorrow."

Within a couple of minutes the phone buzzed, and he had an overseas operator. He told her the number he wanted and then sat and waited.

"I know I just called an hour ago, I'm telling you now. I want the best sent here tonight. Get it done." He hung up. The door opened, and Becky stood in the doorway.

"The DA is on line two. I'll be leaving now, sir." She closed the door behind her.

Fields punched line two. "David is that you?"

"What's so important that I had to leave a meeting?" the DA asked.

"I found out some interesting information about my daughter's case."

"I told you we'd handle this, George. You need to take a step back and let us…"

"If I wait for you to handle this, Reed will be on some island somewhere, drinking cocktails with a flower in her glass. Hell, she may already be there. I found a motive, and I want her caught and put away. I don't care who catches her as long as she's caught." Fields put the phone on speaker and walked over to his bar again.

"You found a motive? That would be great, but I still think we have a good case. What is it?"

"My daughter Lori told me that Emily said she was leaving Carla and moving in with someone else. I bet Reed found out and knew Emily would take all her money with her so she killed her."

"Did Lori say who she was moving in with?"

"No, but I bet it was a guy, and that Reed character couldn't handle that."

"That's a sure-fire motive. I need to talk with Lori."

"Not now, David. She was so upset I had to call the doctor and have her sedated. Possibly we could get together tomorrow."

"That's great, George. That will seal the case and I can get the department off all this overtime and I'll have a fugitive warrant put out on Carla Reed. George, don't worry we'll get her."

"Oh, I'm not worried, David. We'll get her. If there's one thing I know, it's the fact that we'll get her." He hung up the phone and stood in front of the bar. His hand began to shake, and the ice from his glass fell, bouncing off the rug. He threw the glass across the room. "How could she do this to me? Loving a woman? How could she?" He grabbed a glass and the bottle and went to his desk, falling into his chair. "How could she?" he whispered.

Chapter 34

I just wanted to stay under the quilt and ignore the ringing of the phone. I stayed up most of the night reviewing everything I had on the Carla Reed case. Things just didn't add up, and I couldn't put enough facts together to say for sure that Carla Reed was guilty. Aside from the fact that she was missing, and assuming she had run to some foreign land to avoid capture, I hadn't really heard enough to definitely say she had killed Emily.

The phone wouldn't stop ringing, so I dragged myself to the side of the bed with my feet hanging down and wrapped in my quilt. "Hello," I growled.

"What's wrong?"

"I'm tired and cranky and this case is keeping me awake."

"Well, you're going to be thrilled when you hear this, then," Bobbie said.

"Please, thrill me. Tell me you found and arrested Carla, or even better, you know who killed Emily."

"You can wrap yourself in your blanket and sleep for a week, if you want. The DA closed the case."

"You have her?" I asked.

"No, but Fields called the DA and told him his daughter Lori knew that Emily was planning on leaving Carla for someone else. Get this: He told the DA she was leaving Carla for a man. That gives him a motive the captain feels seals the case. He put out a fugitive warrant for Carla and told us we didn't have to keep up the overtime. He's called it, Paula, and he's convinced Carla is the killer. He told me if I talk to you before he does, the case is closed and you needn't continue searching. He's convinced he has all the proof he needs; he knows the killer is Carla, and he can convict her when she's picked up. He feels she won't be able to hide forever. Send him a bill. Sleep in for a day or two. Your job is done."

I was amazed. "You know, Bobbie, when Lori and I talked at the museum, she never mentioned Emily was seeing anyone. And, a man? No way! Emily was seen at an art gallery by Darla, holding hands with another woman. And Joanne told me that some woman got her hair cut and was talking about Emily and another woman. It makes no sense at all that Lori would tell her father it was a man."

"It might make sense if her father told her what to say. That way, he not only gets his family back, but he also gets Carla locked away for life," Bobbie said thoughtfully.

"I'm not closing this case; not yet. Too many things don't add up. I'm going to take a shower. Why don't you stop in at the Blue Hill Cafe and pick up lunch for us? I want to go over everything again. Something is nagging at me. Maybe talking about it will clear a few things up."

"I'm halfway out the door. See you in twenty." Bobbie hung up.

I laughed. All I had to say was *food* and Bobbie was on it.

Thank goodness she worked just as hard on her cases. That's what made her such a good detective. I headed to the shower still wrapped in my quilt. I stayed in the shower longer than usual. The hot water rolled off my face and over my shoulders, giving my back the warmth it so desperately needed. I was leaning my head against the shower wall as the water flowed down my back. I closed my eyes and tried to put all the pieces together. Why didn't Lori tell me about Emily? Why would she tell her father? Why would she say it was a man? The questions just kept coming. By the time I got to the kitchen, Bobbie was already there, setting the sandwiches out and opening a bag of chips.

"You look beat," Bobbie said. "I brought your favorite; roast beef with Swiss cheese, mustard, lettuce, and tomato and, as you can see," she held up a bag of Tri-Sum, "...your favorite chips."

I walked to the refrigerator. "Pepsi or beer?"

"Pepsi. I'm still on duty," she said.

I brought the folder that I had compiled last night and two cans of Pepsi to the table. I sat, took a large swig, and dug into my sandwich. Bobbie did the same.

She looked over at me. "I thought you'd be glad the DA closed the case."

I leaned forward and opened the folder. "I'm still not convinced Carla killed Emily or that she absconded without her money and her things. Things are just too important to her. She spent all kinds of money on objects, and she didn't even know what they were, never mind their worth. I didn't get much information from anybody about her except that she seems to get things done, and she's not afraid of fighting for the prestige she thinks she deserves. She wants to be known. She wouldn't run." I finished my Pepsi and tossed the can into the trash.

Bobbie got up and retrieved two more drinks and picked up the folder.

"You have Darcie's name circled over and over. What's your thinking behind that?"

"She keeps popping up in a negative way." I said, scratching my head.

"How?" Bobbie asked. "Do you think she might have killed Emily?"

"No, but she had a fight with Emily at the Gaelar. And according to Darla, Darcie and Emily didn't speak after that, yet Darcie still hung around at the gallery. Darla didn't think there was a problem and never had to confront Darcie." I thought for a minute. "Another thing I don't understand is Nancy told me Darcie has a college degree, so I did some checking and she actually has a Masters degree in chemistry; then I checked her work history and she's only had menial jobs all throughout her adult life. Her first relationship was with Emily and ever since, all of her relations have been short-term."

"That doesn't really mean anything. A lot of women have short-term relationships until the right one comes along. You know that," Bobbie said.

"True, but all the women she has had relationships with say the same thing. It starts out fine and seems to grow, and then Darcie becomes unkempt and starts having mood swings. I called Joanne and talked to her again and she finally told me Darcie is on an anti-depressant and some other medications to control her moods. She also had been hospitalized for a year some time back."

I picked up the folder and removed some papers. I scanned them then placed them in front of Bobbie. "She's had fourteen jobs in the last four years. She doesn't function."

"You think she killed Emily, don't you?" Bobbie took the papers and began looking them over. "It doesn't make any sense. These jobs are ridiculous for someone with her intelligence."

"Not if she was emotionally unstable. Think about it. She finds someone, attaches herself to them. Things are fine. She's stable and then she decides she doesn't need her meds. In a few days her drugs wear off and she can't control herself or her moods anymore. We should talk to her doctor and find out just how serious her condition is."

"No doctor is going to give you confidential information about a patient. Especially when you have no proof that she's done anything, except, maybe, to follow Emily to a few galleries and a couple of museums. There are no complaints on record. If you're thinking she had something to do with Emily you need to get real proof. Something solid," Bobbie said.

"I'm not saying she did anything, but she does interest me. I think I'll try and get her to meet with me and maybe I'll understand her better once I've talked to her. Another thing that I have to do is track down this mysterious woman that Emily was in love with and find out if she knows anything about Emily's death. You know, I was thinking if Lori knew about this other woman and Joanne knew, she probably told Darcie."

"You think?" Bobbie asked.

"Most partners share everything with each other under the assumption they know it's confidential; you know, just between each other. They don't think their partner is going to go out and tell anyone else."

"But, sometimes it happens. Like Joanne tells Darcie and then maybe Darcie tells a friend and before you know it, Carla hears about it." Bobbie was nodding her head.

"Brings it back full circle, doesn't it?" I said to Bobbie

"Gives the DA's motive more truth is what it does. If Carla knew this, she could have gone into a rage and killed Emily. She tracked down those boys who hurt her when she was young and got revenge. You know, she just might have done it," Bobbie said.

"I think Carla would have gone after the mysterious woman first, and then maybe Emily," I countered.

"You need to talk to the missing woman. I can see how this is keeping you up, but the DA said it was closed. You're off the case." Bobbie looked at me and smiled.

"No! It's not over until I have all the facts. I'm not quitting." I went to the refrigerator and retrieved two more cans of Pepsi.

Bobbie opened the Pepsi and said, "You have a plan. I can see that look in your eye. What is it? You're going to find that woman, aren't you?"

"Among a few other things," I said as I drank my Pepsi.

Bobbie smiled and picked up the wrappings from our sandwiches and threw them in the trash. She headed to the door "I'm off to work. Make sure you call me with any new information and please don't do anything dangerous without calling me first. See ya."

She was gone and I was sitting here looking over all my papers. I was pretty sure Darcie had something to do with this case. I wasn't sure if she murdered Emily, but I did know I was going to find out. I looked over at the counter and couldn't help but chuckle to myself. Bobbie had found the chocolate chip cookies that I was planning on having for dessert. She must have had heavy pockets when she left. Half of them were gone.

Chapter 35

She stopped in the foyer and looked at the billboard. This week only; works by Johannes Vermeer.

She began walking through the gallery stopping at each picture and reading the small card below the picture to the right. She stopped to read the brief history of Johannes Vermeer.

She moved to a section that displayed only three paintings. The small card below the first painting told that he only had three paintings that were dated. *The Procuress* (1656), *The Astronomer* (1668), and *The Geographer* (1669). She admired the paintings and moved on to the next set. Vermeer had two that were historical paintings. A note under one read that it was believed that many religious and scientific connotations could be found in his works.

Darla recognized the woman who often met Emily and walked quietly up behind her. She watched the woman study the paintings; her interest seemed so sincere. She looked at each one, angling her head to see every part of the picture.

"He was said to be a master in the use of light," she said, turning toward Darla.

Darla smiled to the woman. "I didn't mean to disturb you. I haven't seen you lately."

"I've been sad lately," she said as she slowly moved to the next set of paintings. "These are his two townscapes, done in his hometown of Delft."

"I know you've lost a good friend. Emily always smiled when you gave her the rose."

"She always left them on the coat counter," she said, dropping her head.

"How did you know? I thought you left before she did; how did you see she left them on the counter?" Darla asked

"I watched from behind the door. I loved her, and I knew when she took the rose home she would then tell Carla she was going to leave her and we'd be together."

"Did she ever tell Carla?" Darla asked.

"I don't know. She died…" A tear came running down her cheek. She wiped it away. "I don't know if she told her or not. We had plans to meet again but she died before our meeting. I don't think she told her." She moved on to another picture and seemed to drift into it.

Darla was quiet for a short time.

"Have you seen this picture?" the woman asked as she pointed to *Woman Reading a Letter at an Open Window*.

"Yes, it's very nice," Darla said.

"I wrote many letters to Emily and often dreamed that she would read them sitting under a window with the sun shinning in on her. It's kind of stupid, really."

"No, I don't think so, kind of romantic, I'd say. Listen, I have a friend who's investigating Emily's death. I know she'd like to talk to you. Would that be okay? I could call her right now. It wouldn't take long for her to get here. She really wants to find the right murderer and bring peace to Emily, her family, and her friends."

The woman faced Darla. "Does she really want to solve it?"

Darla took her hand. "Yes. She only wants the truth, and she's not interested in anything else."

"Go ahead and call her. I'll take my time and finish looking at these pictures. I'll wait." She turned and walked toward *The Allegory of Faith*.

I parked in front of a fire hydrant and ran through the doors into the gallery. I couldn't believe how fortunate I was that Darla had spotted the mysterious woman and asked her to wait for me. I stopped in the foyer and looked for Darla. She was talking to a woman who was admiring a painting. She spotted me and held up a finger. I sat on the bench and waited. It felt like I waited for at least an hour, but it turned out to be only five minutes.

"Darla, thanks for the call. Where is she?" I was in anguish, waiting to speak with her.

"She's standing in front of *The Girl with the Pearl Earring*. It's the second room on the left."

I got up slowly and began walking through the gallery. I hadn't thought about Elizabeth in, I'd say, twenty-four hours and then this. Darla had said she was in front of *The Girl with the Pearl Earring*, Elizabeth's favorite picture. She had a print hanging in her upstairs hallway leading to the master bedroom. She had talked many times to me about Vermeer and how she liked his works. My stomach began to knot. I stopped and leaned against the wall and told myself, this is business and it's important, and you cannot let yourself be distracted thinking about Elizabeth. I took a deep breath and went into the second room.

She was leaning forward studying the brush strokes near the pearl earring when I spotted her. She was dressed in a suit with basket weave shoes. She was lean, and when she stood straight, she was much taller than I.

"Beautiful picture," I said.

Without turning around, she said, "Some say he had an affair with her."

"He certainly captured her beauty, and his colors have a way of talking to you," I said.

"I can see how someone would love this picture; it's one of his most famous. A book and a movie were made from this picture. I haven't read the book yet, but I hope to someday."

I could see why Emily liked this woman. She seemed kind, quiet and had a love for art, just like Emily. I wondered how hard it was for each of them to find the time to meet and share their passions and if it was worth the time they had had together.

"I'm Paula Graham. I'd like to talk to you, if I may."

The woman turned from the painting. Her face looked tired, and the gray ashen bags under her eyes told me she had gotten precious little sleep.

She held out her hand in a friendly gesture. "I hear you're on the Emily Fields' case. I'd be glad to talk with you." She spoke quietly, but with a surprisingly strong voice.

"Just a few questions and I'll make them as quick as possible," I said.

"Could we go somewhere else? These pictures remind me of Emily too much, and I don't want to feel any worse than I already do."

"Certainly, I know how you feel."

She stared directly at me. "I don't think so, not unless you no longer have the woman you love in your life," she said with an onslaught of sadness.

"You're right. I apologize. There's a small Bistro around the corner. We can go there."

She turned and started walking toward the door

I knew exactly how she felt. When you lose the one you love you don't always recover. You just take one step after another and hope the day ends and the next one begins. I looked at the painting. I closed my eyes for a moment then followed the mysterious woman out the door.

Chapter 36

Joanne opened her door and let out a scream; she ran to the phone and dialed 911. "Someone broke in to my home and tore it apart! It's a mess! Help!"

"What's your name and address?" the operator asked

Joanne quickly answered and repeated her call for help.

"Is there anyone in the house?" the 911 operator asked

"I don't know! I just opened the door and....oh, what a mess! Things are thrown all over the place! Chairs are broken, even my curtains are torn down! Send someone over quickly, please!" Joann was near hysterics.

"An officer is on the way, Ms. Adler. Please go outside."

"Go outside! Why?" Joanne yelled.

"Safety reasons, Ms. Adler. In case someone is still in the building."

Joanne ran out the door and waited on the sidewalk for the patrol officer to arrive.

Not too long after, the responding officer walked out and down the steps from Joanne's condo. "All clear, madam, you can enter now. An officer will go through with you while you make a list of what's been stolen."

Joanne re-entered her building and began walking through her home. She was feeling faint and had to stop to lean against the wall several times to keep from falling to the floor. "I can't believe this! Who would do this?" She was brought to tears. She found a chair and picked it up, placed it back on its legs, and slumped into it. The officer stood next to her waiting for her to stop sobbing.

"Is there anything missing, Ms. Adler? Anything that you can see at a glance that's missing?" the officer asked.

Joanne used the cuff of her shirt to wipe her eyes. "I don't see a thing missing. It's just, everything is smashed."

She reached down and picked up a shattered picture of her and Darcie. She jumped up and grabbed the officer. "Darcie!" she yelled. "Where is Darcie? She should have been here! Oh my God! Something has happened to her!" She shook the officer. "You have to find her! What if she's hurt? You've got to find her!"

The officer called the department and reported a missing person, possible kidnapping or worse. He waited with Joanne until a detective arrived.

Detective Jackson walked through the condo looking at the devastation. He was shocked at the amount of breakage throughout the house. It didn't look like a robbery. Most robbers don't tear the place apart unless they're sure something is hidden in the house. He couldn't find any blood, so if there had been a fight, how did so much get broken without any blood being spilled? He walked to Joanne and knelt beside her. "Do you have any idea where Ms. Chambers might have gone?"

"She wouldn't go anywhere without telling me," she said, looking at the picture.

"Have you had any trouble with anyone who might do this to you?" He asked as he waved his hand around indicating the destruction.

"I'm a hairdresser, you twit! What could I have done to deserve this? Someone must have kidnapped Darcie or hurt her! You've got to find her!" Joanne kicked a couch cushion that lay in front of her.

"Madam, I'm sorry, but I have to ask these questions. Did Ms. Chambers have any enemies that you know about?" asked Detective Jackson.

"No, and the longer you stand around asking me these dumb questions, the longer Darcie might be in danger! You should be out there looking for her!" Joanne said.

"I have the word out already, and we are looking for her, but I need more information to help find her. Understand?" the detective said, getting angry.

Joanne walked away yelling at him to just find her. She went into the kitchen and began calling her friends.

Detective Jackson took one last look and left to go back to the department. Upon arriving at the station, he went directly to Detective Kerry's office. He walked in and took a seat. Putting his feet on the arm of another chair, he asked, "Remember that case about the lesbian who got killed and the other one that disappeared?"

Bobbie looked over at Jackson, "You talking about the

Emily Fields case?"

"Yeah, and the Reed case, we had all the overtime on when she went missing," Jackson said.

"Well, what about it? Reed is still missing. You find something?" Bobbie asked.

"I just left Joanne Adler's condo. Her partner a…," he flipped open his notebook, "a Darcie Chambers, is missing."

"What are you talking about?" Bobbie asked.

"I mean I was called to Adler's condo about two hours ago. The condo looked like a tornado went through it and destroyed everything in its path. There was no blood and way too much damage for just a struggle. The partner disappeared. No sign of her anywhere. Damndest thing I ever saw," Jackson said.

"So what have you done?" Bobbie asked.

"I've put out a missing persons report and I have twenty guys searching the neighborhood and going door to door. It's cold as hell out there. If she's hiding or hurt and out in the open she'll be a frozen brick by morning. I just don't know. I've never seen a mess like that - and with no blood. If she was kidnapped, why was the place such a mess? If she put up a fight why isn't there any blood? And that woman, the hairdresser, she was no help at all. She just kept yelling at me to find her. I don't know what else I can do. All the bases are covered." He dropped his feet to the floor and walked over to the coffee pot. "It's freezing out there, Bobbie," he complained while filling a cup.

"This is strange. What do you know about these two women?" Bobbie asked.

"Not a lot. Adler is a hairdresser and the other is unemployed at the time. She said they weren't having any problems, and Ms. Chambers wouldn't just leave without telling her. Do you think we have some maniac out there killing lesbians?" Jackson asked.

"I certainly hope not, but I wouldn't go around saying things like that, not yet anyway. We need more to go on than just two women missing," Bobbie said.

"That's two missing women and one dead, all from the same group. I'd call that a little strange. Maybe this Reed character is on a killing spree." Jackson got to his feet again. "I have to get going. I've got a lot of paperwork to do, and I'll check and see if the guys have had any luck finding Chambers."

"Jackson, keep me informed. I'm a bit curious myself. If you find out anything we'll have to let the DA know what's going on. He won't be happy, especially if it connects to Carla Reed."

"That's not a call I'd look forward to making," Jackson said.

Chapter 37

We sat at a table close to the front window. People were rushing by, pulling their collars up and their scarves close about their faces. The wind began to blow and the darkness brought in the cold of winter days to come.

"It's going to be a long, cold winter." the mysterious woman said.

"Yes, cold and I'm guessing we'll have a lot of snow to go with it."

The waitress came to our table, and we each ordered a hot chocolate. While waiting for the drinks we were quiet and watched the people traveling the sidewalk.

"Here you are, ladies," the waitress said as she placed the hot chocolates down in front of us.

"Thank you," we both said in unison.

"So tell me," I said, "what's your name?"

"Sam, Sam Adams. And no, I'm not related to the beer." She smiled at the thought.

"I bet you get a laugh every time you say your name," I said.

"I had an uncle named Bud Weiser. He really took a razzing growing up. I think our family had a secret wish to be beer moguls." This time, her smile was authentic.

I hated to ask her about Emily but then, after all, that was why we were here. "When did you meet Emily?"

Sam took a sip of her drink and set the cup down. She began using her napkin to clean the overspill. "I've known her long enough to fall in love with her. She was going to move in with me."

"Did Carla know about the two of you?"

"We talked about how she was going to tell Carla. Emily was scared of what her reaction would be. She felt Carla would try to stop her from leaving."

"Did she think Carla would hurt her?" I took a sip and watched Sam as she thought about my question.

"I wanted to go with her when she decided how she wanted to tell Carla she was leaving. We had a fight when she told me she wanted to tell her alone. I shouldn't have demanded to go. Emily said she was capable of telling her herself. I knew that, I just wanted to be with her to make sure she was going to be safe."

"Do you think she told Carla?"

"All I know is that she's dead, and I wasn't there and I promised I'd always take care of her." Sam shifted in her seat. Then she used her napkin to cover her eyes for a short moment. She kept shaking her head back and forth.

"You did what you could," I said to her. I was the last person to give advice to someone about relationships. I couldn't hold my own together, and here was a woman who felt bad because she wasn't with the one she loved when she died. "She didn't want you there. I'm sure she thought she knew what the right thing to do was, and she wanted to tell Carla herself. If you were there, it doesn't mean things would have been any different," I said.

Sam looked up from her cup. "She might still be alive."

I knew how bad she felt, but she didn't want to hear that from me. Nor would she believe I knew how she felt. I decided to change the subject. "Did Emily have any trouble with anyone else?"

Sam finished her hot chocolate and ran the napkin across her mouth. Setting the napkin down, she waved to the waitress. "I'd like another one, please."

I suggested that we might as well have something to eat. We both ordered a chicken sandwich with fries on the side. Sam ordered her third cup of hot chocolate with her meal and asked that coffee be brought after the meal. I ordered diet Pepsi. I thought to myself maybe I should start drinking coffee. It did seem that everyone else does.

"I thought about your question," she said, through a bite of her sandwich. "She had a blow-out with a girl named Darcie."

"I heard that. In the Gaelar. Emily told her not to follow her any more," I said.

"It was more than Emily simply telling her to stop following her. Darcie must have followed her for months. Then, when we started meeting at the galleries and museums, every time Emily turned around, Darcie was there…acting all surprised to see her. Emily wouldn't introduce us because she was worried that Darcie would call Carla and tell her about us. Not that Darcie was sure there even was an 'us'. But Emily told me Darcie was the one who told her father about her lesbian relationship. That cost Emily a lot of grief with her father. She didn't want to take any chances and didn't want Darcie knowing about us, not before she told Carla. We were real careful not to show any affection when she was around." Sam took a couple of bites from her fries.

"Do you think Darcie saw the two of you holding hands or you giving her the rose?" I asked.

"The rose? I don't think so. I love roses. They're so beautiful, yet if you're not careful with them, they'll bite you. Emily didn't care for roses until she realized why I loved them and wanted her to have them. She was beautiful and at the same time she could be as dangerous as a thorn left on the stem. Did you know if you give someone a rose with no thorns it means…love at first sight? Do you know what I mean?" She asked.

I smiled as I told her, "Yes, I do." I dipped one of my French fries into the little pool of ketchup on my plate. "Do you think Darcie saw anything that might have given her the idea that you two were having an affair?"

"We didn't think so. We tried to be careful, but Darcie popped up everywhere we were, and she might have put it together, or saw something. For example, one afternoon I gave Emily a print called *Meditative Rose* to take home, and Darcie was standing behind us. She had a weird look on her face. Emily had enough, and she and Darcie got into a heated argument that led to some pushing and shoving. We didn't see her after that. Of course, that doesn't mean she wasn't there," Sam said.

"Did Emily ever talk about Darcie to you? Maybe tell you what had happened between them?" I asked as I finished my fries and thought about desert.

"Not much. Emily wasn't one to say bad things about the people she knew."

I shrugged my shoulders. "That's unusual," I said to myself out loud.

Sam laughed; she knew what I meant by that. "She told me they were in school together and she brought Darcie out into the lesbian world. Darcie was crazy about her. But Emily told me they just couldn't seem to get their…mmm; they couldn't tell who was suppose to be the butch, and who was suppose to be the fem. Back in those days, I guess there was a difference. Today you have trouble telling the modern lesbians apart. You know how each generation changes."

"I know exactly what you mean. Old dykes like me are a fading breed," I said.

Sam was nodding her head in agreement. "I miss her."

I wanted to tell her things would get better, but in fact, I believed that they wouldn't. You just find a way to push it deeper inside and hope no one sees how much you hurt. "Do you think Darcie could have killed Emily?" I asked, instead of consoling her.

"Darcie was hurt when she and Emily fought, but I think Carla killed her," Sam said.

I leaned back against the seat and looked out the window. The wind was blowing harder and the temperatures were still dropping as people hustled to their cars. I didn't know what else to say. It looked like I was wrong, and Carla did kill Emily, and I was the only one who wasn't convinced.

The waitress brought the bill and set it on the table. I took it, telling Sam I would call it a business write-off. I signed the credit card slip and made sure I left a nice tip, something that would have made Elizabeth proud. I looked over to Sam who appeared to be sad. I pretended not to notice.

"It was nice meeting you, Sam." I held out my card. "If you think of anything else, give me a call." I passed her my card.

She took the card and put it in her shirt pocket. "Thanks," she said as she walked away.

Chapter 38

My English muffin was burning and I was out of orange juice. I reached into the frying pan and picked the muffin up with my fingers, tossing it onto a plate. It was dark, but I figured I could mask the burnt flavor using enough butter. I threw the empty orange juice carton away and took out my usual.

I sat at my table and pondered the meeting that I had had with Sam Adams. She was going to have to deal with the fact that Emily was gone, and she would have to go on without her. I wondered what kind of a bond they had made in such a short time.

And, I wondered if she would move on quickly, or if she would need a lifetime to forget the few wonderful times they had had together. Sam appeared strong, and I anticipated the best for her.

I wasn't sure what I wanted to do next, if I should agree with the DA or continue looking into the case on my own. I still couldn't believe that Carla had run off without her money.

Most people with no money couldn't survive twenty-four hours on the street. Carla grew up on the streets; that gave her a big advantage. What bothered me was the fact that I didn't believe she would go back to the streets.

I went to shower when I thought I heard the phone, but the warm water wouldn't allow me to leave until I felt all of my muscles relax. When I returned to the kitchen my answering machine was blinking, so I pushed the button.

"Paula, this is Gail at the lab. Call me when you get this message."

I went back to my bedroom and dressed before getting back to her. "Hi Gail, what's going on? I got your call."

"You remember when the autopsy was done on Emily Fields?

"That was a few weeks ago. Has something come up?"

"The M.E. sent us some kind of dust and stone mixture and we couldn't seem to find out exactly what it was at the time. Well, you know me. I kept trying to find the source of the mixture and...I have."

"Well?" I said. "What did you find? Don't keep me waiting."

Gail laughed. "You're going to love this; its cloisonné, or inlaid enamel. Here's a brief story about it, okay? Just listen and you'll see why it was so hard to figure this out."

"All right, let me have it. You have my undivided attention." I sat back with my notebook and pen at the ready.

"Okay, blue is the dominant color which was prevalent during the reign of Jingtai. That's the years 1450 to 1456 in the Ming Dynasty. Now, the making of cloisonné is one that was passed down from Asia to the Chinese." She sounded confident and pleased with herself. "Copper is hammered to form a body, and then colored enamel is used to fill in the design made on the copper body. Enamel is made by melting different materials such as red lead, boric acid, borate, and glass powder. This causes it to become translucent." She stopped to catch her breath. "Then oxidized metals are added to this substance which causes the enamels to change colors. Once this is all cooled, its ground into a powder, then mixed with water, and it forms a paste. From there it is put into the design. Then it's fired. This is done over and over until all the surfaces are filled. Once the final firing is done, it's polished and becomes even. Now that's one of the problems," she said. "After all that, it's plated in gold and silver to keep it rust free. That's why it was so hard to know where the blue stone came from. The combination was what took so long to separate and find. Now, this is what will interest you the most: cloisonné was used for designs on cane handles and staffs."

"Carla had an umbrella basket near her front door filled with antique canes. This is great, Gail. You might have figured out the murder weapon. And the proof it was Carla."

"You still have to find it and prove it," Gail said.

"Gail, you don't know how important this could turn out to be. I owe you one."

"And I intend to collect," she said "Dinner on you next week. I'll call you.

"Dinner it is. Thanks again, Gail." I hung up.

I went through my notes to find the name of Carla's agent that bought her antiques. I needed to go back to Carla's house and count the canes that Carla had near her front door then compare it to her agent's list. I was pretty sure one would be missing, and I'd bet a week's pay it was probably the murder weapon. I also wanted to put the word out to all the pawn shops. I was sure it was worth a lot of money and maybe the killer thought so, too, and had pawned it. I also wanted to call Bobbie and tell her what Gail had found and see if she could get me into Carla's house. I was excited; pieces were beginning to fall into place. If I could find the cane it might have prints on it maybe Carla's, or someone else's.

I placed a call to Carla's antique broker and to Bobbie. Both were out. I left a message for each of them to call me as soon as they could. I went to the kitchen and pulled out some cheese and crackers and returned to the couch. I wanted to review my notes while I waited for one of them to call me. I didn't realize I fell asleep until the phone rang and I jumped a foot and a half and almost fell off the couch.

"Hello."

"Ms Graham, this is Bill Foxwood. You left a message for me to call you. The message said you were a private investigator."

"That's right, I'm working the Emily Fields' murder case, and I'd like to ask you a question."

"I don't see what the Fields case has to do with me, Ms. Graham. I don't represent her."

"I understand," I said, "but you do buy antiques for Carla Reed, and I need to know the total number of antique canes you've picked up for her."

"I still don't see the connection between the two, and without Ms. Reed's permission, I don't think I have anything to say to you."

"Look, Mr. Foxwood, this is a murder investigation, and Carla Reed is the number one suspect and she's been missing for days. The murder weapon may be one of the antique canes you bought for her, and I want to know if one is missing. It's important, and if you think I won't get a warrant for your records, you're wrong. Of course, then I'd have to let the IRS and several other agencies know what you're doing," I quietly added.

"You don't need to threaten me, Ms. Graham. I just needed to know in what reference you needed this information. I'll have my secretary go through Ms. Reed's folder and pull the records you need. She'll send them to you as soon as she can," he said.

"I'm not waiting for the mail, Mr. Foxwood. Have your secretary fax me copies immediately or I'll be there with a warrant in an hour." I waited for Mr. Foxwoods answer, and for a second I thought he had hung up.

"I'll transfer you. She'll give you whatever you need."

I heard the click on the phone and his secretary came on. She took all my information and promised to fax everything within fifteen minutes. I knew none of this information would be useful unless I could get into Carla's house and count the antique canes she still had in the stand.

There was still no call from Bobbie, and the only thing I

could get from the department was that she was out on a case. I went downstairs to my office and retrieved all the faxes from my machine. I went back up stairs and began reading. Carla had fourteen antique canes, each one unique in its own special way. As I read the description on each one, I noticed she owned two cloisonné canes. I was impressed with the beauty of these canes and I was sure that the pictures I was looking at didn't do them justice. The prices her agent paid for them were reasonable and would allow for a good profit, if sold.

    I wanted to get into Carla's house before the day ended, and without Bobbie, I wasn't sure I could get in. I didn't actually have probable cause, just a suspicion. I had another thought. I reached for the phone and called Jackie at the bar. Her bartender, Sandy, answered and it took a few minutes for her to get Jackie.

    The first thing I heard from her was: "Did you find Carla?" She sounded partly relieved and partly anxious.

    "No. I'm sorry, I haven't. The DA has put a fugitive warrant out for her," I said. "He has a witness who will testify that Carla knew Emily was leaving her for someone else." I didn't have the heart to tell her that they were saying she was leaving for a man.

    "What are you talking about? Carla never said a word to me about Emily going anywhere! She didn't know," Jackie said.

    "Listen, that's not why I called. I need to get into Carla's house and I thought maybe you'd let me in," I said.

    "Why would I help you? Can't you just go in or get a

warrant or something like that?"

"I could, but all that takes time, and I need to get in there now. Carla gave you access to a key, so I wouldn't be breaking any law if you invite me in. Then, if I'm right, the chain of evidence doesn't come into question."

"Evidence," she said. "You think that she left some evidence in her house?"

"I think that something is missing and it just might turn out to be the murder weapon. And if there are prints, then it could eliminate Carla and help us find the killer, or prove she's guilty."

There was silence for a minute. I knew Jackie was deciding if breaking Carla's trust with the key would be worth the risk, or if she might be the reason that Carla went to jail for the rest of her life.

"I was just thinking," Jackie said. "That night Carla called me, she said she just went through the house and something was missing. She was coming to see me to tell me about it."

"Did she say what it was?"

"No, just that she'd see me that night. I'll meet you at Carla's place in one hour. Then you can tell me what you think is missing and we'll look. See you in an hour." She hung up.

I was motivated and couldn't wait until I got to Carla's house.

The drive over seemed longer than usual. The cold weather and the rain we had made the driving a little slippery, and everyone was doing the speed limit, which was totally unexpected. Jackie was waiting for me at the front door.

"I didn't want to open the door until you were with me. That way no one could say I took anything out or put anything in the house."

I smiled at her. "You know, you're doing the right thing here. This could clear Carla if it turns out someone else's prints are on the murder weapon," I said.

"Or bury her," she mumbled to herself. She opened the door, and we walked in, flipping the light on. Nothing was moved, and the place was still spotless. I looked over to the corner and saw the umbrella stand filled with antique canes. I counted them. I counted them twice. There were only thirteen, not the fourteen that Carla had bought.

"There's a cane missing," I said to Jackie.

"You think that's the murder weapon, don't you?"

"I'm sure it is. There was enamel and a blue substance embedded in Emily's head, and the lab connected it to a type of enamel that was used in antique cane handles. It's very unusual. Now, if I could find that cane, we might find the killer."

"It's not in this house. Carla would have torn the place apart looking for it if she noticed it was missing. And I'm guessing she did and was going to tell me about it. I remember she said she was afraid it would implicate her as the killer. Now I know what she meant." Jackie reached for one of the canes and held it up high. "Not worth a life," she said replacing it. "Does any of this help?"

"It just might, Jackie. It just might." I started out the door with Jackie following me. "Listen Jackie, I appreciate all the help."

"Just find Carla and prove she didn't kill anyone." She left and got into her car spinning a tire as she drove off.

Once I was home, I checked the answering machine and noticed Bobbie still hadn't called. I headed to the kitchen and decided to fry up some chicken breast strips for supper. I pulled out the Italian bread crumbs and poured the oil into the frying pan. I decided to first put the chicken in an egg before I battered them to fry. It's funny how certain smells bring back memories.

As the chicken was frying I could see Elizabeth standing in front of the stove cooking chicken fingers. She always leaned into the stove and tipped one shoe onto her toes. The chicken fingers were a favorite of mine, and she always cooked a large batch. The phone interrupted my thoughts.

"Hello," I said, trying to sound upbeat.

"Hi, it's me. You called?" It was Bobbie.

"You wouldn't believe the day I've had. Do I have some news to tell you."

Bobbie interrupted me, "You won't believe what happened today. Joanne Adler's condo was broken into and the place was torn apart. Even the curtains were torn down. And that's not all! Darcie Chambers is now among the missing."

"You mean missing as in run off? Or like probably dead? What's going on Bobbie?"

"I don't know, Paula, but something strange is going on. That's for sure."

"I think I know what the murder weapon is," I told her. "One of the antique canes is missing from Carla's collection. I checked tonight. Jackie let me in and I got the list from her broker. We really need to find that cane. I put in a few calls to the pawn shops just in case…"

"Hold on a minute." I could hear the scanner in the background. "Paula, a female body was found down by the river that fits Darcie's description. I gotta go. I'll call you if it's her."

"Call me either way." I slowly hung up the phone and turned back to my chicken. My appetite was fading.

Chapter 39

"Joanne, I'm telling you, people are crazy; they love to tear things up and destroy everything you have." Beth took a breath. "You make sure you check and recheck your stuff; those kinds of people always steal something. They want a souvenir; I'm telling you people are just bad, bad, bad."

Joanne took the phone from her ear and looked at the receiver. "Beth! They made a mess of my house, but there is nothing missing! I looked!"

"Yeah, have you cleaned everything up yet, put things back where they belong? I'm telling you, they took something. People don't go into a house without taking something," Beth said

"Why do you always think the worst about everyone and everything you know? Beth, there are people out there who don't just think about themselves."

"I don't believe that, Joanne. Everyone wants something from someone," Beth said with her usual sarcastic tone.

"Well, I don't believe that, and I pity you if you do. I've got to go. I have to clean this mess up. You could come over and help me."

"Hmmm, I have a customer to call. She might want to see a house today. I'll call you if I can come over later. Look for that missing thing, Joanne. They always take souvenirs." Beth hung up.

Joanne was glad to get off the phone with Beth. She often

wondered what Darcie saw in her. She couldn't believe they were friends.

Joanne began picking up the furniture when the doorbell rang. She thought it was the police again and released the front door to let them in. She opened the door and jumped back placing her hands over her mouth. She was in shock when she ran over to the woman at the door and hugged her tightly.

"What? You thought your friends were going to let you clean this mess up all by yourself?" Jan said. "We're all here to help you. Come on in ladies, let's get started." The women began entering, each stopping to give Joanne a hug.

"I don't know what to say," Joanne said. "I'm so happy to see all of you!"

Jan and Stacy passed out brooms and mops, while some of the other women began setting up Joanne's furniture. All of Joanne's friends and their friends had arrived with the exception of Beth. Joanne knew she was right; not everyone was out for themselves. Real friends are just that, real friends.

Beth laughed when she hung the phone up. She knew she didn't have any appointments but just didn't want to take any of her valuable time to clean someone else's house. After all, she wasn't the one who made the mess. She was lying on the couch watching TV when her door bell rang. Beth wondered if she should answer it in case it was Joanne coming over to give her a ride, so Beth could help Joanne clean up her messy house. She struggled to get up off the couch and slowly made it to the door. "Who is it?" Beth yelled into the door.

"It's me, let me in," Beth heard.

"What do you want? I'm busy. Come back another time," Beth said

"Very funny, Beth. Open the door," Darcie said.

Beth opened the door, and Darcie moved quickly past her. Beth looked out the door, side to side then closed it. She turned around and stared at Darcie. "You look like hell. What have you been doing?"

Darcie kept scratching her head and shaking her hair. "I think I screwed up big time."

Beth was still standing at the door. "Look, Darcie, I have a meeting with a client. I think they're going to buy that big eyesore up on Eastman Street. You know that big ugly one? You should go, and we'll talk on the phone later." Beth opened the door.

Darcie walked over and removed her hand from the knob and closed the door. "You're watching TV, and you have no client. What's with this shit? Are you trying to get rid of me?"

Darcie went to the kitchen and opened the cabinet and removed a glass. She went to the kitchen sink to fill it with water. She slugged it down. Then, she went to sit on the couch. "What are you watching? Anything good?"

Beth moved from the door and stood in front of her. "Why are you here?"

"Because we're friends, and I think I did something really stupid, that's why."

Beth huffed and sat down next to her. "What did you do?" She looked at Darcie.

"I lost my temper and tore up Joanne's condo."

"You did what?" Beth's mouth dropped opened.

"I got mad after talking to Joanne and I kind of messed up the condo. She's going to throw me out, and I thought I'd come here for awhile, at least until she cools off and I can apologize." Darcie gave Beth a small punch on the shoulder.

"You can't stay here," she said. "I don't have enough room. You have to go."

Darcie jumped up, facing Beth. "I thought we were friends! I told you all kinds of secrets, just between you and me! You told me to get rid of my old girl friends, that they weren't right for me! I thought you were on my side!" Darcie was standing over Beth.

"You need to calm down," said Beth. "Are you on your meds?"

Darcie was getting excited and began walking back and forth in front of her. "You told me to get off those pills, that they weren't good for me! Now you're asking me if I took them! Are you nuts?"

"Look Darcie, I'm your friend, but I have to do something right now, and you have to leave. Go make up with Joanne and I'll see you later." Beth smiled at Darcie.

Darcie leaned over Beth as she sat on the couch. Beth's eyes widened and sweat began to bead on her forehead.

"You're a phony," Darcie said between clenched teeth. "You're not really my friend. You used me, you, you, bitch!" Darcie began pacing again.

"Come on, Darcie, we're friends. You know that, don't you? You're just confused with everything that's been happening. Don't we talk everyday on the phone? Don't we share secrets about all those awful people who talk about you? Just calm down and get a glass of water before you go," Beth said, holding her hands out in front of her.

Darcie made a fist and started towards Beth. She stopped just short of hitting her. She stood up straight and started walking to the door. Beth let out the breath she was holding.

"Darcie," Beth said reasonably. "Don't be mad at me. I'll call you tomorrow. Okay?" She smiled.

Darcie opened the door and took a look toward Beth. She then turned and slowly closed the door, locking it.

Chapter 40

"Now you listen to me, and you listen very closely. Don't answer any questions until our lawyer says it's okay. Do not look at anyone but me or our lawyer, and keep your mouth shut unless I tell you differently. Understand me? Lori, I'm talking to you. Are you listening?" Mr. Fields was pacing back and forth in front of Lori as she sat at the dinning room table.

Lori kept her head bent low and every now and then, she would nod as her father continued walking and talking.

"Lori!" he yelled, startling her. "Are you listening to me?"

"Yes sir," Lori said sheepishly. "Do I have to say...?"

"Lori, we've been over this a hundred times or more! You answer whatever questions that you can, and only those. Answer every question that our lawyer asks; just as we rehearsed. Do you understand, Lori?"

Lori began to shake, and tears welded up in her eyes. She quickly wiped them away and looked at her father. "Yes, sir, I understand."

"Good." He looked at her and moved his head side to side. "Go change. I don't like the looks of that dress you're wearing."

Lori left the table and went to her room to change while her father turned to the housemaid.

"I'll take my morning coffee and toast now."

"Will Miss Lori be joining you?"

"No."

A short time later, Mr. Fields and Lori arrived at the courthouse for their meeting with the District Attorney.

"Go right in, Mr. Fields. He's expecting you," The DA's secretary said.

He entered with his daughter following close behind. The office was large and, like most government offices, had several chairs and a large oak desk. The room was covered with book cases filled with law books. The Governor's picture hung next to the President's.

"George, you're early. Come sit down. We'll have some coffee while my stenographer sets up." He pointed to a chair where Mr. Fields sat with his daughter next to him.

The DA buzzed his secretary and had coffee brought in. He poured three cups and passed them out.

"How is everything, George? I hope your lovely wife is doing well."

"She's doing very well David and the business also. When can we get this deposition out of the way? I have a meeting I need to get to, and my daughter needs to return home to be with my wife."

The DA checked with his stenographer, who nodded that he was ready. "I think we can start now if everyone is ready."

"We are," said Mr. Fields.

The DA looked at his stenographer and said, "We are now on record."

"For the record, I am District Attorney David Powers. I am here with Mr. George Fields and his daughter, Miss Lori Fields. This is a deposition given by Miss Lori Fields."

"Miss Fields, are you here on your own volition, without coercion from anyone?" The DA asked.

Lori twisted in her seat then looked at her father. Her father paid her no attention and kept looking forward. He placed his hand over Lori's, and gave a squeeze. Lori flinched.

"Yes, sir," she said.

"Please speak up, Miss Fields," the DA said.

"Yes, sir," Lori spoke louder.

The DA asked the usual questions about name, birth date, address and Lori answered quietly.

"Miss Fields," the DA began. "Did your sister Emily Fields ever tell you that she feared for her life from Ms. Carla Reed?"

"For her life?" Lori asked, looking at her father.

"Did she ever tell you that Ms. Reed threatened her or ever hit her?"

"A long…" The DA pointed to his stenographer and held up his index finger. The stenographer stopped typing and sat back.

"Miss Fields. Lori, we don't want you to go into any detail about long ago, just answer simply, with a yes or no, when possible. Okay?"

He waved to the stenographer, who began typing again.

"Miss Fields, had your sister ever mentioned that she feared for her life from Ms. Carla Reed?"

"Yes, sir," Lori said.

"Had Ms. Reed ever hit your sister?"

"Yes, sir."

"Was she violent to your sister at anytime?"

"Yes, sir," Lori said, beginning to shake.

"Now, Miss Fields, I want you to think about this question before you answer. Did your sister ever tell you that she was planning to leave Ms. Reed and that she was afraid of how Ms. Reed would act once she told her?"

"Yes, sir," Lori said.

"Was your sister worried that Ms. Reed would hurt her when your sister told her she was leaving her for a man?"

Lori was startled and it showed when she threw her head up and her mouth dropped open as her lips mimicked the word man. "What?" Lori asked.

Once again, the DA held up his finger to his stenographer.

"Did you not understand the question, Miss Fields? Would you like me to ask the question in another way?"

"I'd like you to not say a man," Lori said.

The DA looked at Mr. Fields. "George?"

Mr. Fields looked at his daughter. "Just answer the question, so we can get out of here."

"But father, she didn't…" Her father stood up and faced his daughter.

"Lori, just answer the question like we talked about. Then Emily can rest in peace and Carla Reed will go to jail where she belongs."

"I can't," Lori said.

Mr. Fields looked over at the DA and tilted his head toward the door. The DA nodded at his stenographer and they both went into the other room.

On his way out, the DA stood next to Mr. Fields and said, "You need to get this right, George."

Fields turned to his daughter. "What is wrong with you? Don't you want to help Emily? How hard is it to tell them that she was afraid of that Reed character? She's nothing; nothing but a queer bitch that killed your sister."

"Yes, she is a lesbian, and she might have killed Emily, but Emily wouldn't want me to lie and say she was leaving Carla for a man. She just wouldn't," Lori said.

"Your sister was not a lesbian. And besides, we need to clean up the family name. Understand? Now sit down, and when they come back in, I don't want any more hesitations. You will just tell the DA that Emily was leaving Reed for a man and that will be that. Now sit down and straighten yourself out."

Lori leaned her head back and twisted her neck in a semi-circle. The shaking she had felt earlier was leaving her. She stood up and walked to her father, and although she had to look up at him, she no longer felt small.

"No, sir, I will not tell the DA that she was leaving Carla for a man. She was leaving Carla because, finally, she found happiness, and it was with a woman. A woman who made her want to live. And she was going to live with this woman. Not a man. I won't tell such a lie. That would not honor my sister. She was a lesbian and she was proud of it. So, father I will not lie; not for you or anyone else."

Lori turned to walk away; her father grabbed her arm. She stopped looked at her father's hand and, pulling away, she headed for the door.

When she stepped over the threshold, her father yelled, "I wouldn't if I were you!"

Lori turned and glanced back at her father, then, with her head held head high, she walked out the door.

Chapter 41

The doorbell rang, then there was a knock at my door. I wasn't answering the doorbell, the knock, or the phone today. I wanted a day to myself. I wanted to stay on the couch, listening to reruns of Law and Order. I heard the key as it went into the lock, that turn that told me she was entering my house.

"Go away!" I said.

"Not happening. Do you think I don't know what day this is, and just what you'd be doing with it?" Bobbie asked.

"Go away and leave the key on your way out."

Bobbie went to the fridge, got two cans of diet Pepsi, and came over to the couch. She placed the can in front of me. "You're so predictable. You're a date person. All I have to do is look at the calendar and I can tell what you're doing. What are you going to do when every day in the calendar is full? Never leave the couch?"

"I have no idea what you're talking about. Go away."

"Let's see, your mother died on Mother's Day, so you go off by yourself, to who knows where. Georgia died April fifth and you go to a little café in Savanna, where the two of you always went. On her birthday you go…"

"Shut up and go away."

"And today is the day you met Elizabeth, and here you are on the couch. Just when are you going to wake up?" Bobbie said as she sat down next to me.

"It has nothing to do with Elizabeth. I'm coming down with a cold," I said, trying to push her off the couch with my feet.

"You remember the good, and I guess that's a good thing, but you need to remember why you left. Why you got up one Friday morning and walked out of the house. Think about it."

"I don't have to think about it. I know why," I said.

"Then try remembering," Bobbie said slapping my legs.

"Go away before you catch my cold," I said, grabbing a Kleenex and pretending to blow my nose.

"She had no trust in you."

"Maybe I gave her....."

Bobbie punched my leg. "Maybe, hell, you never gave her a reason not to trust you. I worked with you over fourteen years. You're the most trustworthy person I know. I'd put my life in your hands any day. She listened to people who had no idea who you were, and you showed that they out and out lied every time they opened their mouth. Every time; shouldn't that have counted for something?"

"Shut up and go away. Leave me to my one day of misery."

"Let me ask you just one question," she said. "Why did you take this case?"

"Because you pushed it on me."

"No, because you want the truth told whatever it is. The truth is important to you. You've seen too many times when some idiot tells a lie and it escalates and then someone unnecessarily is hurt or ruined, maybe only emotionally, but still ruined," Bobbie said.

I didn't have an answer for her; she was right. The truth is the hardest thing to convince people of. They would rather believe things that make no sense or are too bizarre to be true.

"I have the flu."

Bobbie sat back and closed her eyes. "Dec 30th, Jan 6th..."

"Okay, okay, I'm up! Just stop with the calendar dates." I pushed her with my feet as I got off the couch and shook my head. "Tell me about Darcie being missing, and I'll fill you in on my latest information."

Bobbie was smiling as she handed me my Pepsi. "You won't believe how they found Joanne Adler's place. It was a mess. Nothing was missing, but the furniture was broken and dishes were thrown all over the place. The pantry was emptied and food was thrown all over the kitchen floor. Even the curtains were torn down."

"And Darcie was missing?"

"Detective Jackson told me that Joanne picked up a broken picture of her and Darcie and she started screaming, 'Where's Darcie?' She's convinced something has happened to her."

I was scratching my head in disbelief. "Sounds a little strange; what does Jackson say?"

"He asked the question, Paula. He said one dead lesbian and

two missing. He asked if I thought there might be somebody out there stalking lesbians."

"I don't think so. It still doesn't make any sense that all these women are connected in some way or another. A serial killer or stalker wouldn't pick just this group. He or she would pick at random. All these women are connected, and if we find that one connection, we solve this case."

"You have an idea? I still say Carla is our murderer she connects to everyone."

"Actually, I'm beginning to put some things together, and it's not good. If I'm right, we could have some real trouble coming our way," I said.

"Like we don't already have trouble."

"Is Jackson still working the case?"

"No, he's Homicide, and we haven't found a body. He passed it on to missing persons, and you know how overloaded they are."

"That was a quick pass don't you think?"

"He doesn't want this case any more than the other guys. You can't blame them. The DA is convinced Carla killed Emily, and Darcie missing is just that to them - someone missing."

"They're all tied together. I think one woman killed Emily, and the same woman is involved in the disappearance of Carla and Darcie. I don't think we'll find them alive. Once someone kills, they have nothing to lose by killing again. Course if Carla did kill

Emily she could have killed Darcie and we may never find her and she may not be finished."

"You're thinking a woman and not someone that Fields has brought in?" Bobbie asked.

"No, he wouldn't be worried about Carla missing if he knew she was dead. I think he's still looking for her, and that's why he made the call to the DA about what his daughter knew."

"I'll see if I can get a copy of that deposition. I still have friends in the DA's office," Bobbie said.

"Good, I'd like to see what Lori said. She never told me anything about Emily seeing anyone, never mind a man. Also, I want to talk with Joanne again about Darcie. Then I need to talk with…"

Bobbie began to laugh.

"What?" I asked.

"The one thing I love about you is that you were always logical, unemotional, and detached; ever since you met up with Elizabeth, you've been an emotional basket case. Good to see you thinking with your head for a change."

I heard Bobbie, and if I had to tell myself she was right one more time…I might have to shoot myself.

"I just wanted to make Elizabeth happy."

"And you were only making yourself miserable. You are who you are. It's that simple."

"Nothing's that simple," I said, "Now, get out of here. I

have work to do."

Chapter 42

I called Joanne and found out her salon was closed for the day. I reached her at home, and she graciously invited me over. She lived in a small condo along the river. Her balcony overlooked a ridge leading down to the water. The place was clean and organized. She invited me in, and we sat at the kitchen table. Of course, she set out two coffee cups. I told her black would be fine.

"Have you heard anything about Darcie," she asked. "I'm worried about her."

"I'm sorry, I haven't. Do you think that Darcie was kidnapped?" I asked.

"What else!" She raised her voice.

"You don't think Darcie could have just run away, or went away, for a few days?" I asked.

"When I spoke to her on the phone she was sweet as pie. She was going to cook dinner for us. Nothing seemed wrong, not to me anyway. I'm worried now because she needs her medicines, and they're here. She wouldn't go off for any overnight stay without them," Joanne said.

"May I ask what kind of medicine she's taking and for what?"

Joanne looked around the kitchen, and over by the sink there was a round plate similar to a lazy susan containing several prescriptions. She brought it back to the table and spun it. "It's a lot of medicine," she said, shaking her head. "I don't think she has to take all of these. Darcie knows better than I do. I just try to remind her once in awhile," Joanne said.

I looked at the medicines and began picking them up one at a time: lithium, sodium valproate, carbamazepine, lamotrigine, quetiapine. "Holy moly," I whispered. "Joanne? Is Darcie manic depressive?" I asked cautiously. "Do you know if she's bipolar?"

"She told me she gets depressed sometimes and takes some medication when she does," she said. "She has it all under control. I don't think she mentioned manic or bipolar. Is that important?"

I kept looking at the pill bottles; some of the dates where recent, while others were several months old. "I'm not a doctor," I said, "but these medications need to be taken each day. Skipping these doses can bring on a serious relapse. How has Darcie been acting lately?"

Joanne put her head into the palms of her hands and began rubbing her eyes. "She's been a little weird. We've had a couple of fights lately. I've been thinking of asking her to leave. I just can't take her mood swings. They seem to be getting worse and I just don't want to put up with them. I don't know what to say," Joanne said.

"Has she ever been violent?"

"A few times she swung at me. She didn't hit me, just acted like she was going to. She was always sorry after, crying and begging me to forgive her. I always did. She can be so nice, then all of a sudden she freaks out and Bam! I threatened to call her doctor during the last fight we had. Darcie said she'd get back on her medicine, even go to the out-patient clinic, and everything would go back to normal," Joanne said.

"If she's not taking this medication properly, she could be having all kinds of problems. She might be having a manic episode."

"A manic episode," Joanne repeated. "What does that mean?"

I thought about the question for some time, than decided to tell Joanne what I knew about the medication Darcie was taking or – perhaps - not taking.

"Lithium or sodium valproate," I said as I picked the bottle up to show her, "is used in manic depression or what they now call bipolar disorders. Doctors believe that it's caused by a brain disorder that changes the chemical balance. The unusual changes cause mood swings, excessive energy, and the ability to function normally. That person can become irritable, be reckless, have poor judgment, and demonstrate aggressive behavior. There are a whole slew of things that go on with someone when they're in one of their episodes. When they don't take their medication their brain goes haywire. All I'm sure of is that there's no cure and it's a life long illness. They need to be on medication."

I looked up from the label and noticed Joanne was pale white and looked scared. "I'm sorry. I didn't mean to scare you. A lot of people with manic depression lead totally normal lives. Some just have trouble knowing and understanding that it's the medication and therapy that keep them normal. So they drop the meds and the episodes return. Sometimes they don't even know it. I shouldn't have said anything. As I told you, I'm not a doctor."

Joanne was visibly shaken. "I knew something was wrong. I shouldn't have threatened to call her doctor. She spent a year in the hospital when she was younger, and she's had a fear of them ever since. I probably pushed her into having one of those things you called it, an epi…. An episode; I should have told her she had to leave a long time ago. I never really loved her; I just felt bad for her and wanted her to have a place to stay. I should have known better than to get involved. I screwed up," Joanne said.

"You didn't know," I told her.

"I knew enough. Everyone told me not to get involved. They said she was wacky."

"You can't listen to everyone," I said. "You have to make your own decisions."

"No, this time I should have listened and …" She hit the table with her hand. "I wish I didn't get drunk that night and bring her home. What a mistake that was."

I wasn't going to give her advice. I knew I had said too much already. I needed to ask just a few more questions, and I hoped Joanne was up to them. "Joanne is it possible that Darcie wrecked the house and just left?" I asked.

"I didn't think so when I first came home, but now I'm not so sure any more. I'm all confused."

"Is there a special place in the house that Darcie kept her things? Maybe I could look at her things and see if I can find a clue to a place she might go when she's confused."

Joanne thought for a moment. "She kept her clothes in our bedroom, but I told her she could have the basement if she wanted to keep any of her things that didn't fit in the house. I think she kept a few things down there. She rarely went down there, really. You're welcome to go look if you'd like." Joanne pointed to a door that led down to the basement. It had a pad-lock on it.

I made a call to Bobbie and explained the medication Darcie was on and asked her to see if she could find some old addresses that Darcie might go to. People with bipolar have a tendency to find familiar places when they're off their meds.

Chapter 43

Fall was nearly over, and with the early darkness came the cold; the streets were looking bare, and the people walking about were already wearing heavy coats.

I was watching the wind blow through the bare elms along the sidewalk when I spotted Bobbie pulling up. She jumped from the car, spotted me in the window, and waved for me to come down. I held up my index finger to let her know I'd be down in a minute. I grabbed my jacket and headed for the steps, taking two at a time.

"What's up, Bobbie?"

"If you're right and Darcie's sick and not taking her meds, I found a place where she might be hiding. She used to live over on Braden Street, on the south side. The place is abandoned now, waiting to be torn down to make way for new condos. I thought you'd like to take a ride over there and check it out. Hop in."

I got in the car and we headed south.

"Any luck with your phone calling?" Bobbie asked.

"Nothing. No one has seen her or heard from her since Joanne's home was turned upside down. Most of the women were surprised to hear Darcie was still missing. They all thought she had a fight with Joanne and they had made up by now."

"Was fighting something Darcie did on a regular basis?" Bobbie asked.

"The only thing I got was when she went off her medication

she was extremely moody. It was well known she was on medication, but no one thought she was dangerous or violent. They were surprised to hear I thought she could be violent."

"Really," Bobbie said with a quick glance toward me. "Think you could be wrong about her?"

"Maybe, but I don't think so," I said.

We drove a ways in silence as Bobbie turned into the alley. A vacant building came into sight.

"That's it. She lived on the third floor front. I don't see any windows, and most of the place is boarded up. There won't be any electricity, and the place will feel like a refrigerator. Think she'd be in there?"

"I just hope you brought your flashlights with you," I said, rubbing my hands together to make friction. "It's dark and cold, but I got a feeling."

"Great! A feeling. Here we go again." Bobbie got out of her car and opened the trunk, grabbing two large flashlights. She handed me a portable radio.

"I don't want to call for backup unless we need it, but I want to be ready," she said as she put a radio in her pocket.

We found a side door with no boards covering it and pushed our way in. A cold wave of dry air hit us.

We spotted the stairs and started climbing. "Be careful," I told her. "These things are falling apart." I moved the flashlight back and forth over a step that was cracked and partly missing some wood. We moved slowly and stopped often to listen for sounds. We heard nothing, not even that proverbial mouse you so often hear about. Once we reached the third floor, we checked the room numbers and found we were toward the back of the building.

We needed room three twelve. Bobbie pointed toward the front of the hall with her flashlight and whispered, "This way, about halfway down." I nodded, and we moved on.

The cold and quiet cut through us, and it was good knowing Bobbie was next to me in case anything went wrong. When we arrived at room three twelve, the door was closed. We listened for a time, then I tried the door.

Bobbie got her gun out in case someone popped out of the dark. I swung the door open and moved the flashlight around the room. No one popped out, but Darcie was staying here - or had been. There was a bed with blankets in the corner and some empty canned goods. Mostly soup and beans, things you could eat cold if you had to. I spotted a gold chain in the covers of the bed. I picked it up and noticed the latch was broken. A locket was attached to the chain. I opened it while Bobbie was holding the light over it. When it was opened, I saw it contained a picture of Emily on one side and Darcie on the other.

"They're so young in that picture," Bobbie commented.

"First love is hard to forget," I said. "I remember the women when I interviewed them. Several of them said she always wore this locket. They all knew Darcie and Emily were lovers when they were young, and they all thought they were still friends."

"Well, she's not here now, and it's too cold for her to come back tonight. I'll station a car outside, just in case. Tomorrow I'll set up a stake-out. We'll go through the place in the daylight, and maybe we'll find something that'll tell us where she is."

I looked at the locket still in my hand and decided to put it back on the bed. They could decide what to do with it tomorrow when they brought in the crime scene team. We decided to try the front stairs, hoping they were in better shape than the back stairs.

On the way down, I stopped. "Do you smell that," I asked Bobbie.

"Yeah, I think it's because there's no water and someone's been using the toilets. Or maybe not."

"I've smelled that odor in the morgue. It's death," I said, stopping again to sniff.

"Let's get out of here. I'm hungry and I know a good sub shop not far from here," Bobbie said.

I took hold of Bobbie's arm. "Wait. We should look around."

"No, we should wait for daylight."

"Smell that? That's the smell of death; we need to look around now."

Bobbie was sniffing. "I can't tell. It could be dead rats. We'll get the lab down here tomorrow and they'll figure it out."

When we reached the bottom of the steps, I stopped. "Is

there a cellar in this place?"

"Oh no, no…we're not going into a cellar without better lighting. Let's go," Bobbie said.

The front door was boarded up, but the window next to it was opened enough to fit through. Bobbie started to pass me the flashlight. "Hold the flashlight for me while I squeeze through, then I'll hold it for you," she said, turning and looking for me.

I was already halfway down the hall, looking for a cellar door.

"Damn it, Paula!" she was saying as she caught up to me.

"The smell is stronger here. There!" I pointed to a heavy steel door, just down a few steps to a landing. "Help me move these crates that are blocking the door." I slid one across the floor and went to move another.

"There's nothing here, Paula. Who would move these crates every time they wanted to get into this room?"

"Let's look anyway. It's a feeling I have."

Bobbie started moving the crates, mumbling the entire time. "Okay, let's open it up so we can go and get something to eat."

Bobbie held the flashlight and had her weapon out once again. I opened the door. The smell of feces backed both of us up a few steps.

"The sewer must empty in here," Bobbie said.

We both stepped forward and moved the lights across the room.

"Oh my God," I whispered.

Bobbie pulled her portable radio out of her pocket, "This is Detective Kerry. We need an ambulance at thirteen Braden Street South, Stat!"

Chapter 44

The scene was like a horror picture straight out of the movies. On a metal table with holes drilled in it, lay a body. A homemade saline bag hung on a hat rack, and a tube was feeding something into the arm of a body. She was lying in her own feces, and the bugs feeding on her body had made so many sores, she couldn't be identified.

The first medic had to leave to vomit before he could help the others move the body. One of the medics said he was afraid to move her out of the sheet. He thought her bones might break if she was handled wrong. They wrapped her in the sheet she lay on, and then slid her carefully onto a straight board. One of the medics cried out when he tightened the strap to hold her on the board and heard a bone break.

"If this is that Reed woman, I can't believe she's alive," said one of the medics.

"She might be better off if she didn't make it," said the other.

It took them almost an hour to get her into the ambulance. Bobbie was outside setting up a perimeter and trying to keep the press away.

I followed the wiring from the light switch and found it hooked up to a small generator. As I looked around the room, I had trouble believing any human being could do this to another. A bucket full of broken needles was tipped over near the metal table.

The walls were covered with frost and mildew.

In the corner there was a cane. I went over and looked at it, making sure I didn't touch it. I was sure it was Carla's missing Cloisonne'. Next to the cane was a broken, mangled picture. Shards of wood and splinters were spread across the floor. I used my jacket sleeve to move the frame around. I could see it was the picture that Sam Adams had given Emily. There wasn't much left of it, but I could see a petal part of the rose that floated in a clear blue sky.

Bobbie came down to inform me that the crime scene had arrived and we should get out of the way. I was shaking my head and looking around the room.

"I've never seen anything like this before."

"Let's hope we never do again," Bobbie said.

We walked past several crime scene investigators, carrying cameras and cases filled with instruments to help them find the clues which would put this person away for a very long time.

The officers keeping the crowd back were busy. Bobbie and I were almost to the car when her Captain called her over to his car. "Be right back," she said, as she left me at her car.

I got in and started the car to warm me and the engine up. I was still in shock. I was pretty sure the body in that room was Carla Reed but I couldn't swear to it. The body looked like it weighed almost nothing, maybe sixty pounds. Her arms were covered with bite marks--as was her face. I was amazed she was still alive and doubted she would be for much longer. I wondered how much she had suffered. I rested my head against the head rest, rubbing my brows over and over. I thought for a second I was going to vomit.

Bobbie returned to the car. Once in, she started hitting the steering wheel over and over with her fists. I waited until she stopped.

"That was unbelievable," I said in a low voice.

"There's more," she said.

I looked over at her. "More! What else could there be?"

"After you called all the women asking about Darcie, the station got a call. It seems Jan remembered seeing Darcie's car in Beth Winslow's complex. She didn't think anything of it because she knew they were friends and she didn't know anything about Darcie not going back to Joanne. Like all the others she just thought Darcie was in one of her funks."

"So they picked up Darcie."

"No. They found Beth's body. They said she was beaten to death."

"Jesus," I whispered. "We should go to the hospital to wait. Maybe Carla, if it is her, and I'm pretty sure it is, will come around and we'll get an Id from her. Bobbie, we have to catch this woman," I said, as I looked out the window, knowing Carla would probably never come around.

"It's not likely that she'll recover. I could post a guard near her room and you could wait at home. The hospital will call us,"

Bobbie said.

"No, I want to be there."

"I'll drop you off and go check on the murder of Beth, see what they know. I'll be back later," Bobbie said.

I nodded and kept looking out the window. The night was clear. Every star gleamed, and the moon was almost full. I still couldn't process the hate that someone had for one individual. I didn't even notice the car was stopped in front of the hospital until Bobbie nudged me. "We're here," she said.

I got out and waved to Bobbie as she left. The air was crisp, and the wind calm. I kept taking several deep breaths. Then I couldn't stop shaking. I found a stone wall and sat down, trying to calm myself.

I must have been sitting there for about a half hour when a nurse came over and asked me if I was alright. I nodded and stood, stretching and taking another deep, clean breath. I thought I could still smell the stench from that room on me. I took my jacket off and dropped it in the trash disposal in front of the hospital. I couldn't wear it another minute.

The walk down the hall was a mixture of fluorescent lights and the smell of rubbing alcohol. The nurses moved quickly and efficiently up and down the halls and in and out of the rooms. I went to the waiting area and left a message at the desk to have the doctor see me when he knew something about the patient's condition. I drank four Pepsi's and ate what tasted like a three year old Milky Way. I was exhausted and stimulated at the same time.

I sat back and closed my eyes, my head rested on the crown of the chair. I began thinking about Carla. Here was a woman who had grown up on the streets, trusting no one, with a family that threw her out at age eight. She found a way to eat, sleep and survive amongst the worst of the worst. She found away to climb out of the streets and start a business. All she wanted was a little respect and admiration from the women's community. Granted, she didn't know how to do this appropriately, but she had no one to teach her, either. Now, here she lay in the hospital, all alone, no family, no partner, and no friends…accused of murder that she may not have committed.

Then it dawned on me that I should call Jackie. Carla did have a friend, at least that's what I hoped. Suddenly, I felt someone standing over me and I opened my eyes.

"Are you the one who left a message about the woman who was brought in by the police tonight?" A tall slim man, nearly bald, in blue scrubs was asking.

I blinked several times and stood up. "Yes sir;" I said. "I was there when she was found. I need to know if she's going to make it. Is there any chance at all?"

The doctor waved me to the chair, and we both sat down. He was looking for the right words to say. He wiped his forehead with the small blue cap he had in his hand.

"It's the woman you've been looking for, Carla Reed. She

was identified by a tattoo she had on her back. I can't believe she's alive," he said quietly. "The number of anti-depressants that have been fed into her body convinces me that if she does live, she may never be normal. The brain can only take so much, just like the heart will only handle so much. It'll take days to estimate the damage done to her body and mind if she lives. Also, if she does begin to come back, the pain will be so excruciating, that alone could kill her. To be honest, she may be better off just slipping away." He sat back shaking his head. "I've never seen anything like this before, and I've been in the ER for twenty-two years."

"She's a strong woman who has been through hell before. She may fool everyone."

"Let's hope she remembers her way out of hell because that's where she is now," the doctor said.

"What can I do?" I asked, looking at the doctor and noticing the exhaustion on his face.

"You can wait and pray, if you've a mind to. I don't give her much time, though, so if she has family or friends, you should give them a call," he said as he got up to leave. His slow, tired walk showed the twenty-two years he had spent in the emergency room.

I picked up my cell phone to call Jackie and noticed the battery was dead. I went to the desk and asked if I could use the phone. The dowdy old nurse didn't even bother to pick up her head to speak to me. She simply pointed across the room to a pay phone.

"Great, now let's hope I have some change," I said aloud to

myself.

Sitting next to the phone was this old man, who watched me go through all my pockets looking for change. And of course, I didn't have any.

"Young lady," the old man yelled, while waving his hands around in the air. "Come over here and use this contraption I have." He pulled a cell phone from his pocket. "My son insists I keep this here thing on me all the time. Don't know what good it is. I can't figure out how to use it. I've been around over eighty years, and always got things done without one of these. I just carry it for my son's sake." He handed me the phone. "Don't care if you forget to give it back either," he said, laughing.

I took the phone and called Jackie. I told her what I could about Carla, and told her if she wanted me to, I'd wait for her to get here to explain anything else I was allowed to discuss. She was quiet while I spoke and when I finished talking to her, she told me she'd be there within the hour. I really didn't know what I could tell her. I decided to step outside for a smoke and think about how this case has developed. I made the decision to go back to Joanne's and look in the cellar. I needed to see what Darcie was hiding. I called a cab and headed to Joanne's.

Chapter 45

Halfway down the stairs I had to stop and hold my breath; the stench radiating from below was so bad I almost chocked on the bile creeping up my throat. I started breathing through my mouth and took the last few steps. The floor was covered with trash to the point where you couldn't see the floor. There were several benches against the far wall, covered with plastic tubing and what looked like needles. I waded through the trash to the bench. I couldn't believe what I was looking at. Darcie had made makeshift IV bags. They were labeled with red ink. Some said saline solution, others were labeled with anti-depressant. There was plastic tubing connected to the bags and each tube ended with a needle attached. There were several bottles of alcohol rub, some with the caps still off. To one side, I found a plastic baggy filled with hypodermic needles, while others were filled with tablets. There was a small hot plate and a few pans with a couple of beakers. It looked like a drug lab.

I began thinking I needed to call Hazmat to contain all these chemicals. I saw chlorine bottles in a corner and several liquid vials unlabeled. I slowly moved back, went upstairs, and called the Hazmat Team. I asked Joanne to wait outside with me until they arrived.

"What's down there?" Joanne asked.

"I'm not sure. There were a lot of chemicals and I don't

know enough about stuff like that, except the wrong mixture can cause serious damage."

"Oh, you mean all that stuff in the bags and bottles lying around?"

"Yeah, you know about that stuff? What it is?"

"I don't know exactly what it is, but it's safe. Darcie has a Masters in Chemistry and she said she's working on some special project that will make her rich and famous one day. She's always making different chemical combinations. She told me not to go down there because I could knock something over and it would ruin her tests. I'm sure she wouldn't make anything dangerous. I don't think you need the Fire Department or that team you called for," Joanne said.

"Let's just see what the Hazmat Team comes up with and then we can go from there. Okay?"

We sat on the steps leading into her condo. She was quiet, and I didn't know what I could say to her that would make things better. I certainly couldn't tell her how we found Carla and it looked like Darcie could be responsible. So I just sat beside her as quiet as she was.

The Fire Department arrived first, followed by the Hazmat Team and the Police Department. I recognized one of the officers as he walked up to me.

"Hi John," I said.

He nodded to me. "What do you think we have here Ms.

Graham?" He asked.

I hate to be called Ms. Anything. It always makes me feel older than I am. I played along. "I went into the cellar and there were all kinds of drug paraphernalia so I backed out and called you guys," I said.

John patted my shoulder as he walked by me. "Just like old times," he said. "I'll let you know when it's safe to come in." He walked away following the Hazmat Team.

It took about two hours before John came out and said it was all clear. He pulled me aside.

"You won't believe the drugs that are down there. Every kind of pill you could imagine. The rest of the stuff, well, I just don't know for sure. It looks like a medical ward waiting to blow. We'll have to wait until the lab tells us. I've never seen such trash in a makeshift lab. You can't tell the rugs from the dirt. It's awful. The smell is odd, too. It just might be the trash, hard to say. The Hazmat Team is bagging everything. You might as well go home and drop by the lab tomorrow. I'll make sure Gail gets this one. I know how you prefer the best."

"Thanks John," I said.

Joanne was sitting on the steps crying when I approached her. "Do you think Darcie ruined my house? Is she selling drugs? What's down there? Whatever she's doing, when you find her, you tell her not to come near my place ever again."

"We don't really know anything yet, Joanne. Your place is

safe to go into when you're ready."

"I'm going to my friend's house. I already called her. I want this place cleaned and sterilized before I come back. I want all of Darcie's stuff gone. Gone!" Joanne walked to the driveway to wait for her friend. She turned and yelled, "Tell them to lock up when they're done."

John and I looked at each other; we both understood. Her privacy was taken away, and someone she thought she could trust had betrayed her and she wanted no part of it. I waved goodbye to John and headed for home.

Chapter 46

I called the lab.

"Hello, Paula. The answer is no. I haven't even gotten to the evidence. It doesn't have a priority stamp on it, so it was placed into the bin with all the other cases. My hands are tied. We're buried down here, and the DA is screaming for evidence on another case."

"Of course, he doesn't want any new evidence messing up his case against Carla Reed," I said.

"You think this is about Reed?"

"I'm beginning to think this Darcie Chambers has a whole lot to do with this case. She went missing, ended up staying in an abandoned building where Carla was found. Then all this drug paraphernalia turned up in the cellar where she lived. I need to know what it is. I'd like to track her down and find out just how guilty she is."

"It'll take weeks to run all the tests to find out what everything is, and I'm swamped and understaffed," Gail said.

"Can you just take a look and give me an idea? Something to go on; I'd like to know if she's selling drugs or making it for someone. Maybe Emily found out about it and was going to call the police or told Carla. I don't know, and I just need an idea so I can start asking questions at the right place."

"Listen, even if I just look and give you a guess, it won't

hold up in any court and you know that."

"Gail, I can't wait weeks. Another life might be in the balance. Can you just give it a quick look and call me? I just can't wait that long." I was working on the sympathy card hoping Gail would fall for it. I heard a slight huff, then a small giggle.

"You're something else, my friend. You think that pleading crap would work on me? I'm busy, and the DA will have my butt if I dropped this other case to help you. When you know he told you your case was closed," Gail said.

"Then you'll do it?"

"Yes, I'll skip lunch and take a quick look, but no promises. I'll call you after lunch. Paula, you owe me big time."

"Thanks. I'll be home waiting for your call. I knew you'd help me out. You can't resist a good case any more than I can."

"No, you knew I didn't like the DA." I heard her laugh as she hung up the phone.

I dug up all my PDRs and any other book I had on drug interactions and settled down on my couch to do some research, waiting until Gail called. I knew Gail, and she would find out anything she could on the evidence brought in from Joanne's cellar, even if it took longer than her hour for lunch. I wanted to know about saline solutions and what all those beacon glasses could be used for. I opened my book and started reading. It was after two when the phone rang.

"Hello."

"It's me. I can give you just a general idea of what I think all this stuff is," Gail said.

"I got my books and my pen and paper. Go."

"Okay, the saline marked bags are just that, saline. The bags full of pills were all old anti-depressants. There were several paxil, all over three years old. Some Zoloft, I'd say at least two years old. Then there was some Remeron, Wellbutrin, and Effexor - all were old. It looks like she saved every medication that she took."

"You mean didn't take," I corrected. "What about the plastic tubes and beacon glasses and Bunsen burners, what are they for?"

"Well, I'm only guessing at this time, but it looks like the saline was set up to be used as a hydrant."

"Hydrant?"

"It's used to keep someone hydrated, so they don't die before the doctor can care for them, like in transportation to the hospital or in the hospital, when the patient can't drink or eat for some reason."

"Could these drugs be used to torture or keep someone hanging on to near death?" I asked.

"Pretty much. There was a mortar and pestle in the evidence. It was used to crush pills into a fine powder, and the beakers and tubes were a set up to make the drugs into a liquid. This Darcie certainly knew her chemistry mixtures and what they could do," Gail said.

"Could they be keeping someone knocked out so they could be moved, or put someone in a coma? Or used to kill someone?"

"All of the above my friend, and more, depending upon the combination used, how much, and how often. How smart do you think Darcie is?"

"Maybe smart enough to fool all of us," I said quietly. "She's manic. That alone is scary enough, but combine that with a Masters in Chemistry...now that could be deadly. Thanks Gail, for everything."

"Remember, Paula, none of this is official until a complete report is made, and that won't be until all the test are done and filed. That could take weeks."

"I know. But you might have helped solve this case. I'll keep you informed. Thanks again." I hung up and leaned back into the couch. "Shit," I whispered.

I picked up the phone again and called Bobbie. She answered her own line.

"Detective Kerry," she said.

"Bobbie, I need your help. Darcie Chambers killed Emily, and she's the one who put Carla in a coma."

"What do you need?" Bobbie asked.

"I think she went off her medication or maybe mixed some and has had a bad reaction. Maybe she's became paranoid or depressed or both. I'm not sure what it was, but something set her off, and I believe she got into a fight with Emily and lost control. Then I think she blamed Carla, and we know what happened to her. I'm sure she tore up Joanne's house, so I need to find her before someone else gets hurt or killed," I said.

"So what do you want me to do?" Bobbie asked.

"I need you to put out an APB on Darcie."

"Already done. You know the DA isn't going to like this," Bobbie said.

"He hired me to find out who killed Emily and that's what I'm going to do. In the long run, he wants the truth like all of us. He'll back us in the end."

"I'll call you as soon as I have something."

"Thanks. I'll be waiting for your call."

A couple of grilled cheese sandwiches sounded good. Then I'd sit and wait, hoping she wouldn't have time to kill again.

Chapter 47

I believed Darcie would return to the vacant apartment building to see if Carla was still alive. Most of all, I believed that once she realized her locket was lost, she'd come back to find it. I wanted to stake the place out for a few nights. The sun was rising when Bobbie pulled up and honked the horn.

"Jump in! We'll have breakfast at the *Café Du Paris* over on Arlington Street, and I'll fill you in on what we think happened at Beth Winslow's place," Bobbie said, pushing the passenger door open.

"I have things to plan. I don't have time right now."

"Sure you do. The Café is a great place for breakfast, and I'm sure you haven't eaten breakfast yet. Besides, we have a lot to catch up on."

The café was quaint; it had a glass front window where patrons watched the foot traffic in Boston Commons as they enjoyed the wonderful food. Here, people could sit on patio chrome chairs, lean their elbows on the chrome and glass tables and wile away some time outside the hectic Boston grind. On the walls were hung pictures of Paris, mostly done in oils, but none had been done by the masters. The room was small, but the fluorescent lights made the room bright and airy. You ordered from the counter and you picked up your own meal. There were no waiters or waitresses.

Bobbie loved this place mainly because the bakery section

was her favorite, and rightly so. Their pastries were excellent, and the fruit juice freshly squeezed. We ordered breakfast.

Bobbie ordered three pieces of the Texas French Toast with extra butter and plenty of pure maple syrup. On the side, she ordered three pieces of extra crisp bacon and a large orange juice. And we can't forget the pot of coffee with extra cream. I ordered the short stack of pancakes, no butter, and a diet Pepsi. I dug in. I couldn't remember what or when I had last eaten, and the pancakes were delicious.

"What did the scene look like at Beth's?" I asked as I took a swig of my Pepsi.

Bobbie was finishing her bacon. "The Crime Scene people had a fit." She began smiling.

"What's so funny?"

"It's not really funny, but even before the Crime Scene guys could get in they had the Animal Shelter Rescue Squad there. There were cats everywhere, puppies in the back room behind a baby gate, cages of birds. You might remember that Beth was some kind of animal spokesperson or savior. I don't know, one of those things. Anyway, the crime scene was trampled by humans chasing animals and animals running throughout the whole house.

"Detective Jackson said when the team arrived they threw up their arms in disbelief then started yelling at all the Animal Rescue people. They, in turn, started yelling back, and the animals all began barking, screeching, and the cats were sending out all kinds of messages. It was a real zoo there. Get it, a real zoo!" Bobbie started laughing.

"That must have made Jackson's day. All that evidence destroyed. What are they planning on doing?"

"Jackson got the murder weapon with Darcie Chamber's prints all over it. He doesn't care what they did to the place. But I bet he had a private laugh about it," Bobbie said.

"What was the murder weapon?"

"You won't believe this," she said, as she finished her juice and poured her coffee. "Beth had a cane that she kept near the front door and besides Darcie's prints there's more blood than anyone could imagine all over it."

"A cane," I whispered. "I remembered she told me her arthritis was bad at times and she needed a cane occasionally."

Bobbie took a sip of her coffee, staring at me. "You can't blame yourself because Carla's in the hospital. You had no way of knowing she was connected to Darcie or that Darcie was a killer. So don't go there."

I took my last bite and started pointing my fork at Bobbie. "I know that, I was just thinking. I wonder what pushes someone like Darcie to kill her first love, kidnap Emily's partner and torture her, but keep her alive! Then kill her best friend?"

"You know what? I don't really care. My job is to find her and bring her in, that's all. The *why* is for all the shrinks. I'm sure her lawyer will be getting a good one when she comes to trial,"

Bobbie said.

    Bobbie was right. When Darcie is caught and goes to trail, she'd have doctors coming up with all kinds of reasons as to why she had killed. I was guessing the lack of proper medication or supervision of would be her biggest defense.

    "I wonder what her doctor's thinking right about now."

    Bobbie looked at me seriously. "Whatever doctor she had, he's not thinking about her at all. They won't even admit that someone's their patient. Not unless some attorney gets a subpoena and forces them to testify. You know yourself they don't want to get involved. Bad for business to have a patient become a killer."

    "I know. Listen, I'd like to run something by you."

    Bobbie set her coffee down. "What?"

    I tapped my fork against the table. "I'm thinking Darcie might come back to the abandoned building. If not to get her things, then just to check on Carla, to see if she's still alive. After all, she's been keeping her alive for weeks. She must have a reason."

    "Crazy people don't need a reason," mumbled Bobbie.

    "Even if she doesn't care about Carla, she'll care that she lost her locket. I think she'll come back looking for it."

    "You're dreaming!" Bobbie said. "She's seen all those cops hanging around the place and pulling everything out. If not, she must have heard it on TV by now. She's not going to take any chances this late in the game. I bet Darcie is halfway across the country by now. And why the hell would she care about some locket with her and Emily's picture in it? She killed her!" Bobbie sat back against her chair with her arms stretched out.

I thought about that for a minute. "I still think she'll come back. She has no place to go. This is her home. Right now, she's confused and off her meds. There must be some routine she follows when she's alone. I'm guessing it's…she stays in familiar territory. Maybe we should warn her other friends again," I said in passing.

"I already did that. Everyone we knew that she was close to in someway was notified not to let her in and to call us if they saw or heard from her. I even included her doctors, although each and every one wouldn't even admit they knew her," Bobbie huffed.

"I'd still like to stake out the place for a night a two."

"Fine, but she won't come back, and I'm not sitting in a car all night with you. It's too cold," Bobbie said.

"I didn't ask you. I'll watch for a couple of nights while you and the department try and find her. I'll keep in touch with you by cell phone. Now, take me home so I can get some rest before tonight."

"Okay, but you have to call me," she said pointing her finger at me. "I'll keep a car there until you show, after that you're on your own."

"Alright, take me home. I'm tired and I'm getting cranky," I said as I smiled at her.

"You're always cranky," she replied. "Let's go." She stood and started putting on her jacket.

I spotted the bill, "Did you leave a tip?" I asked.

She laughed out loud and headed toward the front door.

Chapter 48

The alarm went off at six that evening. Fumbling to hit the off button I was tempted to just throw the clock out the window. At last, I found the right button, and the buzz of the alarm quit. I bagged up the clothes I had been wearing when we found Carla and put them into the trash can. I took a long hot shower which helped eliminate the smell I was sure still lingered on my body, and a quick walk through my place spraying Febreze seemed to help clear the air in the loft.

I made two sandwiches and threw in a small bag of chips and a couple of diet Pepsi's into a backpack. I tried not carrying a weapon after I left the force, but tonight I was taking my nine-millimeter semi automatic pistol with me. I always carried a Beretta; it's small and easy to handle. It only weighs 2.55 pounds fully loaded, carries fifteen rounds and has a velocity of twelve hundred feet per second. It was my choice of weapon when I joined the force. I loaded the magazine and set one in the chamber then tossed it into the backpack as I threw it over my shoulder. I looked around my loft and wondered what, if anything, was important. I shook my head, walked out, and locked the door behind me.

I met with the two Police Officers who staked out the empty building and was told they had seen no one entering or leaving the crime scene since the CS team left late that afternoon. They were happy to be relieved and headed out before I was back in my car.

The weather was in my favor tonight; it was clear and not excessively cold. I didn't have to keep starting my car to keep warm.

I parked between two buildings, giving me a good line of sight to the main door of the vacant building. The street lamps were out, and the alley itself gave off very little light. After a while, my eyesight adjusted and I was able to see any movements. There were none after four hours of sitting still. I stretched several times, pushing back against the seat of my car. My legs were stiff, and my Pepsi was almost gone. A knock on the passenger window made me jump, and when the door opened, I had my weapon pointed straight at the door.

"Easy, it's me," Bobbie yelled. She threw in two bags and crawled into the seat. "I couldn't resist coming by and saying I told you so." She began emptying the bags. "I brought you a roast beef sandwich the way you like it, mustard, lettuce, tomato, and Swiss cheese." She passed it to me. "Oh, and a Pepsi." She opened the can and handed it to me. Bobbie opened a bag of potato chips and unwrapped her own sandwich. I wasn't sure what it was but it was juicy and already dripping on her coat.

"Couldn't stay away?"

Bobbie was using a napkin to clean up the drippings on her coat. "No I just had nothing else to do for a few hours and I thought I'd drop by and see how you were doing. Any movement?"

"None. Any leads on Darcie's whereabouts?" I asked as I

enjoyed my sandwich.

"We checked with everyone she knew and no one has seen her in the past few days. No calls to her doctor or anyone else. Zip, nada, nothing! I think she was staying in Beth's house for a while."

"I'm probably wasting my time sitting here, too," I said. "You have any real evidence on Darcie?"

"Lots! We know she killed Emily and kidnapped Carla, and she killed Beth. The proof is solid. The DA's happy about knowing who killed Emily because that gets Fields off his back. But he wants Darcie in custody immediately, if not sooner. He mentioned you a time or two," Bobbie said smiling.

"Something set Darcie off again when she killed Beth. We need to find her soon, before someone else gets hurt."

"She's long gone, I'm telling you," Bobbie said as she finished her food.

"Thanks for the sandwich and the company, but you should go home and dig out your little black book and call one of your friends to go see a movie or something," I said with a wink.

"I haven't got the time."

"You're not getting any younger," I reminded her.

"Yeah, yeah, yeah," Bobbie was saying as she picked up all the wrappings and shoved them into a bag. "You sure you don't want company?"

"Go. I'll call you in the morning."

"You call tonight if anything happens!" She said pointing her finger at me.

I nodded and waved goodbye. I watched in my mirror as she left the alley, and then I settled back and began watching the empty building. I didn't want to start day-dreaming. I was afraid I'd miss something if I didn't stay alert. The night moved slowly, and I was glad to see dawn showing itself over the far corner of the building.

After a long hot shower, I made the call to Bobbie and listened to the 'I told you so' then went to bed. I set the alarm for six p.m. once again. I wasn't ready to give up yet.

This night was much like the night before, except it was much colder. I parked in the same place and made myself comfortable for the watch. I heard a bottle hit the road and grabbed my pistol. I spotted movement straight ahead of me and watched carefully, holding my pistol close. I had one hand on the door handle as the shadow moved closer. Suddenly, my cell phone rang and I jumped, hitting my head on the roof of my car. "Son of a b…" I said rubbing the top of my head.

Then, as I looked out the windshield, directly in front of my car stood a man. He didn't move; he stood there, just staring at the windshield. I waited for a couple of minutes then waved at him. He waved back and then moved on kicking the bottle. I looked down at my weapon and began nodding my head. I checked my phone and noticed it was Bobbie who had called me. I was dialing her number when my phone rang again. It caused me to jump again.

"Hello," I said.

"Good thing you answered," she said. "I was calling a squad car to check on you."

"I'm fine. This homeless guy was walking toward my car and I jumped and bumped my head on the roof."

"Don't tell me you weren't paying attention!" Bobbie began yelling.

"Calm down, I saw him out there, but you called just as he was walking toward me, and it made me jump. I'm paying attention. Nothing's going to get by me tonight. It's as quiet as last night. You might be right after all," I said.

"Hate to say it again, but I told you so. Why don't you go home tonight? I can get a car to watch the place one more night if you want."

"No, I'm fine and wide awake. I might as well stay the night. If Darcie doesn't show tonight, I'll call it off," I said.

"Listen, Paula, I can't get by there tonight, so be careful. I have a homicide across town, and it'll take most of the night to clean it up."

"Stop worrying. I'll call you in the morning and you can give me your famous line," I said laughing.

"Gotta go, call me." She hung up.

I went to sit back again and hit my Pepsi bottle and it spilled all over the seat, wetting my jeans. I was now sitting on a wet seat in wet jeans and feeling really uncomfortable. Staying all night on a ten percent chance that Darcie might show was something I wasn't looking forward to, but I was determined to stay, wet and cold.

I stepped out of the car and took a rag and began wiping off the seat. I thought I heard a noise and stopped for a second and listened. Nothing. I returned to cleaning up the seat and got back into the car and tried to get comfortable. The night seemed longer than the last and except for the homeless man kicking a bottle, nothing was happening.

After several hours, I felt stiff and cold so I decided to get out and stretch. I put my gun in my back pocket and pulled my coat over it. The alley was peaceful, the wind was still, and the crisp air felt good. I did a few stretches and decided to take a short walk around the building. Not my best idea. The alley was dark, but you could still see enough to know where you were walking. I got to the front door of the building and took a glance around and listened to the night. I could hear the traffic and the bustle of the town, but nothing here. I had walked around to the back and saw and heard nothing, except the voice in my mind repeating Bobbie's 'I told you so.'

I decided it was getting too cold to stay outside and began to return to the car. As I turned the corner, I heard a window open in the building across the alley. I leaned into the shadow of the wall and checked the building. I followed the lit windows up the side of the building to the third floor where I noticed the window was cracked.

I saw a woman looking into her mirror and then promptly

leave the room. I took a deep breath and rested my head against the building. "Damn," I whispered to myself.

I closed my eyes and felt the weight of the world hit me in the chest. My heart began thumping and my hand automatically went to my chest. I grabbed my coat, closing my fist around the front; I closed my eyes again and told myself over and over to calm down, breathe. I was remembering Elizabeth, and it was tearing me apart; I was losing it.

Slowing my breathing, I thought back and remembered that warm evening we barbequed pork chops. That night I went out to cover the grill in the back yard. It was warm and the stars filled the sky. You could see whispering white clouds, their tails flaring at the end. I thought about how happy I was. I didn't have a care in the world. I covered the grill and turned only to see Elizabeth positioned in the window. She was standing in front of the mirror in our bedroom. I watched her slowly turn to the front then look over her right shoulder and then her left and then back to the front again. She then slipped her blouse over her shoulder. Elizabeth moved from side to side watching every move she made in the mirror. My God, I thought, how beautiful.

She moved with the grace of a swan, the arch of her neck the curvature leading to her shoulder. She removed her blouse and stood facing the mirror. I could see her back and the shape of her spine, the strength in her shoulders, and the shape of her rib cage. She was beautiful and she was with me. How happy I was at that moment. I could have stood there all night watching the woman I had fallen in love with.

Suddenly, there was a sound. I went to open my eyes. Slam! I was too late. The last thing I remember was hitting the ground hard.

Chapter 49

Bobbie heard it over the radio that a call came in from a woman living in a building connected to the Braden Street alley. She said that someone had been attacked. Bobbie put on her siren and arrived at the scene within thirteen minutes. She spotted several police cruisers and an ambulance. The reporters were setting up at the end of the alley and the patrolmen were having trouble keeping them back. Bobbie pulled her car up onto the sidewalk and bailed out, running through the alley. She could see several people kneeling over a body, while an IV bag was being held up high. "Move," she was yelling, as she pushed through the crowd. "Get out of my way!" Bobbie pushed an EMT aside and knelt near the body. There was blood everywhere, and the clothing was soaked in it.

"Is she alive?" she yelled, as she grabbed Paula's hand.

I squeezed her hand. "I'm alive," I said almost inaudibly.

Bobbie looked around. "Get her into the ambulance! What's keeping you? Get moving! Go!"

She held onto Paula's hand as the EMTs moved her onto the backboard and then into the ambulance. Bobbie leaned over and whispered, "I'll be right behind you. I've got to check something."

All I was able to do was give her hand a weak squeeze as it slipped from mine.

Bobbie closed the doors to the ambulance and tapped on the back of the truck. She watched the ambulance drive away with its lights and siren. She stood rubbing her forehead for a short time then turned and went back to the scene.

"Who's in charge here?" She asked with determination.

An officer walked over to her. He nodded and flipped his note book open. "We received a phone call from Mrs. Murphy." He pointed to the third floor window. "Her window was cracked, and she heard someone screaming and noises that sounded to her like someone was being hit with something hard. She yelled down that she was going to call the police, and that scared the attacker off, probably saving Ms. Graham's life. She called the police and we were here within five, and when we recognized it was Ms. Graham, we made sure you were called."

Bobbie started walking around the area. "Do we have any idea who did this?" she asked.

"We found bloody footprints here." He pointed to where Paula was found. "And a two by four covered in bloody prints was thrown over here. It's been bagged and tagged. A few bloody fingerprints were found here on the corner of the building. It looks like the attacker slipped and grabbed a piece of the building to keep his or her balance," he explained.

"Has all the evidence been sent to the lab?"

"Everything. Mrs. Murphy did say she thought she heard a woman's voice, but the alley was too dark, and the shadows blocked any clear look. She couldn't tell if the attacker was a woman or a man."

"I'm pretty sure I know who did this, and I'll find her," Bobbie said. "Thanks officer. You can go now."

The officer left the scene, leaving Bobbie standing there staring into a pool of blood. She was trying to figure how Paula got caught unaware. It wasn't like her. She decided to take a quick walk through the empty building, just in case Darcie was still here, if it had been her who had returned that night. Finding nothing disturbed in the building, she headed to the hospital.

Bobbie was thinking about all the questions she wanted to ask Paula. Why did she leave the car? Where was her gun? And most importantly how did someone catch her off guard when she already had one experience that night? She decided to turn on the lights, and she pushed the gas peddle all the way down.

Bobbie pulled up in front of the hospital, the blue and red lights still flashing. She bolted from the car and ran through the sliding emergency doors that almost didn't open fast enough for her to fit through. She arrived at the reception desk and plastered her badge against the window. "Graham," she yelled as she flattened her badge tighter against the glass.

The nurse was watching the frantic detective with caution. "Down the hall to the right," she replied.

Bobbie took off heading down the corridor. "Down the hall to the right," she was mumbling. "Fourteen rooms in this ER and she says down the hall to the right."

Bobbie quickly stopped at each room, opening the door and

taking a quick glance inside. The first room had a woman and a baby sitting on the examination table. The second was empty. Bobbie noticed a few doors down there was an officer stationed outside the door. She ran to the door and attempted to pass him.

"You can't go in there," the tall, overweight officer said.

Bobbie slapped her badge against his hefty belly and walked by him and into the room.

"How is she?" Bobbie asked.

The doctor was standing in front of the patient and turned. "Excuse me?" The doctor said, facing Bobbie.

When the doctor moved, Bobbie was startled. Sitting on the examination table with a thermometer in his mouth and a bandage over his nose, was a prisoner in handcuffs.

"Where's Paula?" Bobbie asked the doctor.

"Who? This is Stanly Mepes," the doctor said, looking confused.

"The woman the ambulance just brought in! She was injured in an alley a short time ago," Bobbie said, becoming extremely frustrated.

"Sorry. I can't help you; we've had people in here all night. Must be a full moon. As I said, I haven't seen her."

"Great," Bobbie said, heading down the corridor once again. She opened the last door and made her entrance. "Are you alright?"

Chapter 50

Bobbie grabbed and shook my leg. Then she started with a barrage of questions. "What the hell happened? Did you know you were in trouble? Why did you leave the car? Wasn't there some homeless man hanging around? Didn't you think he might be a problem?"

I tried picking my head up so I could see Bobbie, but the doctor pushed down on my shoulder. "Don't move. I'm trying to put these stitches in, so they won't leave a large scar. You have to stay down and be still."

The doctor turned to Bobbie. "I'm afraid you'll have to leave."

I wanted to tell the doctor that that wasn't going to work, but again, he told me to stay still. I tried a smile instead.

"Forget it! I'm not going anywhere. What about these stitches? Is she going to be okay? Someone better tell me something, and I mean now!"

I could feel Bobbie's grip on my leg getting tighter.

The doctor gave the nurse the needle that was being pulled through my brow. "Finish this," he said to her.

I could barely read the name tag on the nurse's uniform, Nurse Bellitti. I wondered if she knew what a bad scar could do to me. After all, what if the future women in my life didn't like scars? I almost laughed out loud when I realized what I was thinking. Like there would be a future. "Forget it, Paula," I mumbled to myself. "Lay still."

Meanwhile, the doctor had placed his hand on Bobbie's arm and was trying to lead her out of the room and into the corridor.

Bobbie looked at the doctor's hand. "Do you know it's illegal to grab me? I could have you arrested for assaulting an Officer of the Law. Now let go of me and answer my questions." Bobbie's voice was firm but casual.

The doctor stepped into the hall with Bobbie following.

He leaned against the wall. "Your friend is going to be fine. She has several contusions on her back between the shoulder blades." He reached over his shoulder pointing to the approximate place the bruising would be. "She has a couple of cracked ribs, but they'll heal on their own. You don't have to worry about them. She also has a few scrapes and scratches on her chin and cheek. I pulled several small stones and plenty of dirt out of the cut over her eye. We'll check that often to make sure that she doesn't get an infection. That was the stitching I was doing before you interrupted. And she has a concussion that will give her a headache the size of Manhattan. She should be watched for twenty-four hours either here or at home, but she should not be left alone," the doctor said.

"So you're saying she will be as good as new?" Bobbie asked, looking up at the ceiling as she thanked the Lord.

The doctor smiled. "A few days of rest and a little pain medication and she'll be fine. I wanted to admit her, but she refused. If I were you, I'd make sure she was kept quiet for a few days. She doesn't need to be chasing after anyone in her condition."

"I understand; I'll make sure she stays at home and rests for a few days. I'll personally stay with her. When can she go home?" Bobbie asked.

"Let Nurse Bellitti finish up and we'll get the paperwork ready for dismissal. I'd say she'll be ready within an hour," the doctor said. "Oh, and make sure she doesn't drive for at least forty-eight hours."

"Thanks Doc, I'll keep that in mind," Bobbie said, knowing she has never had that kind of control over her friend. Paula had a mind of her own, and if she decided to do something, broken ribs and a concussion weren't going to stop her.

Bobbie went to the vending machines and got a cup of coffee. In the waiting area, she took a seat and planned a way to gently ask Paula why she had taken such a risk. The sweat built on her forehead as she thought to herself: *I could have lost my friend tonight.*

* * * *

My head was pounding, and the stitches felt like fire. I struggled to sit up. Slowly, I swung my feet over the side. The bed was raised to a height where my feet didn't reach the floor, so they simply dangled there. I had my arms down by my side, and I pushed down on my hands thinking I could slide off the bed and onto the floor. I felt dizzy and almost fell forward, so I scooted back some. I kept my eyes closed and my head down. The amount of energy that took had me covered in sweat already and deeply regretting the fact that I had tried to sit up. My back ached, and I was sure my head was about to detonate at any moment.

Bobbie came through the door so fast the it slammed against the wall. I was so startled that I almost fell off the bed. My eyes popped open while Bobbie was heading toward me with her lips pursed and her fists balled up.

"What were you thinking? What were you doing out in an alley without calling back-up?" She was yelling.

The yelling sounded like a thunder- storm rattling around in my head. The noise sent sharp pains down through my neck.

"Bobbie, you have to stop yelling. I'm fine," I said as quietly as I could. "My head hurts."

Bobbie puffed up. "Stop yelling! I haven't even begun to yell. Are you stupid? You knew someone was in the alley. The homeless guy should have made you aware of possible trouble. You know better. What the hell were you thinking? Why in God's name did you get out of the car? Why didn't you call me? You could have been killed!" Bobbie kept yelling.

I tried moving, but the thought of it made me nauseous. I lay back, trying not to move my head. "The doctor said I'd be fine in a couple of days," I said in a whisper.

Bobbie settled down and came to sit at the foot of the bed. She moved closer to me, pushing on my legs. I was praying (and not for the first time) that she wasn't going to try and give me a hug. My back cringed just thinking about the pain I knew I'd feel if she leaned over to embrace me.

As she sat there, I could see the worry and concern she had for me. Finally, she asked the question I had feared was coming, and had I hoped she would have put off for at least a day or two.

"So what happened? It's not like you to be caught off guard, especially when you're on the job. You're way too smart to get yourself in a spot uncovered. I need an answer. What went wrong?" Bobbie stared at me, waiting for the answer.

"I know things went wrong," I whispered, hoping my own voice wouldn't cause my head to shriek with pain.

Bobbie waited patiently never taking her eyes off me. I knew the time had come, and I was going to have to explain why I wasn't aware of the danger and why I was leaning against the wall in that alley. I dreaded it. I was at fault, and it had almost cost me my life.

Chapter 51

I bit my tongue and closed my eyes. I put my finger tips alongside my temples and rubbed in a circular motion. Taking a deep breath, I told Bobbie what happened. I included everything from the time I left the car to my day dreaming about Elizabeth while leaning against the building. Bobbie never interrupted and listened intently until I was finished. This took some time because I had to stop often due to the nausea and the pain. Every movement and every breath took an effort.

Bobbie looked deeply into my eyes then began yelling. "You did what?"

"I screwed up," I said. My head stung from her penetrating shrills.

"You're telling me you almost got killed because you were day dreaming about Elizabeth. Are you out of your mind?"

Bobbie wasn't getting any calmer. Her voice was on the rise, getting louder and louder. I have to admit, anyone yelling at me makes me get extremely angry, then I turn everything inward, and I become non-responsive to things going on around me. She got up and moved to my side.

"Well!' she yelled.

Nurse Bellitti hurried into the room when she heard Bobbie yelling. Bobbie turned toward the nurse, who was standing at the door. "Get out!" she yelled. The nurse began to walk further into the room. Bobbie pulled her badge out and flashed it to the nurse. "Get out now!" The nurse shrugged, turned, and left the room. I began to groan.

Bobbie returned to my side, staring down at me, still waiting for a response.

"I'm sorry, what else can I say?" I managed to say without too much pain.

"Sorry? Sorry doesn't cut it, pal. You're investigating a murder. A murder, do you not get that? You can't be despondent over a woman you left. You could have been killed! Wake up!"

I struggled to sit up and slid off the bed, barely keeping my balance. I faced Bobbie. "Back off! It won't happen again!" I was feeling like I would pass out at any moment.

"Damn right it won't. You're off the case, Paula, as of right now," Bobbie said angrily

"Nice try, Bobbie, but you're not my boss and you can't do that. I'm close or I wouldn't be here. It had to have been Darcie that hit me. I won't quit until she's brought in," I said, weaving back and forth.

"I don't think so, Paula. You're mind is somewhere else, and this is not working out for you. I didn't realize myself how messed up you were over Elizabeth. Maybe I was wrong to bring you back to work so soon. I made a ..."

I lunged at Bobbie. "I can do this!" I yelled.

Then I fell back against the bed, grabbing my head. The bile crept up into my throat and I covered my mouth trying to swallow instead of vomiting. Bobbie moved forward and held my arms, helping me back onto the bed.

"You've got two choices Paula: one… get over this woman and move on. Two…get out of the business. I suggest the latter."

I knew Bobbie was right (again) but I truly loved Elizabeth, and everywhere I went I saw things that reminded me of her. I couldn't shake her memory or move on. I hung my head as Bobbie stood next to me, preventing me from falling from the bed.

"I love her. I always have and I always will," I whispered.

The rage returned to Bobbie's voice. "That's just great! In that case, why'd you leave her?"

I knew that question had been coming even before I had finished talking. I wished I'd never opened my mouth. "You know why," I murmured.

"Oh I get it. You're going to give me that BS excuse. How does it go? You were sure she'd realize that she did love you even though she told you she didn't. Or, that one day she'd wake up and see that you're the one." Bobbie started flaring her arms around. "Or, how about this? Maybe one day she'll climb a mountain and yell from the top. 'I love Paula.' Or maybe one day, she might trust you implicitly. All BS," Bobbie said, as she lowered her arms to her side. Calming considerably, she softened her tone. "What was it you said to me right after you left Elizabeth?"

I sat quietly, feeling the pain, only this time I wasn't sure if the pain was from my injuries. I was ignoring Bobbie's questions. "Yes, I thought all those things," I said, beginning to feel sick.

Bobbie was quiet for a moment. It was a silence I was beginning to cherish. Then Bobbie took a huge breath and sighed. "I know you thought you had enough love for the both of you. But it doesn't work that way. Life's not that easy; you have to work at any kind of relationship. It takes two to make a partnership work. Remember what you said the night after you left Elizabeth? When you were sitting at my kitchen table?"

I knew what she talking about. It's hard to forget the time your heart was breaking and you didn't care if life continued or not. I sat at Bobbie's kitchen table in tears. I had walked away from the woman I had loved more than life that morning, never looking back and not thinking about the heartache I would have or cause.

The night before I left, Elizabeth and I were cuddled once again on the couch. We were having a conversation about all kinds of things. Then, out of nowhere, Elizabeth told me she had never believed that I truly loved her. The pain that shot through me at that moment was something that I will never forget. It hurt so bad I couldn't do much but make some stupid joke about the time we were together. We lay there several more hours watching TV; I remember nothing about the shows. All I could do was think about what she said and try to hold back the tears and pain that kept building within me.

We went to bed, and as she slept, I stayed awake, running the same sentence over and over in my head. I couldn't understand why she'd say something like that and I couldn't come up with anything that I had done to make her feel that way. I was in love with Elizabeth from day one, and I thought of all the things she knows, she knew that. I couldn't sleep, and I knew at that moment I couldn't stay in the house any longer. I said to myself and later to Bobbie the one thing I couldn't do anymore was lie to myself. I didn't want to talk. Not now.

I tried shifting in the bed giving myself time to answer Bobbie. "Get away from me," I said.

Bobbie threw up her arms and paced across the floor. She pivoted on her foot and pointed at me. "You're a dreamer. You think life is like a TV show and everything ends with the lovers running into each other's arms on the beach. I just don't understand what the problem is. She doesn't love you, you're gone. So listen to her words and get over it! Did she try to talk to you when you left? Did she give a damn?" Bobbie's voice began rising again.

Somehow, I had jumped out of bed and had my hands on Bobbie's shoulders trying to push her into the wall. "Shut up! Shut up!" I was hollering in her face.

Bobbie left my hands on her shoulders. She didn't push back. Her eyes filling as she looked at me. "You're hurt now, but it will go away. You need to box this crap up, all these feelings that will only keep hurting you. Put all that emotional stuff away like you used to be able to do, before Elizabeth. Or give up your license, and I mean it. I'm not going to your funeral. She'll never believe in you," Bobbie said.

She gently pushed me back to the bed, where I sat down. I could hardly speak, my throat was closing and my emotions and heart were running rampant.

"I just wanted to be....."

"You know what?" Bobbie said standing near the bed. "I don't give a shit, deal with it. I'm through. You're hopeless." She headed toward the door and slammed it behind her.

I watched the door, but she didn't return.

"I just wanted to be wrong. Just once I wanted to be wrong and find out she did love me."

I hurt in more ways than I could count. I lay down across the bed and closed my eyes. Suddenly the door opened and Nurse Bellitti came in with a wheel chair.

"Are you ready to go home?" She asked.

"Ready as I'll ever be," I said, trying to hide my tears.

The nurse gathered up my belongings and set them on the corner of the bed. I didn't see my gun. I assumed Bobbie took it so no one at the hospital would be tempted.

"Where's your friend?" She asked, looking around the room.

I had no idea, but I was getting out of here no matter what. "She's getting the car," I said.

She wheeled the chair near the bed and helped me get into it.

"We'll meet your friend out front," she said, as she began pushing me to the door. Outside, she kept looking for Bobbie and her car. "You sure she's coming?'

"I'm sure. The car's probably parked out back. She'll be along soon, I'm sure. You can go back inside. It's okay."

The nurse kept looking around, then back at the hospital doors. "I'm not supposed to leave you."

"Go. I'm fine, honest. It'll be all right. Bobbie should be here any moment."

"Are you sure?"

"Yes, go."

The nurse took one more look and left me sitting outside. I sat there another ten minutes. Bobbie wasn't coming, and I was getting awfully cold. I looked toward the door. I didn't want to go back inside; I wanted to go home. I was bewildered, and wondered how I was going to get there. My car wasn't here, and if it was, I didn't have the keys. Then I realized I had my cell phone and I could call a cab. As I was dialing, my luck began to change. A cab pulled up and dropped off a visitor.

"Hold that cab!" I yelled.

"Chair yours?" He asked.

I shook my head no and made an attempt to get up. The driver took my elbow and helped me into the cab. I gave him my address, and when we arrived at the shop, I noticed Sheila was closing up, so I asked the cabby to go around to the back. He was nice enough to help me up the back stairs. I made sure to give him an extra tip for his kindness.

Chapter 52

I was holding on to the sink in my kitchen. The glass of water I tried to drink ended up on the floor because I had the shakes. I put my head against the counter, wishing the nausea would go away. I couldn't keep from shaking, and I wasn't real sure I could make it to the couch before I fainted from the excruciating pain in my rib cage. I was going to take a pain pill when I realized I had taken a cab home and I hadn't stopped to fill my prescription. Okay, folks. It's time to try and get to the couch.

I tried holding on to everything and anything I could as I crossed the room. The counter in the kitchen only went so far. I reached for the kitchen table, then a chair. I still had to cross the room to get to the couch. I closed my eyes and tried to picture myself getting to the couch in one quick movement. Ready? Go! I headed to the couch and I landed on the floor with a thump just a few feet from it. The pain was unbelievable, and I felt the darkness covering me. The next thing I knew, Bobbie was helping me to the couch and covering me with my favorite quilt.

"You came," I said. I could barely focus on Bobbie.

"Hush, close your eyes and rest. I'll be right here."

"I need my prescription filled. I'm in pain," I whispered.

"Okay, you rest and I'll run down to the pharmacy and have it filled. I'll be back as quickly as possible. Stay on the couch and don't get up until I'm back."

"All right, but hurry," I said.

I wasn't sure how long she was gone when I heard someone knocking on the door. I thought Bobbie must have left her key on the table.

"Hold on, I'll be right there," I tried to yell. The knocking kept up with urgency. "I'm coming! Hold on."

I struggled getting up. Holding my rib cage, I took my time getting to the door. I opened it. "Forget your..." I backed up slowly, raising my hands as far as I could.

There stood Darcie with my gun pointed straight at my chest. "Darcie," I said quietly, still backing up as she walked forward, never taking the gun off me. Her eyes were large and a deep dark color. Her face was bleach white and had a crazed look on it. I had no doubt that she could pull the trigger at any time.

"Darcie, what can I do for you?" I asked, hoping my demeanor was calmer than I felt, and knowing my knees were getting weaker by the moment. Darcie said nothing; she stood silent still pointing the gun at me.

I had a slew of thoughts going through my head and thinking about how long it would be before Bobbie got back, was one of them. I wondered if she would be in time to save me or not. Was I going to be able to keep standing or was I going to pass out? The look on Darcie's face made me believe my time was short. I decided to try and keep her talking, provided I could get her to talk at all. If she ended up killing me, at least I wanted to die knowing some answers. I was never going to leave questions unanswered again. Well, at least not in my lifetime.

"Darcie," I said quietly. "Darcie, can I ask you something?" I waited a moment to see if she was hearing me. Her hand began to shake. I took a step back. "Darcie, why did you kill Emily?"

I wasn't sure if those would turn out to be my last words. But I had already spit them out.

Darcie's trembling got worse and the gun dropped a little. She quickly pulled her arms up and straight out. "I didn't mean to," she said, her voice quivering.

"I'm sure you didn't. You were friends right?"

I had to keep her talking. Darcie was weaving all over the place. The gun kept dropping and then she'd raise it up, over and over. I knew from experience that even the lightest weapon gets heavy when you're anxious. All your muscles get tense and sore. Then the weapon keeps getting heavier and heavier. That could be dangerous. Often that's when the person gets to the point where they pull the trigger. I wanted to give Darcie the opportunity to vent without making her angry.

"This, this woman took my place and Emily wouldn't spend time with me at the museums anymore," she was saying. "She took roses from her, but she always threw them away. I saw her, honestly, she threw them away."

She started waving the gun. "Darcie, its okay," I said. My knees were getting weak, and my ribs hurt so bad, I thought I might throw up.

"It wasn't!" She yelled. "Beth told me! She told me Emily was no good for me, that she would get rid of me the second she found someone else. She was right!" She said pointing the gun straighter at me.

I had to think of something to say quickly. "Right," I said. This calmed Darcie down for a short time.

The thought of 'where the hell was Bobbie' kept running through my head. Maybe she was never here, and I had only dreamed she was. If that was the case, I had to plan on taking Darcie down by myself--- and soon.

"Tell me what happened, Darcie. Just tell me in your own words," I said. "What happened?"

She started pacing in a circle. I hoped she didn't realize the door was still open. "I used to go to all the museums and I'd see Emily there. You know, we used to be together a long time ago," she said. "Then this other woman came along. And...and Beth warned me about her. Emily took this print from her, *a rose*. She acted like she was going to leave Carla." Darcie began mumbling to herself. She was making no sense, and her voice began to drop, making her words come more from her gut.

"Darcie, tell me about the print," I said, thinking it would get her talking again.

"She always left the stuff. Only this time she was all excited and took the print home with her. I was so mad, I confronted her at the museum and she told me she never wanted to see me again."

Darcie began crying and her words were harder to understand. I could see she was hurting. This was not the time to say anything to her. I waited, holding my arms tightly against my rib cage.

After a short time, Darcie looked at me and brought the gun up and at me again. I winced.

"She deserved what she got," Darcie said. She was angry now, and I was afraid she would pull the trigger at any time.

"I thought you said you didn't mean to kill her."

Darcie stopped short of pacing back and forth. "I didn't. I went to her house to apologize. When she opened the door, she was on the phone. She said 'hold on' then told me to get lost. She turned her back on me, and before I knew it, I had a cane in my hand." She tried wiping her eyes with the back of her hand. "I couldn't stop."

I knew time was getting short. Darcie was jumpy, getting edgier. She went from crying and babbling things I couldn't understand to yelling in a rage. I knew I had to start looking for an opening, to grab Darcie, and perhaps subdue her.

"Why kidnap Carla?" I asked.

This made Darcie start waving the gun everywhere. "I wanted her to suffer like I was," she said. "She thought she was so much smarter than me. All that fancy stuff in her house, her own business. I'm smart as her!" She yelled. "I could have had my own business if I wanted! Who did she think she was?"

Darcie was shaking her head back and forth. I took a couple of steps closer to her. She was beginning to get caught up in her own rage.

"Beth told me she was a hard worker. I'm a hard worker!"

I needed one more question answered, and I prayed I had time for it. "Darcie? Did you kill Beth?" I took another step closer to her.

"She lied to me!" She yelled. "She said she was my friend! She was just using me! I trusted her! I listened to everything she said to me! I believed her!" Darcie stomped her foot with each word. "I told her all the secrets I knew about everyone; all she did was use those things for her own benefit!"

Darcie's face changed, showing this strange, disoriented feature. I tried moving a hair closer. She raised the gun at me. I stopped. I was close enough now that if I made a quick jump, I could be on her, and with my training and background, I hopefully would be able to take the gun away from her. Would my body hold up? Probably not, but what could I do?

"I asked her for help and all she said was 'take your meds Darcie.' Can you believe that?" Darcie's voice was shaking and rising. "She said go home and make up with Joanne and everything will be okay. She only used me, told me crap about everyone just because she wanted to run her mouth. Can you believe it? She never really was my friend. I have no one," she said.

I was standing within three feet of Darcie when she became calm. She slowly looked at me, pointing my own gun straight at me.

"And you!" She yelled. "You took Car……"

I made my move. I jumped toward her, grabbing the barrel of the gun and pushing it up toward the ceiling. Darcie was shocked, but held onto the gun. It went off, the first bullet hitting the ceiling. We began to grapple and ended up on the floor, both of us still holding onto the gun. She was like a mad man with the strength of a bear. Another shot went off, hitting the wall. We rolled several times, neither of us letting go of the gun. And with one last ditch effort, I managed to get on top of Darcie, holding her arm with the gun above her head. She began punching my side as I tried to take the weapon away. I fought through the pain knowing if I didn't, I would die. I got into a position that allowed me to hold her down with my knees and be above her. At that time, I hit her hard enough that she let the gun go.

I rolled off her and came up on one knee, pointing the weapon at her. She was barreling down at me with the force of a crazed woman. I fired twice. Darcie fell back and groaned. I thought I heard the last breath leave her body as I fell forward, my face hitting the floor.

Chapter 53

Two days later I woke up in the hospital with two doctors and Bobbie standing near the window. I could hear them whispering. Bobbie, as usual, was doing most of the talking. I slowly moved my toes, I felt my fingers moving and then I tried lifting my head. I pulled my hand from under the covers and waved as I said, "Hi."

Bobbie moved toward me. "You were in a coma for a couple of days. They were a little worried when you weren't awake this morning," she said.

"I'm a little stubborn," I said smiling.

Bobbie laughed. "That you are."

"What happened?"

"I'm not sure. I came back from the pharmacy and found you and Darcie on the floor."

"Did I kill her?" I asked as my eyes closed, and I fell back to sleep.

It was almost a week before I was able to get out of bed and grasp what had happened. I had killed Darcie with two shots to the chest. When I fell, my cracked ribs actually broke, and one punctured my lung.

I was able to remember most of my conversation with Darcie and I told the story more than once to Bobbie and to the DA. The case was officially closed. The DA came by the hospital to personally thank me. On his way out of my room, he reminded me to send the city the bill.

The doctor informed me that when I could get up and walk around, he would let me go home. I was up and pacing the halls every chance I got.

The next day I was limping down the hall and spotted Jackie. She was sitting in the solarium. I hadn't given Carla Reed any thought lately. I expected to get a call one day telling me that she had died. I walked in and sat next to Jackie; she was staring at one of the plants on the nearby table.

"It's a type of ivy," I said. "Does well inside but fails outdoors."

Jackie gave me the once over and said, "I heard what happened to you. At least you got the bitch who did this to Carla. How are you?"

"I'm fine. How's Carla doing?"

Jackie hung her head and shook it back and forth. "She's still hanging on by a thread. It's awful. I have to fight every day with the nurses to turn her so the bed sores don't get infected. She has pneumonia, and the antibiotics aren't working. The doctor was rattling on about the mixtures she was fed, and her body built up immunity to them, or some crap like that. They have something new to say every day. Mostly, they tell me they have no idea why she's still alive. I think they've given up trying to help her and are just waiting for her to die. They say she'll never be normal if she lives." She sighed deeply. "I don't know what else I can do," she whispered.

"You're doing it; just being by her side everyday. It's all you can do."

Jackie swiped a magazine off the table. "She doesn't even know I'm there."

"Sure she does."

Jackie stood up and turned to face me. "No she doesn't," she said, turning to walk away.

Chapter 54

Bobbie called all my friends together and tried to have a secret combination welcome home and first solved case party. The secret was short lived.

I watched the caterers setting up their tables; white table clothes and fancy punch bowls. I couldn't believe Bobbie went to this much trouble. I wanted to kill her. Bobbie was doing her usual griping and bossing everyone around. She was determined to control every aspect of the party. She stayed away from me after we had had a small confrontation about surprise parties. I hate them.

Around eight, the place looked wonderful and our friends had begun arriving. Bobbie was the official meet and greeter, handing everyone a glass of champagne as they entered the door. For the next few hours everyone mingled and patted me on the back for a job well done.

I was tired and hurting. I excused myself and went into the bathroom.

I was leaning over the sink splashing water onto my face when I noticed the two small ceramic turtles. I held them in my hand, staring down at them. These turtles were a joke between Elizabeth and me. There used to be an ad on TV with these two turtles. They called themselves the Slowsky's. Elizabeth and I started saying "that's us." We're the Slowsky's; never in a hurry. I splashed more water on my face. God, I missed that woman. Everything that I went through these last few weeks would have meant so much more if I had had her to share everything. I wanted to be able to share the highs and lows, to share the excitement of the chase, and the terrible ending. I wanted someone who cared about me and my career. All this was gone, and I wasn't able to fix it.

Looking into the mirror, I saw Elizabeth standing over my shoulder. I swung around with a smile. Then, slowly I turned back to face the mirror; it was only my imagination. I was alone.

Bobbie knocked on the door and entered. "Are you ok?"

I kept looking in the mirror.

"You're kidding, right?" She was beginning to get perturbed and it showed. All I could do was shake my head. "You're in here thinking about Elizabeth when all your friends, your friends, Paula, are out there showing you how much they care about you. And where are you? You're in here daydreaming. I can't believe it."

"I can't help it, Bobbie. That woman changed my life, and I can't seem to get back to where I was. There's a memory everywhere I turn. I keep thinking how I want her here when I come home. How I loved talking to her, cuddling on the couch."

"Look, I know you're hurting, tired, and think you're alone. But you're not. You've been through hell these last few weeks. I'm sorry I fought with you when you were in the hospital. I was scared you were going to die, and I didn't want to lose my best friend. Not that I wasn't right giving you hell! But I picked the wrong time to argue with you." She patted me on the shoulder. "Paula, believe me when I say you have to let her go."

"You know what Bobbie?"

"What's that?"

"The only problem I have with that is my heart doesn't know how to lie."

Bobbie drew a deep sigh and walked to the door. She opened it and started to leave, then turned toward me. "You know what, Paula? Neither does Elizabeth's."

I still thought I saw Elizabeth over my shoulder. I reached up with my hand and placed my finger on the mirror. I could feel her close to me. I closed my eyes and tapped the mirror softly as I pictured Elizabeth smiling.

"Good bye Elizabeth. You'll always be in my heart."

Printed in the United States
201942BV00004B/4-21/P